"Y'know, time was when the serial killers women. Now they're taking out bodybuilders

When promising young bodybuilder Paul murdered, DI Claire Summerskill and DS Dav in the unfamiliar territory of hard core gyms and weights, supplements and steroids. But when the one thing linking the growing list of murder victims is that they are the last men you'd expect to be victims, Summerskill and Lyon are faced with their toughest case yet.

"Bodies Beautiful" is the second in the Summerskill and Lyon series of police procedural novels.

BODIES BEAUTIFUL

Summerskill and Lyon, Book Two

Steve Burford

A NineStar Press Publication

Published by NineStar Press
P.O. Box 91792,
Albuquerque, New Mexico, 87199 USA.
www.ninestarpress.com

Bodies Beautiful

Printed in the USA
First Edition
July, 2018

Print ISBN: 978-1-949340-19-8

Also available in eBook, ISBN: 978-1-949340-17-4

Warning: This book contains depictions of violence.

For Duncan. Always at the scene of the crime.

Chapter One

7:00 P.M.

Pain.

Fierce fire across his chest, up his arms, burning the muscles. More intense than any he had ever known.

It was...awesome!

"Go, Paul!"

"C'mon, man!"

"Push it."

"*Push it!*"

With one last, titanic effort and with a strangled, inarticulate bellow, Paul Best pushed the massively stacked barbell that last, all important, near impossible centimetre up over his heaving chest, locked his arms, held for one second, two, then let go. The men on either end of the barbell staggered as they took its weight, hauled it back, and let it drop with a crash on the support framework behind Paul's head.

"Sweet!"

"Brilliant, mate!"

"Un-be-fuckin'-lievable!"

Face flushed, near blinded by his own sweat but grinning like a loon, Paul lay momentarily exhausted on the bench, gasping like a landed fish, and accepting his mates' extravagant praises. A new gym record. A new personal record. A whole one point two five kilos over his last best weight, way beyond anything any of the other guys in that gym could bench-press.

But still not good enough. It was never good enough.

Paul waited for his heart and breathing to slow back to something like normal, dragging a towel one of the guys had thrown at him across his eyes to clear the sweat. The small crowd of enthusiastic admirers who had surrounded his bench drifted back to their own workouts, some inspired by what they had just seen; a couple completely demoralised. Still grinning, Paul sat back up on the bench and accepted the water bottle held out by one who had stayed, one of the two men who had taken the weight from him. "Thanks, Rob."

His mate stood to one side, shaking his head in amazement. "That was just *beyond,* man, y'know?"

Paul wiped the towel across the top of his pumped chest and under both armpits before hanging it around his thick neck. "Was, wasn't it?"

"Want me to spot some more, or do you want to stretch off?"

Paul squinted at the clock on the far wall. "Nah," he said, standing up from the bench. "Think I'll just grab a shower and get going."

Rob frowned. "You sure?" It was a standing joke at the Heavy Metal gym that Paul would be there all the hours God sent if he could, and the staff frequently almost had to throw him out at closing time which was still three hours away. Even Paul might not have anything left to give after that last display, but hitting the showers without stretching off? That was like... Rob struggled for an appropriate comparison but couldn't find one. Similes weren't really his thing. But whatever it was like, it was wrong. Paul Best didn't cut corners in the gym.

"Okay." Rob sounded uncertain. "Fancy a shake then? I've got some of the new protein formula from that show up in Brum. Doesn't taste like shit. Pure protein. That's what it says on the label. I mean," he added, "it doesn't say, *doesn't taste like shit,* just...well, y'know what I mean."

"Nah, mate. Thanks all the same. Save it for tomorrow, yeah?" Paul pointed his finger at Rob as if aiming a gun, winked, and made a clicking sound with his tongue. "Things to do tonight, y'know?"

Rob shuffled his feet uncomfortably. "Oh yeah. Right."

Paul laughed. "You in tomorrow?"

Rob nodded vigorously. "Course."

"Good man!" Paul thumped his friend on the shoulder then made his way across the crowded gym to the small changing room and shower area. All around him, standing, sitting, lying and squatting, men, and some women, pushed, pressed, pulled and lifted barbells, dumbbells, kettlebells and, in one instance, a sandbag. Soft grunts, gasps, and the occasional guttural cry punctured the air which was heavy with sweat and muscle rub.

He stopped just short of the changing room door. On the bench there lay a man, stretching out his arms and pectoral muscles, eyes closed, psyching himself to press the impressively loaded barbell resting over his head on its stand. Either side of the stand were two other men, ready to lift the weight up and over to him and stand by in case he needed their help.

Paul came and stood over the man on his back. To the untrained eye, he might have appeared as built as Paul himself. His skimpy vest, like Paul's, did little to conceal his massively overdeveloped chest and arm muscles. But with the eye of the obsessive, Paul could see the differences: the lack of definition here, the extra eighth of an inch of fat there. And the weight this man was going to try to press... Paul's grin became positively wolf-like. It was heavy all right, heavier than anything else anyone was pressing in the gym right then. And a good five kilos short of what Paul had just shifted.

"Warming up, Danny?" Paul said, just loud enough for everyone around to hear.

The man on the bench hissed in what might have been a reaction to Paul's words or might have been part of his mental preparation. He opened his eyes but stayed staring at the ceiling. He nodded once to the men on either side of his head. They heaved the weight up from its rest, brought it forward until the bar was over his chest and he could grasp it, waited until they were sure he had a firm hold, arms locked, then let go and stepped back. For a moment, the weight stayed right where it was. Then, very slowly, teeth bared in a rictus of effort, his breath a series of sharp hisses, the man on the bench let the bar come down until the metal was just resting across his heaving chest. With a cry like a yelp of pain, he then thrust powerfully upwards. The bar moved, an inch, then another. On either side of him, the helpers shifted uneasily. Veins stood out on the forehead of the man on the bench as he strained against the weight. The bar moved another inch, then part of another. Then inexorably sank back downwards. The two standing men stepped in, seized the ends of the barbell, and hauled it back into its place on the stand.

Paul laughed out loud. "Bad luck, Danny," he yelled, as he threw open the changing room doors. "Like to stick around and help you out but things to do, people to see. You know how it is." He turned and stood for a moment in the doorframe, arms held out at his side as if inviting everyone there to gaze adoringly at his powerful body. "I mean, you know how it *was*. Keep taking the tablets."

Dan Thompson lay on his bench, gasping like a man who had run a marathon, while his training partners shuffled uncomfortably off to one side, avoiding any eye contact with him. "Prick!" Dan gasped. "Fucking little prick!"

The door swung shut behind Paul but didn't completely muffle the sound of his mocking laughter.

In the changing rooms, Paul pulled his sweat-sodden vest up over his head, tossed it to one side, and stood in front of the mirror, admiring his body in the almost dispassionate way a car enthusiast might admire a sports car he had built from scratch. Biceps pose. Triceps pose. Quad flex. Yeah, looking good. Looking big and looking *really* good. And burning Thompson had felt good too. So good it had just about made him forget the nagging in his gut. But not quite.

Rob's confused surprise at his early exit from the gym had been a laugh but tearing himself away from his training so early had not been easy for Paul. Not at all! The obsessive compulsion that was part of his life, that was almost *all* of his life, that drove him through the pain and privations of bodybuilding day after day, week in, week out, was all but impossible to ignore. Besides, it would have been cool to hang around and bask some more in the mingled admiration and envy of the other guys there.

But when sweet deals came along, you had to make the most of them. And tonight's deal promised to be so sweet Paul would be able to keep himself in allegedly delicious protein drinks for many months to come. And not just milkshakes. He whistled happily to himself as he took one last admiring look over his shoulder at the reflection of his flared lat muscles and enviable narrow waist before padding off to the showers.

AS FAR AS Dave Lyon was concerned, there were two questions you just shouldn't ask on a first date. Not that this was a date.

Was it?

Meeting someone you'd made contact with via a mobile phone app wasn't going on a date, was it?

So, what was it? A getting-to-know-you session? A hookup? A quick shag?

No, no, and... Dave paused. *Definitely getting ahead of myself there. And anyway...* He glanced down at the jacket and tie he was wearing. *Like this says, "Wanna shag me?"*

He'd been working late at Foregate Street station, helping his immediate boss, DI Claire Summerskill, get on top of the backlog of paperwork that had been set to overwhelm her when the text had come through on his phone, and he'd had no time to go back to his flat to change. Not that he'd have known what to change into if he had. The other guy's profile picture had been a head and shoulders shot, with no indication if he was a T-shirt and jeans or bow tie and cummerbund kind of guy. *This,* Dave thought, not for the first time that evening, *is a bloody ridiculous way to meet anyone.* He toyed with the idea of taking his tie off to try to strike a balance between smart and casual. *Which'll look really cool if he comes in and sees me doing it. "Nice to meet you. D'you mind if I start taking my clothes off now? It'll save time overall."*

Leaving his tie on, Dave scanned the bar again. He'd been the one to name the meeting place and had deliberately chosen somewhere outside Worcester city centre. It minimised the chances of bumping into colleagues or, worse, anyone he might have advised, cautioned, or arrested recently in the course of his duties. Which was why he found himself in a small pub he didn't know, halfway between Worcester and the nearest town, Malvern. On the map it had appeared ideal but, in reality, had all the charm of a bus shelter.

He drummed his fingers on the small bar table he was sitting at. It was already ten minutes after the time they'd arranged (although how many minutes either way did "ish" actually mean?) and there was still no sign of "Al." Dave realised he was mentally putting speech marks around the man's name. Who used his real name on a gay mobile app? And it was then, as if to ironically underscore his thoughts, a man's voice called out behind him. "Lenny!"

So much for my bloody surveillance skills.

The new arrival had come in through an unnoticed side door and was now striding towards him, hand held out. Dave rose. "Al." The man's handshake was reassuringly firm. He wasn't fat, he wasn't bald and, given the pub's admittedly dim lighting, he even looked around the age he'd claimed to be in his stats. A good start.

"Alan, actually," said the other guy with a small laugh.

"Right. And it's Len," said Dave, wondering why either of them was being so particular with his lie. "So... What can I get you to drink?"

"WHAT HAVE WE got to eat?"

Claire Summerskill, key still in the front door which she had just pushed open, regarded her eldest boy sourly. "Hi Mum," she said, with sarcastically assumed jollity. "Good to see you. Hard day at work? Come in. Take the weight off your feet, and I'll make you a lovely cup of tea while I run your bath."

Tony Summerskill rolled his eyes but dutifully stepped up, pecked her on the cheek, took her bag from her and hung it on the hallway stand. "Sorry, but I am starving!"

"Where's your dad?" said Claire, taking her coat off. "He was supposed to be getting your tea tonight."

Tony was already on his way up the stairs heading back to the teenage sanctuary of his bedroom. "Emergency meeting. OFSTED. Or OFCOM." He shrugged his shoulders. "NATO? Something like that. Sounded stressed."

I'll give him bloody stressed! "And where's Sam?" Claire called up after him.

"He's up here. Starving too!"

"Can I have beeeeeans?" came a plaintive cry before a curly head thrust itself through the bannisters on the landing and beamed down happily at her. "Hello, mummy."

"Hello, love. I'll be up in a..." But four-year-old Sam had already pulled his head out from between the wooden poles and run back to his room to continue with whatever was currently gripping his young imagination. "You are old enough to make your own food you know, Tony," she shouted up at her eldest. "And to feed your starving brother."

"True," Tony conceded from the top of the stairs. "But only when there's something in the house to cook in the first place. Which there isn't. And I couldn't go out to hunt and gather any because..."

He jerked a finger over his shoulder from where the happy cry of, "Beeeans," was repeated.

"But the food shopping..." Claire began before realising too late the trap she had dug for herself.

"Was your job this week," Tony completed for her. "It's written on the fridge door. Can't blame Ian for that."

Claire frowned slightly. She'd noticed the way Tony had taken to referring to his stepfather as "Ian" rather than "Dad" lately. There might not be anything to it, but— "Shit," she muttered to herself as she reached for the coat she thought she'd done with for the day.

"Shiiiit!" came a happy echo from upstairs.

8:00 P.M.

Walking down the street, feeling fine. T-shirt so tight it might have been sprayed on. Sleeves cut so high they were hardly deserving of the name. It was getting chilly. Most guys would have had on a sweater or a coat, but when your body was packed with this much muscle, it tended to keep itself pretty toasty. And hey, if you had it why hide it away?

People told Paul he swaggered. He told them that was bollocks. When you looked this good, you didn't need to swagger. And when your lats were this wide, it was bloody hard to walk any other way.

"Yo, Paul! Heard about the bench press at the gym. Sound!"

Paul turned, clocked his mate, Daz, and gave him a thumbs-up and a broad smile, but kept walking. Worcester was a small city. News travelled fast, very fast via social media. But not all of it, thank God. If tonight's little job ever got out... Paul considered briefly. Actually, he didn't give a shit if it did. And in any case, given who was involved, that was highly unlikely, wasn't it?

He pulled his phone out of his back pocket, not without some difficulty given the tightness of his jeans, to check the time. Eight o'clock. Better ease off a bit. Wouldn't do to be too early. Could raise some awkward questions.

Paul slowed his walking pace as he carried on to his destination. But he still swaggered.

"I HAVE TO admit, Lenny," Dave's new friend leaned across the small table and lowered his voice, as if the four other people in the tiny pub were dying to hear what they were talking about, "Alan's not my real name."

"No?" Dave did his best to fake at least some surprise.

"Nah. Not even Al." He paused, waiting for Dave to pop the question. "It's Duncan," he said when Dave didn't.

Dave raised his nearly empty pint glass in a toast to the other man. "Hi, Duncan."

"Hi."

There was another pause. They both knew this would have been the moment for Dave to admit he wasn't actually "Lenny." "So, why Al?" Dave said.

"It's after the song. Y'know." Duncan paused, and when Dave said nothing, "'You Can Call Me Al'."

"Ah. Right." Dave considered this. "You a Paul Simon fan then?" he ventured.

"No."

"Oh. Okay."

They considered their drinks. "So. You really Lenny then?" Duncan asked.

For a moment, Dave considered saying that he really was. But then what if this did...go further? At what point did he come clean? Second date? First shag? The morning after? *Sod it.* "Actually, I'm Dave."

"Right!" Duncan beamed and returned the toast. "Hi, Dave." His forehead furrowed in thought. "So, why Lenny?" Dave went to answer, but Duncan flapped his hands. "No! No! Wait, let me guess." Duncan leaned in even more closely—closer than Dave would have preferred—and peered at him as if close scrutiny of his handsome companion's face might yield an answer. Dave sighed inwardly. All part of the game he supposed. Duncan clicked his fingers. "That guy from the book. *Mice and Men.*"

"Of *Mice and Men*," Dave corrected automatically.

"Yeah. That one."

"Big, stupid Lenny from *Of Mice and Men*?"

"Yeah." Duncan's smile quickly faded as he realised the possible insult. "No?"

"No. But thanks for the comparison."

Eager to redeem himself, Duncan pressed on. "Lenny Henry?"

"I'm not black."

"Lenny Bruce?"

"I'm not Jewish."

"Lenny Face?"

"I'm...not even sure who that is."

"It's an emoticon."

"Really? No."

Duncan sat back in his chair and laughed. "I give up."

"Lenny the Lion," Dave said, almost apologetically.

Duncan considered. "I have no idea who that is," he admitted.

"A puppet," Dave said, beginning to wish they were talking about almost anything else. "It was an old family joke. Because my surname's... Well, my gran on my mum's side used to call me that. She thought it was hilarious." He ground to a halt before admitting, "No one gets it anymore." He'd thought it was mildly witty and amusing when he'd chosen it. As a conversation piece, it was, he now realised, complete rubbish. He would never use it again.

Duncan laughed again, uncertain. "Right."

And that should have been a cue for them to talk about families. Or lions. Or whether they came here often. Or any damn thing. But Dave was just a fraction of a second too slow, and before he could stop him, Duncan asked the first of the two questions which, so far, Dave had managed to keep them away from.

"So, *Dave*, what d'you do for a living?"

"SO. HOW WAS your day?"

Claire's husband, Ian, sank down at the kitchen table and leaned back. "Bloody awful."

"Tony said something about OFSTED," Claire said as she dished out the beans.

"OFQAL," Ian corrected. "OFQAL tells us what we have to do. OFSTED comes along every three years to tell us how wrong we're getting it. There's been major reworkings of core syllabi. Again. Science department has completely cocked things up, so we all had to stay behind and get told off." He regarded his plate dismally. "Beans?"

Sam chortled. "And how about you?" Claire asked Tony. She genuinely wanted to hear about her son's day, but she was keener not to sit through another of Ian's rants about educational reforms. Well, he never wanted to listen to her bitching about police initiatives, did he?

"Same old, same old," Tony mumbled.

"Done your homework?" Ian asked.

Tony gave an exaggerated sigh. "Yes, I've done my homework."

Claire groaned inwardly, recognising the lie with a mother's instinct, and anticipating the ructions it would eventually cause. "And how about you, Trouble?" she asked of her youngest, the only wholly happy face at the table, albeit one now covered in tomato sauce.

"Had beeeeans," he proclaimed.

"No, I mean what about at school?"

"Had beeeeans!"

Claire groaned. "We are so in trouble with social services if they ever find out."

The family continued its meal in more or less silence for another minute or so.

"I led a multi-million-pound drug bust today," Claire said finally.

"Really?" said Tony, showing signs of actual interest in his mother.

"No." Claire's tone was acid. "I spent eight hours reviewing incident forms and filing case notes." She reached for a bottle of beer. "But thanks for asking."

"POLICE! WOW!"

Dave gave a thin smile. *Please don't say it! Please don't say it!*

Duncan leaned in close again. "So, did you bring your handcuffs?" he asked in a low, mock-thrilled voice.

He said it.

"'Fraid not. I do, however, have a standard issue Taser if you're up for something really kinky."

Duncan laughed, with just enough uncertainty to suggest he wasn't sure how far Dave was joking. "No, but seriously," he began.

"What do you do?" Dave asked hurriedly. He had no interest whatsoever in knowing. He hated the fact that as soon as guys learned what his job was, they made all kinds of assumptions about him based solely on that. He hated even more that, very often, those assumptions were right. He nevertheless realised he did exactly the same about them. Couldn't he and Duncan enjoy at least a brief moment of spurious excitement at the thought that one of them might be a film star while the other was a shy millionaire? Anything other than a police officer and...

"I'm in retail."

So much for spurious excitement.

"Not very interesting, I suppose," Duncan added with a self-deprecating shrug.

Dave's small smile could almost have been taken as denial.

"Not as interesting as your job."

Dave thought of the day's paperwork.

"Guess we'll have to make our own excitement then, won't we?" Duncan said. "Another round?"

"Cheers." Dave watched Duncan as he made his way to the bar. His jeans and jacket hit the right note of smart casual that Dave had missed. *No tie. Should I take mine off now? Too much of a signal? Got to stop thinking about it. Feels like it's choking me!* He focused on Duncan to take his mind off the apparently shrinking tie. *Nice enough guy. Not much of a spark. But...* He studied Duncan more closely as he stood at the bar ordering their next round. *Neat little arse.* Okay, he concluded, he could probably spend another hour or so in pleasant enough fashion in this pub, just making human, non-police contact with another gay man.

Just don't ask the other question!

9:00 P.M.

Paul picked his way cautiously through the shadows. It hadn't been this dark last time he came, he was sure of it. Hadn't there been a light or something in the stairwell? Paul was massive. He took shit from no one. He only had to look pissed off at another guy to make him back down. Trouble was, he was also just the smallest bit...wary of the dark.

He came to the door. To his irritation, it was locked, and not just in the way he'd expected. It was chained, the padlock old-school and heavy.

"Hello?" His voice echoed, in a way he was bloody sure it didn't in daylight. He steeled himself and called out again. "Hello."

There was a sudden sound behind him. He whirled round, fists clenched tight, pumped biceps bulging...and dropped his hands the instant he saw who it was. "Thought there was no one here for a minute," he said, his adrenalin rush giving his words an unwanted edge. It wouldn't do to sound scared. Definitely not good for business.

There was a flash of light reflecting off metal. The key to the padlock. "Let's go in, shall we?"

Paul laughed, keen to completely erase any suspicion he might have been spooked, but a little louder than he intended. "Yeah, let's! After you."

10:00 P.M.

Claire lay in bed and groaned. Then she threw her arm across her eyes to keep out the damn light. "How much longer?"

Ian didn't even turn from the sheaf of papers he was reading. "I've just got to get this last section mugged up for tomorrow. If I don't, Alex is going to rip me a new one."

Claire sniggered. "Alex? He's your deputy head, not a mafia boss. The worst he'd do would be to tut, wag his finger, and give you more time."

"I may not be out chasing criminals all day," Ian said testily, "but my deadlines are every bit as important to me as yours are to you."

Behind her shielding arm, Claire rolled her eyes in exactly the way Tony had rolled his eyes at her earlier. She recognised the tone of tetchy, wounded male pride. "I've not been chasing criminals. Not today." She thought of Alex, the rather quiet, desperately serious man who was her husband's line manager. Then she thought of DI Jim Rudge, her former line manager, and Chief Superintendent Clive Madden, the superior officer she reported to now. Now there were two guys who could really rip you a new one. She sighed. She wondered if Ian even knew what that meant. "You're going to ruin your eyes, you know."

"I don't need glasses." Ian's tetchiness was even more pronounced. "It's like I've said before, we just need..."

"...a brighter light in here. Yeah, yeah."

There was an uncomfortable silence for a minute. "Why don't you read your book?" Ian said. "I'll only be a few more minutes."

Claire briefly considered the latest soft-porn bonkbuster on her bedside table. Ian's sister, Sal, had foisted it on her. "It's great!" Sal had said. "A real page-turner. It's about this woman who, y'know, does it for money." Then she'd given Claire a small wink, pretending she'd done it so none of the men present could see, and added, "And it's a bit of a turn on too."

Claire had got one chapter into it and felt physically sick. The tastefully packaged, watered-down S&M had been so far removed from the lives of either the working girls or the victims of sexual violence she had dealt with through her work. The book had been on her table unopened for several weeks now. She decided that tomorrow she'd give it to the local second-hand bookshop. It was Christian Aid, but they seemed to like that kind of thing.

Unexpectedly, she found herself wondering what her sergeant, Dave Lyon, was getting up to right then. Hadn't he said something about a date? No, not a date. Dave had gone so far out of his way to avoid that word she hadn't been quite sure, at first, what he'd been talking about. She knew he'd broken up with his boyfriend, Richard, soon after starting at Foregate Street station, but then he'd told her that Richard hadn't really been a boyfriend at all. *If he was a suspect in an interview room, I'd be extremely suspicious of someone so bloody fussy over words.* Well, whatever it was he was up to this evening, she wished him well of it. It'd be a waste if he wasn't up to something spicy, a good-looking guy like him. She'd make a point of asking him tomorrow. She smiled sleepily. She'd also make a point of calling it a date and asking if he'd found a new boyfriend. That would get right up his nose. Be a good way to start the day.

Claire yawned pointedly and stretched out in the bed. Her toes came into contact with the bare skin of her husband's calf. *Lucky, lucky Sergeant Dave.* She turned to Ian. "Don't suppose...?" she murmured.

"Not a chance," her husband replied, turning a page of his papers. "Go to sleep."

"NEARLY CHUCKING OUT time," Duncan said with a small smile.

"Is it?" Dave checked his watch. Rather to his surprise, the time had flown by quite pleasantly in idle chat. After the usual show of interest in handcuffs and a casually phrased question as to whether Dave had ever been involved in any salacious investigation into the wrongdoings of celebrities, which he'd rebuffed with a firm "no", Duncan had seemed happy to move on from talk of Dave's job. They'd chatted about films and music and local matters, and Dave had had to admit to himself, there had been a little chemistry there after all, though it was more of a slow burn than a flash and bang kind. Not that he'd completely ruled out a bang yet. He sank the last of his pint. "Better be making our way then?"

Duncan finished off his own drink. "Yeah."

They stood and regarded each other over the bar table and its collection of now dead beer glasses and empty peanut packets. They'd reached that point. *Shall I? Could I?* Dave wondered. *Nice enough. But is enough...enough? Back to his place? But what if it's miles away? Back to mine? But what if he wants to stay the night? Will I be able to cope with him at six tomorrow morning when I'm having to get up and get out? I mean, he's all right, but...*

And then Duncan asked the second question.

MIDNIGHT

Paul lay, eyes open to the stars overhead. They were cold and distant. It was dark, but that didn't bother Paul anymore. Neither did the icy metal under his back nor the ruin of the once crisp, white T-shirt stretched across his powerful chest which had, such a short time ago, been the envy of the cheering gym rats.

"Hey, you!" came an angry voice from a short distance away. "What d'you think you're doing?" There was the crunching of someone approaching, scrambling down the embankment and across the gravel towards him. "Get up off there now, d'you hear me? You young idiot. You want to cause an accident? You want to get yourself kil—"

Ted Garnham, station master at Worcester Shrub Hill train station, came to an abrupt halt and stared down in horror as he saw, close to, the violated body that lay across the railway tracks. He was instantly and copiously sick.

01:00 A.M.

Mobile ringing. No nonsense, standard ringtone. Dave's eyes were open after the second ring. For just a moment there was the thought, *Duncan? Please God, no.* But then he remembered. He and Duncan had not exchanged numbers. The number on the phone screen was enough to clear his head and bring him to fully focused wakefulness. "DS Lyon." He listened to the terse report from the night's duty sergeant and was out of bed and reaching for his clothes before it had finished. "I'll be there in ten minutes," he said. "Yeah, well there isn't going to be much traffic about at this time of night, is there?" He tucked the mobile under his chin as he was struggling into his trousers. "You've called DI Summerskill?" He sighed at the answer. "Then call again and leave it ringing."

Shaking his head, Dave ended the call, threw the phone on the bed, and finished dragging on enough clothes to be warm and decent.

AND I-I-I-I-...WILL always love you-oo! Will always love you-oooo!

Claire shifted on the bed. Oh, that song had got her into such trouble. Had she ever been so stupid, so...young? So much in love? Of course she had. She groaned. Turned over. Tried to drag a pillow over her head. Had to block out the song. No. Had to change the ringtone on her mobile, that's what she had to do. Or get Tony to change it for her. She didn't know how to do it. Bloody song. Bloody mobiles.

Mobile!

Claire lurched upright in her bed and snatched for the phone, sending the steamy paperback on the bedside table flying across the room in the process. The damn thing was playing at full volume. It must have been ringing for ages to get so loud. Next to her, Ian swore blearily, still more asleep than not, and pulled the duvet in tighter around himself. With a jab of a finger, Claire silenced the emoting diva. "Summerskill."

After several seconds and two requests for clarification, she was up to speed and clambering out of her bed, ignoring the muffled protests of her husband at being dragged back into the waking world. "I'll be there straightaway," she said to the desk sergeant. "I don't know. Fifteen minutes?" The person at the other end spoke again. "Yes, I'm sure he said he could do it in ten but it's easier for men, isn't it?" And she ended the call and threw the phone down on the bed.

"Lives nearer too," she muttered to herself as she picked her way over her and Ian's clothes left scattered on the bedroom floor. "I should have said he lives nearer."

01:30 A.M.

"Traffic!" She made her way down the overgrown bank that led to the rail track.

Dave snapped his notepad shut. "Always heavy at this time of night," he said drily. She saw him half raise a hand and go to say something, perhaps to warn her? Her face dared him to try it, and his possible warning turned instead into an indication of where she needed to go. As if she had to be told.

"He's been moved, hasn't he? Why?"

Dave indicated a man in a heavy coat and peaked cap sitting on an abandoned sleeper. A couple of uniforms were talking to him and one was handing him a cardboard cup of something hot. "Andrew Garnham," he said, consulting his notepad. "Duty station master. The body was across the rails. First rule of the job apparently—clear the track. Whatever you find."

Summerskill knelt down beside the body. Around them, SOCO officers had set up lighting, taped the area off, as much as they could without obstructing the rail line, and had begun their work of meticulous investigation.

"Gave him a nasty shock when he found it," Dave added. Claire winced at the use of *it* but said nothing, too focused on what lay in front of her. "Even more of a shock when he moved it."

"I'll bet it did," she said softly. "What the hell has happened here?"

Dave flipped his notebook closed and took in again the macabre sight his boss was contemplating. "It looks as if someone has tried to cut his head off."

Chapter Two

"HARDLY WORTH GOING home," Dave said three hours later as the preliminary SOCO crew were packing their bags, and a still shaken Mr. Garnham was being led off.

"That's because you haven't got kids," Claire snapped. "See you at 8:30 as usual." And she left. Her bad temper was in no small part due to the prospect of a difficult day ahead after precious little sleep but also to the complete lack of anything even approaching evidence on the scene. The location and the time had practically guaranteed a low chance of witnesses while a cursory inspection of the CCTV situation confirmed the scene of the crime was a virtual blind spot. The body had been photographed, examined in situ, and taken for post-mortem. The cause of death was fairly obvious, but Claire prayed the examination would reveal something about the method which in turn might yield up the ghost of a lead to the killer.

AT HALF EIGHT precisely, a quick shower having done little to make up for his lack of sleep, Dave pulled up outside his boss's house, turned off the ignition, and waited. In the couple of months since his start at Foregate Street, he and Summerskill had fallen into a pattern of Dave picking Claire up most mornings. Partly, it was common sense: Claire's house was practically midway between Dave's current flat and the station. Partly, it was also economy: "Car-sharing's green," Claire had said, and Dave had hoped that meant a sharing of the cost of the petrol. It hadn't. Mostly, though, it was just a way of getting DI Summerskill into Foregate Street Station and to her desk on time. In many ways, Dave had quickly found, this was the most demanding aspect of his job. Given the night's events, he'd doubted today would be any different. But he had still underestimated just how late she would be.

When Claire did finally emerge from her small detached house, it was with a truculent Tony in tow. "Sorry," she said as she bundled the fourteen-year-old into the back of the car, though her tone wasn't particularly apologetic. Dave was amused to notice she automatically put a protective hand on the top of Tony's head as she shoved him in, just as she would have done with someone she was arresting. "Can we drop him off at the school on the way?"

"Course," Dave said, starting up the engine and trying to remember just which of the speed cameras on the way to Foregate could be trusted not to pick them up. "Morning, Tony."

"Dave." Tony gave a brief smile in reply before lapsing into adolescent morning moodiness.

"Thought you went in with your dad?"

"That's supposed to be what happens," Claire said, "but someone wasn't able to drag himself out of the bathroom this morning."

Tony plugged himself into his phone, Claire glared out of the window with occasional murderous glances back at her son in the mirror, and Dave focused on the speed cameras. The journey passed in uncomfortable silence.

When they arrived at the front gate of Monastery Grove High, Tony opened the door and went to leave without a word, but Claire turned around and stopped him with a hand on his leg. "See all your mates over there? You make me late again and I swear I will get Dave to put on the lights and siren, and as you get out, I will kiss you and wave goodbye to you for as long as you are in sight. Now go. Right," she said to Dave, as soon as her stunned offspring stumbled out of the car, "now get us to the station before Madden tears us a new one."

With a small but satisfying squeal of tyres, Dave pulled off. "Tear us a new one?"

"It's what everyone says these days." Claire pulled down the passenger sunshield to check her makeup in the mirror. "Get with it."

"YOU'RE LATE," SAID DI Rudge, the instant he saw them.

"You're right," Claire replied.

Jim Rudge grunted as he strode past her on his way out of the tiny office they shared at Foregate Street station. "Hope you got your filing done last night, girl. Madden's got a stick up his arse over it."

"I bet he's none too thrilled about the wrong kind of body on the tracks too," Dave said quietly.

"Yes, I did the paperwork," Claire said, "and did you cover for…?"

"Of course," Rudge called back over his shoulder, already halfway down the corridor. "Don't I always?"

Which was, she had to admit, only the truth. A valleys girl from Pontypridd, Claire didn't take crap from anyone. Her mam used to say she *took no prisoners,* but they'd all agreed she ought to stop saying that after Claire entered the police force. Compared to Jim Rudge, however, there were times she felt like Mother Theresa and Florence Nightingale rolled into one. Possibly the most cussed bastard she'd ever met, in the five years Claire had known him, she'd watched Rudge grow more and more dog-in-the-manger in the face of endless reform and escalating bureaucracy. She'd seen it harden into a personal crusade against a twenty-first century that was slowly but inexorably leaving him in the cold. But for all that, Rudge was still the only one of her immediate colleagues who had anything important in common with her other than being in the service. He had a family, two sons, and a wife he'd been married to for over thirty years, and Claire had never heard him say a bad word about any of them. And by now she'd lost count of the number of times Rudge had twisted the truth with their superintendent when she'd turned up late for work because one of the kids had been ill or she'd been on the school run, or Sam had hidden the car keys or one of the hundred and one other things that happened to a family on a daily basis. Rudge understood. "Catch you later," she yelled after him.

"Make coffee," came back from around a corner.

"In your dreams." She followed Dave into the office. "Morning, Jenny. Terry."

DS Terry Cortez made a nod back in their general direction and a vague noise that might have been a greeting intended for both of them and might not, muttered something about following his boss, and exited the office.

"Busy, busy, busy!" said WPC Jenny Trent cheerily as she walked over to Claire's desk and dumped the small pile of files she had been carrying into the inbox.

"When is it not?" Claire said, though she thought it hadn't been quite so busy until she and Dave had shown up. She picked up the top sheaf of papers and brightened at the official tag it bore. "Say what you like," she said mostly to herself. "But he's bloody quick. When he wants to be." She grabbed the coat she'd only just slung over the back of her chair and turned to Dave. "C'mon, you."

Dave rose reluctantly from his computer that was still booting up. "I haven't checked my emails yet."

"That thing is more out of date than Jim's fashion sense. It'll take another hour yet to get going. Let's get the day's low point out of the way first thing. Time to see my favourite person in the whole world."

"Thought that was me," said Dave and Jenny at exactly the same time. *Laugh, damn you!* Claire thought. But neither of them did.

THE THREE OF them stood in the white room around the table with the body on it.

"So, what," Claire asked softly, "did that?"

"At a guess," said Dr. Aldridge, the station's chief medical officer, "I'd say about three hours in the gym every weekday and most Saturdays too for about the last three years. Ah," he added, in response to the DI's withering expression, "you mean the neck."

"Yes Doctor, the neck."

Aldridge turned from one to the other of the police officers, seeing Lyon's close observation of the body. "Your type, sergeant?" he inquired breezily.

"I generally prefer them living," Dave replied, his eyes fixed on the body, giving no sign that he, like his boss, thought this man was an unmitigated prat. "This...injury," he continued, indicating the mashed muscle and bone, "it wasn't caused by a train, was it?"

"My dear sergeant." Aldridge mounted the high horse he always kept so close at hand. "Something has nearly severed this head from this body, but the operative word there is *nearly*. If a train had indeed run over it, there would be no connection at all. Pardon the pun."

"The body was left with the head across the rail, though," Claire said, recalling what the station master had told them only hours earlier. "And if the body hadn't been discovered before a train had come along, the head would have been completely cut off."

"And even I wouldn't have been able to tell that this neck had been not so much *cut* as *crushed*." Aldridge paused to regard the two of them, obviously hoping for some kind of revolted reaction to his description.

"*Crushed*! By what?"

"Some kind of beam or bar, I suppose. Metal presumably, or possibly something with a plastic sheath given the lack of natural fibres in the impact area. I'm inclined to metal given the tensile strength needed to create that kind of damage. Three to four centimetres in width. Any narrower and it would probably have cut right through. As it is—" and he reached down and tipped the head forward "—he's just about hanging on in there. Always best to keep your head, eh?" He let it fall back, none too gently, onto the autopsy table.

Summerskill bit her lip. Was it testosterone, she wondered, that made men react like this? Weak jokes to show that the blood and violence didn't get to them? In Aldridge's case, she suspected something more too. The man was one of life's perpetual adolescents who seemed to believe that one way to a woman's heart was to gross her out. And, regrettably, his job gave him ample opportunities to do it. She even suspected it might have been his major motivation in choosing his career. *Or am I being unfair?* She considered him, saw the way he was watching her closely, eager for signs of a reaction. *No,* she decided. *He really is a complete and utter dick.*

"And how," she asked with dangerous slowness, "could somebody drive a bar that hard into a man's neck?"

Aldridge mimed swinging an imaginary weapon. "I don't think they could. Frankly, it's inconceivable that any man—" He laughed slightly and gave a small mock bow in Summerskill's direction, as if conceding a point she hadn't made. "—or woman, could have the strength to do it. Besides, the angle is all wrong. The crush line is straight as a die. Whatever came at him—" He mimed a karate-like blow at Summerskill's neck and she refused to so much as blink. "Came perfectly horizontally."

"So, what are we talking about?" Lyon asked. "Some kind of device?"

"A...guillotine?" Summerskill ventured, hardly able to believe herself what she was suggesting.

"A guillotine, Inspector?" Two months on, and Aldridge was still putting a slight emphasis on her title as if suggesting he couldn't quite believe this attractive, blonde, relatively young woman could hold such a rank in the service, or as if it was some private joke the two of them shared.

"You've got a better idea, Doctor?" And somehow, when Claire used his title, she managed to make it sound like she couldn't believe that either.

"I'll admit, at the moment, no. But I'd be curious to know where you think you're going to find a guillotine in Worcester these days." He tapped his chin pensively. "There's always museums, I suppose, though we do tend to focus more on the English Civil War in these parts rather than the French Revolution. But, as I believe I said, this man was killed by the high impact of some kind of bar rather than a blade. Death came from choking rather than severance of the spinal cord." He hesitated, as if the picture he was conjuring up was too unpleasant even for him to make a joke about. "It...wouldn't have been easy. You'll have seen the state of the fingers and nails. This man died struggling. But show me the man who would willingly lie under a guillotine. Apart from Charles Darnley, of course." He smiled from one to the other of the grim-faced officers as if inviting them to take him up on his challenge or at least ask him who he was talking about. Claire had no idea. She guessed Dave knew. Neither of them gave him the satisfaction of asking. Aldridge shrugged and continued with the job at hand. "No restraint marks, on wrists or arms, though he must have been conscious when the blow landed even if he wouldn't have remained so for long." Aldridge took a long breath as he tried to imagine the scene. "It's hard to picture anything appearing so forcefully out of nowhere, and yet our boy here seems to have been standing, or lying there, just waiting for it to happen."

"An accident then?" Claire was unable to conceive of some device or situation so absurdly dangerous a lad would be prepared to stick his head into it on the off chance nothing bad would happen.

"Whatever it was, it didn't happen at the train station," Lyon said. "There was remarkably little blood at the scene." He turned to Aldridge who signalled agreement. "So the actual scene of the death must have been pretty messy."

"Clothing? Effects?" Claire asked.

Aldridge turned from the table to retrieve a large clear plastic evidence bag. He shook it at them as if he were tempting them with a giant bag of sweets, and Claire found she dearly wanted to hit him round the head with it. She took the bag from him and peered through the plastic. "T-shirt. Jeans. Shoes. Not much here. Cold night to be without a jacket."

"You look that good, you don't wear that much," Lyon said. "What? I wouldn't."

"And such a large body mass would generate a certain amount of its own heat," Aldridge added.

"Nothing else? No personal effects?"

Lyon consulted the file. "One key, presumably for a house or flat, not for a car or bike, no jewellery, and one card."

"Bank card?"

"Gym membership," Aldridge said, handing over a second, much smaller plastic bag with a theatrical flourish. "Which given the musculature isn't exactly unexpected, is it? That's how we know his name."

Claire took the bag from him and peered at the card through the plastic. "Paul Best," she said, seeing the grainy computer-generated thumbnail picture of the dead lad next to some kind of barcode, surmounted by what she assumed was the name of his gym. "Heavy Metal. Cute."

"It's over on the Blackpole industrial estate," Dave said.

"And nothing else? No money? And who goes out without their phone these days?"

"Stolen, you reckon?" Dave asked.

"Yeah. They could have been in some bag or jacket that was taken, either for what they were worth..."

"Or to stop us searching through his texts and call records."

"If there was a wallet, why wouldn't this card have been in it, along with all the other credit cards, loyalty cards and the like?" Claire straightened. "Okay, I guess we head off to Blackpole and Heavy Metal. It's our only lead at the moment until blood or prints come through." She turned back to Aldridge. "Thank you, Doctor. We've already taken up a great deal of your undoubtedly valuable time. We'll not hold you up any longer." She signalled to Lyon who folded his notebook shut with obvious relief and made to leave.

"Aren't you going to ask me about his hair?"

Summerskill and Lyon stopped in their tracks, then turned back together slowly to the man in white with his hands in his pockets and a smugness that would have tested the patience of a saint.

"His hair?" Claire repeated, uncertain whether or not she had heard correctly.

"Come, come, Inspector," Aldridge said with mock surprise. "As a woman, I did think you might have had an eye for such things. Or perhaps..." he began, turning to Dave. The expression on Dave's face was warning enough, even to a man with skin as thick as Aldridge's, not to pursue that thought any further. The doctor quickly made his way back to the table bearing the pale body and stood at its head. When he spoke, it was in the world-weary singsong all in his profession seemed to adopt when dictating their investigations to recording devices or police officers. "Victim, Paul Best. Male. Caucasian. Height, five eleven. Weight, 193 pounds, an estimation due to the degree of blood loss. Extremely muscular development. Age, early twenties. And yet—" At this point, he abandoned his monotone for something approaching glee. With the flourish of a second-rate conjurer, he leaned over the boy's head and, with gloved fingers, lifted back from the forehead the fringe of dark hair. "You will observe the receding hairline here and here—" he indicated the temples with jabs of his finger "—and the area of reduced hair coverage, especially around the crown area here."

"So he was losing his hair. Tough when you're so young but no big deal. Rarely a cause for suicide let alone murder."

"Coupled with," Aldridge went on, blithely ignoring Claire's comments, "this and this." He swept his hand first across the shoulders of the corpse and then, after raising the pale green sheet that covered most of the corpse, down the thigh.

Reluctantly, the two police officers stepped in closer again to see more clearly. "Acne?" Lyon volunteered uncertainly.

"He is young," Claire said.

"Not that young. Premature male pattern baldness. Post-adolescent acne and tits the size of watermelons, all signs of..."

"Steroids," Lyon concluded.

"Well done, Sergeant," said Aldridge, unable to conceal a touch of irritation at having his reveal taken away. "Ever thought of a career in autopsy?"

"I don't have the personality for it."

Aldridge's sarcastic smile wavered. He knew he'd been insulted but was faced by two poker faces that weren't owning up to it. "It also causes shrinkage in the genital area," he said with asperity. He placed a hand on the corner of the cloth that had, as was custom, been placed across the waist of the otherwise naked corpse.

"We can take your word for that," Summerskill said quickly before he could pull the cloth back.

"Oh come, come, Inspector. I'm sure we've all seen our fair share of cocks in our time. Haven't we, sergeant?" He smiled at Dave.

"We have," said Dave, "but I think we can rely on your experience to correctly identify genital shrinkage."

Aldridge dropped the cloth with ill grace. "In point of fact, everything was fairly average down there. But the hair and skin make me pretty certain that when we get the blood back, we'll find young Herakles here was dosed up to the eyeballs on some steroid or other."

Claire wondered. There had to be a reason why someone as obnoxious as Aldridge was kept on, and maybe this was it. He might have given them an early lead. "They alter moods, don't they? Steroids. Make people more aggressive."

"'Roid rage," Aldridge said, rolling the r's. "Increased levels of testosterone or testosterone analogue bring out the caveman in all of us. The girls love it." Again, he glanced at Dave. "And some of the boys too."

"Nothing more of a turn-on than a bald caveman with bad skin and a tiny dick," Dave said.

"Works for me," Summerskill said. "Thank you again, Doctor. Let us know as soon as the blood work comes through. C'mon, you." She led the way out of the autopsy room, Dave following her. "It's off to the gym." She pushed her way through the theatre's double doors. "Do us both good to ogle a few scantily clad men pumping iron."

"That's all we are to you, isn't it?" said Dave. "Meat."

"Damn right."

Chapter Three

"YEAH. THAT'S PAUL. One of our regulars." The sullen, heavily built young man behind the shabby desk scowled at the two police officers showing him Paul Best's gym card. "Why? He in trouble or something?"

"Is that likely?" DI Summerskill asked smoothly.

"Dunno."

"Why would you ask?" DS Lyon added.

The young man, whose clumsily handwritten badge declared him to be Marc, shook his head. "Just...you know." He pointed at them. "You're police."

"Yes. Yes, we are," said Claire. This guy was confirming all of her prejudices about males who spent time in gyms pumping their muscles.

"He's not in here yet," Marc said, as if reluctantly trying to undo a bad impression by offering useful information.

Claire shook her head almost imperceptibly at Dave. *Not yet.* "Would he normally be here by now? It's still quite early, isn't it?"

"Not for Paul. Hardcore, he is. He's in here morning and evening most days. Hates to miss a workout. 'S how you get on, innit?" He flexed his own impressive biceps, left all too visible by the skimpy gym vest he was wearing, and nodded at Dave, as if the other male would instinctively understand his point. Dave nodded back, as if this was obvious to anyone, and avoided Claire's sardonic eye. "He done something then?"

"I'm sorry," Claire said crisply, "but I'm afraid we can't say at the moment. We were hoping though that you could help us with some details. I presume for starters you'll have his address on file?" She indicated the computer sitting on the counter between her and Marc. Even by Foregate Street's out-of-date IT standards, this one was antique. She doubted the peeling sticker on its side—*Bodybuilders do it on benches*—helped its efficiency.

Marc blinked, his sullenness now tinged with uncertainty, and his eyes slid past Claire's shoulder to the gym beyond his desk. "Yeah well, you see, we're not supposed to do that sort of thing, y'know? Give out information I mean. Data Protection, y'know?" he added in a rush, as if the suddenly remembered phrase was some kind of protective talisman, bound to work with officers of the law.

Claire regarded him steadily, forcing him to stop glancing out into the gym and to meet her level gaze. "I know about Data Protection," she said, with the unspoken but still clear postscript, *and I don't give a damn.*

The lad chewed his lip but held his ground. "Okay, I'll just go and ask, yeah? I'll be right back." And he moved quickly from behind the counter, haring off across the gym floor in the direction of a door with frosted glass panes at the far end. The shorts he was wearing were as tight and relatively tiny as his vest, and Claire got a good view of his behind as he scurried away from them. She wasn't a great one for muscles, but she did like a good arse. And this boy, she had to admit, had a great arse. *And my sergeant and I are as one on this*, she thought, as she caught Dave also tracking the lad's pleasing posterior.

Marc disappeared behind the opaque glass door and, as they waited, the two police officers took the opportunity to turn around from the entrance counter to have a proper look at the establishment they found themselves in.

Heavy Metal gym was housed in a large industrial unit and was, as its name suggested, packed to the gunnels with metal. Very large pieces of very weighty metal, in battered and chipped plates and bars and dumbbells, stacked and piled on racks and stands, or just leaning against walls. Scattered, apparently haphazardly among them, were a number of worn and patched benches in a variety of colours and material coverings, the whole space rendered seemingly even larger and more confusing by the endless reflections in floor-to-ceiling mirrors that covered all of the available wall space.

At this early stage of the day, the gym was comparatively empty. Only half a dozen men working out in pairs, one man straining to lift or press or pull some barbell, dumbbell, or pulley, his mate standing crouched at his side or in front or behind him, ready to give a helping hand, or take the whole of the weight if necessary, as well as shout out some blunt motivation. "Fucking push it!" one of them was bellowing right into the purple face of a loudly grunting mate seated on a bench, whose veined arms visibly trembled with the effort of pressing two massively loaded barbells over his head.

"God, that takes me back," Claire said.

"What? To the last time you were in a gym?"

"No, to the last time I was in labour. Great nurses."

With one terrific roar, the man battling the dumbbells forced them up as high as he could, locked his arms for a second, then after a quick grunt to his partner who skipped out the way, let them fall crashing to the gym floor. Claire had thought he couldn't see her watching him, but to her embarrassment, she suddenly realised he was watching her in the reflection of the mirror in front of him. He grinned at her, then stuck his tongue out and flexed his arms.

"Yeah, right," she muttered. "Does he think I'm impressed just 'cause he's pushed a couple of doorstops over his head?"

"There may be a bit of overcompensating going on there," Dave suggested softly.

"You mean like Aldridge said: Big muscles equals small dick?"

"No. I was thinking more of his age."

"Ah." Claire saw what Dave was getting at. Contrary to her expectations, not all of the men working out that morning in Heavy Metal were youngsters. None was as young as Best, apart from Marc, the lad behind the desk. Some were well into middle age, and the overly friendly guy in the mirror trying to impress her with his deltoids had to be at least in his fifties. "Isn't he a bit...old?" she ventured.

"*A bodybuilder is a thing of beauty and a boy forever,*" Dave said.

"What?"

Dave pointed to a curling poster on the wall to one side, showing a picture of Arnold Schwarzenegger in a posing pouch, flexing his biceps over the motivational quotation. Next to it was a companion poster showing a woman wearing not much more than Arnie, flexing muscles many men would have killed for above another inspirational motto. "*You don't stop training because you get old. You get old because you stop training.*"

Claire peered closely at the picture. "Is that real?" she said suspiciously. "I mean, can a woman even *get* muscles like those?"

"A woman can get whatever she wants. If she wants it badly enough."

Summerskill and Lyon turned quickly to face the source of the voice. Walking towards them from the direction of the now open door at the far end of the gym, with Marc trailing along gloomily behind, was a woman who seemed even more out of place than the inspector and her sergeant. Claire estimated this tall, slim woman was in her late thirties, revising the estimate to possibly early forties as she drew nearer. She was stylishly though simply dressed in a dark grey jacket and skirt, her blonde hair pulled back in a ponytail. She held out a hand. Claire noted the nails were beautifully manicured and the woman hadn't hesitated to offer the hand to her first of all.

"Susan Green," she said.

"Detective Inspector Claire Summerskill." Claire indicated her companion. "Detective Sergeant Dave Lyon."

"How can I help you, Inspector?"

Cool, Claire thought. Even when completely innocent, most people couldn't suppress a slight feeling of panic or guilt when police turned up unannounced. It was always a relief to deal with people who didn't make a fuss. "Would you be...the owner of this gym?"

Susan Green's lips curled in a slight smile. "I would be." She said no more, but the two women understood each other. Behind them, men grunted and groaned in a primal struggle of muscle against metal. *Yes,* Susan Green was saying wordlessly, *I, a woman in a deceptively simple but expensive dress and immaculate makeup, am the owner of this spit and sawdust temple to testosterone.* The older guy who'd tried to impress Claire a moment ago gave a particularly suggestive grunt as he powered his way through another set of exercises. *Crazy, isn't it?*

"We were hoping you could help us. Do you know this man?" Claire nodded for Dave to hand over the membership card Aldridge had passed on earlier.

Susan took it. "Paul. Of course." She handed it back. "What would you like to know?"

"I'm impressed," Dave said.

"Why?" Sue Green asked calmly.

"You recognised him immediately. I mean, how many members do you have in this gym? Do you know them all? Or is there some reason why Paul Best's name stands out?"

Susan arched a perfect eyebrow. "That's a lot of questions, Sergeant. Well, to answer hopefully all of them, I am, these days, a businesswoman, and a good businesswoman should know the names of her clients. And yes, these are my *clients,*" she stressed, as if answering an unspoken question. "Don't let this fool you." She indicated her jacket and skirt. "You've caught me dressed for a meeting, but when it comes to my gyms, I'm very hands on."

"You work out yourself?" Claire said. There was a great guffaw from behind the desk. Both Summerskill and Lyon turned to Marc who was making no effort at all to hide his huge amusement at the question.

"Yes, Inspector," Susan said, giving Marc a look of mild reproof that curbed his outburst. "I do indeed work out." And she gestured at the poster Summerskill and Lyon had been inspecting just before she came in.

For a moment Claire didn't understand. Then the penny dropped. "That's you?"

"A few years ago, I'll admit, but yes." Green was apparently not fazed by Claire's obvious surprise.

Not wishing to appear as if she didn't believe, but unable to help herself, Claire stepped up to the poster to get a closer look. The hairstyle was different, and the muscular body was far from what she would have imagined was under that smart jacket, but yes, now she could see. She read the small print under the toe-curling motivational message. "*Susie Green— Miss Midlands Lightweight*" and a date that fixed the poster as some ten years old.

"Wow," she said.

"Wow," Dave echoed flatly, though he had not reexamined the picture. "But, coming back to the matter in hand."

Susan Green glanced at him before addressing her answer to Claire. "Yes. Paul Best. Probably the main reason I know his name is because...well, he is going to be a name, if you know what I mean."

"I'm not sure I do."

"Paul's nickname is 'The'." Susan paused at the police officers' uncertain reactions. "As in, 'The Best'." She gave a small shrug. "Yes, I always think it's a bit too tricksy to catch on but who knows? Anyway, he's got the genetics and the drive. He's already won several junior bodybuilding competitions. There's no doubt he's going to win more, and by more, I mean the big competitions. And after that...?" She spread her hands to suggest the many possibilities.

"Another Arnold Schwarzenegger?" Dave ventured, glancing at the poster next to the one of Susan Green herself.

"Well, we can all dream, can't we? We all should." Green dropped her hands and her attitude became more serious. "Though I'm wondering whether you being here asking questions means that might all be academic right now. Is Paul in some kind of trouble? He's not...?" She let the unspoken question hang.

Claire knew the point had come. "I'm sorry, Mrs. Green..."

"Sue. Please, call me Sue."

"Paul was found dead in the early hours of this morning."

For a moment, Sue looked away from them into the gym, though Claire doubted she was seeing the men and machines in there. Claire took the opportunity to check out how Marc was taking the news. He still had that slightly angry turn to his face as if life was an annoying puzzle. She suspected this was pretty much a default setting.

"Was it...?" Claire turned to see that the other woman was facing her again. "Was it an accident? I mean, I assume it was an accident."

"I'm afraid it seems not. We don't know the full details yet. We've only just started our investigations."

"I see," said Sue Green. She took a small breath as if collecting herself. "Well, I guess here is as good a place as any to begin. Heavy Metal was practically a second home for him."

"We're assuming you'll have his real home address on your records," Dave said.

"Yes. Yes, of course. Marc, could you dig out Paul's details and let these officers have them?" She turned back to Summerskill and Lyon. "I'm afraid it will only amount to where he lives, though."

"Bank details?" Dave suggested. "Does he pay his fees through direct debit?"

"Paul was one of our...cash clients," Sue said diplomatically. She discreetly indicated the other men in the gym. "Not all of my clients have bank accounts, sergeant."

"What about his mates?" Dave asked.

Marc had ducked under the counter and brought up a tatty cardboard box filled with old-fashioned filing cards. He'd started picking through them in a slow manner, suggestive of a lack of comfort with the written word. At Dave's question, he looked up from his card search, then to his boss who gave him a nod and a small reassuring smile.

"All the lads here are mates," Marc said. Summerskill and Lyon waited. "Though I guess Rob was his best mate," he finally suggested. "Spotted for him all the time."

Claire's brow furrowed. "Spotted?"

"Helped him," said Sue. "The lads who stand-by to take the weights, lift them on and off the stands, are called spotters."

"And do all these lads get on?" Dave asked. "Have there been any disagreements lately. Arguments? Fights even?"

"You said Paul was very successful," Claire added. "Did that make any of the others jealous?"

"No. They all just...work out together."

"We'd still like their names, please," Claire said, "and if you don't mind, Mrs. Green—Sue, we'd like to come back a bit later when they're likely to be here, so we can ask a few questions."

"Of course, Inspector." Sue turned to see how Marc was doing, then gave Claire an apologetic look when it became clear the lad was still laboriously making his way through the cards. "If we were at my other gym, I'd offer you a drink, but I'm afraid Heavy Metal doesn't run to lattes or cappuccinos."

As if to underscore the truth of her words there was a strangled cry of, "Fuck! Yeah!" from behind them as a pumped bodybuilder pressed a ridiculously overloaded barbell over his head, followed by a crash as the weight fell back to the ground. Sue Green raised her eyebrow in his direction and there came a small, "Sorry."

"You have another gym?"

"In Worcester? Yes. The Venus and Adonis. It's in the city centre, top floor in the Shambles Arcade. It caters to...a different kind of clientele. More family orientated." She gave Dave a very small smile. "That's where you'll find your direct debit gym-goers, Sergeant." She turned back to Claire. "More women too."

"Wouldn't do to have big weights like these smashing down in a top floor gym," Dave observed.

"Just because there are more women there doesn't mean the weights are all much lighter, Sergeant. I think you'd be surprised what some women can manage." For the first time, Sue Green really looked at Dave. Claire wondered whether it was a professional appraisal or whether she was just noticing for the first time how handsome he was. She seemed thoughtful. "Yes, I truly think you would. Do you work out, Sergeant?"

"Afraid not, Mrs...."

"Sue. I thought not."

Claire coughed to cover her amusement at both the comment and Dave's obviously narked reaction.

"Lack of time...Sue," Dave said stiffly.

"You should find the time... Dave, was it?" She appeared to hesitate over the name, though Claire had little doubt she remembered it well enough. "Although I imagine all that running around after men helps keep the weight down."

"I'm sorry?"

"Criminals, I mean."

"Less running around than you'd think," Claire said. "It's all the sitting around doing the paperwork that puts the pounds on."

And now Claire found herself the object of Sue Green's professional appraisal, and she desperately tried to think of something to say that would dodge any negative comment about her own less than gym-toned appearance. She was damned if she'd give Dave the satisfaction. "I suppose I should make more use of the station gym," she said quickly.

"We have a gym?" Dave said, unable to conceal his surprise.

"I think Cortez said something about one once. It may have a machine in it. Or something."

"Yes, well, we all need more than just a machine to help us get what we want," Sue said with professional briskness. "Guidance and encouragement for starters. Perhaps we could have a talk one day about setting up a membership deal for your station. Group discount, that kind of thing. You join either of the gyms in Worcester and you are automatically a member of the other, and of my other gyms too. And the discount extends to husbands and wives. Partners too," she added, with a small smile at Dave. "If you were to sign up for the new Fitness First project..." She appeared to realise now might not be the right moment for a sales pitch. "After all...this is cleared up, of course. I'm sorry. Sometimes I get a little carried away. Let's call it professional enthusiasm. And it still hasn't sunk in. What's happened."

Any further embarrassment was prevented by Marc finding and handing over the information he had collated to Dave who thanked him and clipped it into his notebook.

"Okay, well, we'll be back later if that's okay, Sue?"

Sue Green smiled warmly. "Of course, Inspector. A pleasure to meet you. You too, Sergeant." She shook each of their hands in turn. "Although I obviously wish it had been under happier circumstances."

"Indeed." Claire turned to Dave. "Come along then, Sergeant. Back to the station. Maybe if we jog, we can burn off a few unwanted calories."

"Not in those heels, ma'am."

The two officers left the gym.

"COW."

"What?"

"Sarky cow," Dave amended.

Claire regarded her sergeant as he drove them back to Foregate Street. His manner was calm, but the words were emphatic. "What's brought this on?"

"All those little digs. 'Chasing after men'."

Claire chuckled and thought. "And...?"

"That bit about partners. 'Husbands, wives, and *partners.*' That was directed at me."

"Ri-ight." Claire waited. "And?"

"Well, it was pretty obvious, wasn't it?"

"What? That she thought you were gay?"

"Yes."

"But you are."

"It's not for her to go making comments about it though, is it?"

"She was hardly making comments. The bit about partners was...inclusive."

"And the bit about chasing after men?"

"That was just funny."

"And how was she to know anyway?"

"I don't know. Could be it was the way you minced into the gym?"

"I do not mince."

"No, because you are so 'straight-acting'." Claire already knew how much this description annoyed Dave. He'd taken the best part of an hour once, during an ultimately failed stakeout, to explain to her, in detail, how that phrase, so well-used on gay contact sites, was just a kind of internalised homophobia. She smiled to herself. Sometimes, yanking Dave's chain could take the edge off an otherwise grim day.

"I don't act anything. I just am."

"Cue for a song!"

"And I am *not* into musicals!"

Claire sighed. "No, you're not. I do wonder sometimes if you're actually a straight cop in some kind of deep undercover mission. Look. Sue Green is what it says on the tin. She works with people, a lot of very different people by the sounds of it. She'll have had to get used to reading them, that's all."

Dave sniffed. "Woman's intuition?"

"Which I believe in about as much as you believe in gaydar. No, *businesswoman's* intuition. That's a whole other kettle of fish. Added to which, you did ogle that lad's arse. Either she saw you or someone else did and told her."

Dave considered. "I did not *ogle*. But it was a nice arse."

"Shame the lad it's attached to is thick as a brick."

They drove on in silence for another minute or two. "Nearly broke my fingers when she shook my hand too," Dave said.

"Yeah well, that's because you're so limp-wristed."

"PAUL BEST!" JENNY proclaimed, waving a printout triumphantly in the air as Summerskill and Lyon walked back into their office at Foregate Street.

Claire pretended not to notice that Jenny had jumped up from the edge of Terry Cortez's desk where she had been perched, almost certainly sharing the printout information. "He's got a record?"

"Yup. Prints came back positive."

"And?"

"He's a bad boy."

"Really?" Claire found she was disappointed, feeling almost let down in some absurd way. Not that it made the slightest difference, of course.

Dave reached across and took the printout from the WPC and began to scan it. "Originally from Bristol. Lived with his mum on the Lockleaze Estate. Bit rough. No dad on the scene, no brothers or sisters. Done a couple of times for bunking off school. Couple of warnings for fighting—late night, chucking-out time, that sort of thing. One overnighter which is where the prints came from. Girlfriend trouble once. Again, got a bit of a talking-to by the local plod."

"Violent?"

Dave skimmed the notes further. "Hard to tell. I don't think so. Bit of a temper on him, but I'm guessing when a big lad gets his hair off he can come across a lot more alarming than most. There's no record he ever actually hit his girlfriend, or anyone for that matter." He dropped the paper on his desk. "That was over a year ago. Just before he came up here." He looked at Jenny. "*Bad boy* is overstating it a bit."

Claire leaned forward at her desk. "So, girlfriend not around anymore?"

"Doesn't seem to be. Perhaps that was why he left Bristol, to make a break and a fresh start."

Claire was doubtful. "Sue Green thought he was destined for greatness in the bodybuilding world. Is Worcester the sort of place a bodybuilder comes to follow his dream?"

From across the office came a barked laugh. "You kidding?" Sergeant Cortez said. "There's got to be better gyms down there than here. You might leave Bristol to go to Birmingham maybe, but Worcester?"

"Bit of an expert on the local muscleman scene, Terry?" Claire asked.

"Terry works out, don't you, Tel?" Jenny said.

"A Heavy Metal man?"

"I train in Birmingham," said Cortez, a note of defensiveness creeping into his voice. "Closer to home. Better facilities. Plus, I'm less likely to bump into someone I've banged up."

There was a general murmur of understanding.

"Well, Susan Green did all right for herself," Claire said, "and I presume she was based in Worcester when she was competing, so maybe there is something about the place that's good for muscles." She turned back to Cortez. "You ever been offered steroids at this gym of yours, Terry?"

It had been a flip question, more joke than serious enquiry, but to her surprise, Claire was sure, for a moment, she saw something in Terry's eyes. Wariness? Annoyance even?

"The most stimulating thing I'll take before a workout is an energy drink," he said.

"Right." Claire noted that neither she nor Dave had been able to resist a quick peek at Terry's hairline. Seemed strong enough.

"I've been told there's a gym in the station," Dave said.

"There's a weights room," Cortez said quickly, as if pleased to have at least a partial change of topic. "Down in the basement. I mean, I guess that's what you'd have to call it. It's got two weights in it. One of them's used to prop the door open. Part of an initiative back in the nineties, apparently."

"Initiatives!" Jenny exclaimed with scorn, adding quickly before anyone could ask her what she meant by that, "So, don't fancy getting your kit off, Tel, and working out down there? Showing us your pecs and glutes?"

"I get better results from a proper gym, thank you very much."

"Not tempted to try Heavy Metal?" Dave asked. "Some serious equipment there."

"So I've heard," Cortez said coldly, "but it's not the kind of place I could take Debs to."

"Ah, the pneumatic Debs!" Jenny grinned. "You train with her then, Tel? You pump together, do you?"

"When we can," Cortez said, deliberately ignoring the almost single *entendre*. "Which isn't often given her mad work patterns and my long shifts."

"Tell me about it," Claire said with real feeling. "Debs is a trolley dolly," she added for Dave's edification.

"An air stewardess," Cortez said, in the way of someone who'd had to make the correction many times previously.

"You know, it must be nice running a gym," Claire mused out loud, leaning back in her chair. "Sitting around all day, watching every other poor sod get exhausted."

"Like being an inspector, you mean?" Jenny said. "And on that note..."

She turned and left the office with the list of names Summerskill had got from the gym to run some preliminary background checks on. In less than two minutes, Terry followed her.

"Didn't know Cortez had a girlfriend," Dave said as he took his seat at his desk.

"Didn't you? He talks about her all the time."

"Can't say I've noticed."

Claire glanced across at her sergeant who was apparently absorbed in logging on at his computer. Yes, Cortez did talk about Debs all the time. Just not when Dave was around. Claire knew all about Debs, and all about Jenny's various, brief boyfriends, and Jim Rudge's family, because they were a team and talked about these things all the time. Or at least, they used to.

When a new guy joined any team, there was always a period of readjustment. People weren't quite as open as usual until they'd got the feel of the newbie. But it had been nearly two months now since Dave had joined them at Foregate Street. Did that still make him a new guy? He was sharp; he was funny, in a dry kind of way; he was damn good at his job. They should all be bantering just as much as they used to, ripping the piss out of Terry and Jenny about their respective love lives and generally reminding themselves there was a world apart from the one where young men ended up pulped on railway tracks. But they weren't.

Claire thought back to her conversation with Chief Superintendent Madden when he'd first sprung the station's new recruit on her, the product of one of those "initiatives" that Jenny had been so pointedly contemptuous of a minute ago. One of the first things that had struck her then was Dave's relatively slow career progression. A university graduate; nothing but positive results in the policing he'd done from uniformed years to the present day. He could have been an inspector like her. Should have been, even. But here he was, her sergeant. She knew the unspoken assumption as to why he hadn't been promoted, but even Dave had been reluctant to accept that was the reason. Now she found herself wondering. Was it because he was gay? Or was it because Detective Sergeant Dave Lyon was just a bit too...prickly?

Dave looked up from his screen and caught her studying him.

"Just wondering," she said. "How was your date last night?"

Dave blinked, caught out by the unexpectedness of the question. "It wasn't a date."

"You found him on your mobile, you said?"

"Ye-es."

"You met him at the Halfway House?"

"Yes."

"You wore your tie?"

"How did you...?"

"I am the inspector here." *He'd never have had time to change after he left me.*

"Yes, I wore my tie."

She leaned back and folded her arms. "Then it was a date. Did it go well? He your new boyfriend?" *Gotcha! "Date" and "boyfriend" in under twenty seconds.*

"No! I mean, yes, but very definitely no!"

"I've known multiple murderers to be less evasive."

Dave sighed. "He was...okay. We had a drink. We got on. End of."

Claire waited. Dave said no more. "What? That was all?"

"Pretty much."

"You didn't...go home?"

"Yes. Just not with each other."

"Did you get a kiss?"

"No, because there wasn't a convenient bike shed we could hide behind and, oh, neither of us was a teenager."

"And I thought a shag was the gay equivalent of a handshake."

"And I think that's getting pretty close to some kind of actionable gender orientation abuse."

Claire considered. Had she pushed her teasing just that bit too far? What if she had? She didn't tiptoe around any other special groups: she was damned if she was going to start now with gay men. Especially with those who worked under her. Besides, he needed it. *I'm on a mission.* "So sue me," she said.

"And what would I do with that small fortune?"

Claire smiled to herself. She hadn't misjudged him.

There was a pause. Both of them had turned back to the bright screens on the desks in front of them, but with an instinct honed in dozens of interview rooms, Claire could sense Dave wanted to keep talking. She waited.

"The thing is," Dave said, "I reckon there are two questions gay men shouldn't ask each other when they're...meeting for the first time."

"You mean, on a date. Sorry, couldn't help myself. Okay, I know the one is definitely, 'What do you do for a living?'" They both nodded in sympathy. They'd had that conversation before and knew each other's strategies for dealing with it. "What's the other one then?"

Before Dave could answer, the door to the office opened and Jenny leaned in. "Writeups from SOCO," she said, throwing a pale green folder onto Claire's desk. "And Madden wants to be filled in now on progress so far with Best before he has to face any reporters."

Claire picked up the folder. "Later," she said to Dave as she got to her feet. The station's CS was not a man to be kept waiting.

"Right," said Dave, returning to his computer.

Chapter Four

HEAVY METAL WAS a considerably busier place when Summerskill and Lyon returned to it that evening. Even before opening the steel door that led into the gym, they could hear the grunts of exertion and clash of metal plates. "Brace yourself," Dave said. He pushed the door and they stepped in.

As before, the gloomy Marc was on duty at the desk. "Long hours," Dave remarked after saying hello. Marc grunted and went to find Sue Green.

Unlike earlier, this time there was barely a bench or weight station unoccupied. The average age of those working out was considerably lower than it had been in the morning, though there were still one or two older guys, including the one who'd tried and failed to impress Claire with his delts. Dave saw him watching Claire again though in a more guarded way than before, probably because he now knew she was with the police. *Maybe that'll mean he'll keep his tongue in his mouth.* He noted one or two others staring across at them and then quickly pretending they hadn't, trying to make it seem as if they weren't more than ordinarily curious. *Word's got around. Good. Let's see who gets nervous.*

"Hello again!" Sue Green was striding towards them. Gone was the power suit of the morning. Now, the gym owner was dressed in bright red training bottoms and a T-shirt with the gym logo, a hugely stacked barbell acting as a hyphen between the words *Heavy* and *Metal*. "I took the liberty of letting some of the guys know you'd be wanting to have a word. I thought that was probably best." As before, she addressed herself mainly to Claire. "I hope that was all right?"

"Very helpful," Dave said.

"I also made a note of one guy who...well, he'd normally be here, but he suddenly decided he didn't want to train this evening after all. When he knew the police would be dropping in."

"We shouldn't make assumptions..." Dave began.

"Thanks, Sue," said Claire. "That might be useful." She handed the piece of paper to Dave.

"To be honest," Sue went on. "I don't think there's a...what do you call it? A link? Connection? Dan's not...*was* not a mate of Paul's. I just think he's got...other things on his mind. I thought I'd better let you know, though. To be on the safe side."

"We'll check on it, thanks," Dave said. "Just to be on the safe side."

"I guess you'll be wanting to start with Rob?" Sue said. "He was Paul's best mate."

"And he's come to train? Having just heard his mate was dead?" Dave asked.

Sue regarded him coolly. "He didn't know Paul was dead, Sergeant, until I told him. He agreed to stay and talk to you, to help. He's in my office. I thought you might like to use it while you're here." She led the way across the gym floor to the door from which they had seen her emerge that morning. "I say 'office.' Broom cupboard would be nearer the truth."

"It is much appreciated, thank you," Claire said.

Sue showed them in, and they immediately saw the accuracy of her disparaging description. Little more than a corner partitioned off from the main gym, the office offered a table, one chair, and just about enough room to squeeze in three people. Four if they were small or extremely good friends.

"YOU THINK SHE'D like to stay in while we question the guys?" Dave said after Sue had shown them in and gone to fetch Rob.

"Still got your Y-fronts in a twist? She's being helpful. You're not thinking she might be a suspect, are you?"

"Are you saying she isn't?"

"Do you honestly think a woman could have killed a man like Paul Best, in the way he was killed?"

"She said herself, *"You'd be surprised what a woman can do."* And she's got muscles."

"Inspector?" The door to the office opened and the subject of their discussion put her head round. "This is Rob." Sue Green stepped back to let the lad shuffle in.

He was dressed in a frayed T-shirt and shabby tracksuit bottoms, and it was immediately clear Rob shared the same kind of pumped physique as every other member of this gym. Its powerful masculinity made for a strange contrast with his obvious nervousness and discomfort.

"If you need me," said Sue, "I'll be at the desk with Marc."

Claire gestured to the one small chair. "Please, do sit down."

Dave took out his notepad. With a sinking feeling, he wondered how many of Heavy Metal's members Sue had lined up for them to interview. The gym was packed. This could be a long evening.

Claire began. "Hi. I'm Detective Inspector Claire Summerskill, and this is Detective Sergeant David Lyon."

Dave considered the lad sitting in front of them as Claire began her line of questioning. No one could have missed his apprehension on entering or the way he'd immediately focused on Dave, obviously assuming he was the senior officer. Neither could anyone have mistaken the slight lessening of his apprehension when it was the small blonde woman who had announced herself as being in charge. If he could have chuckled, Dave would have. *Sucker. She's Welsh. There's a reason their flag has a dragon on it.*

With Rob's attention on Claire for the moment, Dave took the opportunity to have a closer look at the young man. He took in the cheap T-shirt with its faded, meaningless logo, the not unattractive face...and the muscles. There were, Dave thought, a lot of muscles. He wasn't, on the whole, into muscle Marys. If pushed, he'd have been happy to talk at length about how it was personality and intelligence that were the important qualities. But it had been well over a month now since he had split up with Richard, and if you had to choose someone for a meaningless but stress-reducing shag then it would be someone with a good body, wouldn't it? And in this room, they were all so close together he could practically feel the heat radiating from Robert's pumped muscle mass. Maybe he wouldn't be thinking this way if his meeting with Duncan had worked out differently. But then again...

Dave took a deep breath and forced himself to focus on his notebook and not on the distraction of Robert Taylor's biceps.

Claire was wasting little time on commiseration. Time was short and there was a lot of work to be done. And besides, Dave thought, she wasn't good at commiseration. "So how long had you known Paul?"

Dave searched Rob's face for reactions. Nervous, definitely, but also dazed. He almost certainly hadn't had time yet to take in the news of Paul's death. Dave knew from personal experience it could be days, weeks even before the truth of a loss like that hit home. If, that is, Rob and Paul genuinely had been close friends. If they had been friends at all.

"About a year and a half, I guess." Rob licked his lips. "Not long. I mean, we were mates, but not like best buds. I mean... Why are you talking to me?"

Dave gave a reassuring smile. He felt sorry for the lad, and not just because his inspector was giving him a hard time. He was already beginning to form a picture of young Rob Taylor's life, and it didn't have a whole lot in it apart from working out in the gym and getting big. "It's okay, Robert," he said. "Rob?" The lad gave a hesitant nod. "Rob. This is just a routine inquiry. We're trying to find out as much as we can about Paul, to help us understand him, help us find out...what happened."

Rob's eyes widened. "Then he was killed, right? I mean, someone killed him! Jesus."

"This seems to have come as a great shock to you," Claire said calmly.

"Of course it has, man!" Rob exploded. "I mean, like, nothing like this has ever happened to me before, has it? I mean, people getting killed an' all. It's like, it doesn't happen in real life, does it?"

"I'm sorry," Claire said quietly. "So, how did you first meet?"

"In the gym."

"Here? Heavy Metal?"

"Yeah. We just got talking, like."

"What. About the weather?"

"About training?" Dave offered.

"Yeah." Rob turned his attention and directed his answers to Dave. "We were both lifting the same kind of weights. He asked me to spot for him, so I did. Spotting's when..."

"We know," Claire said quickly. "Go on."

Rob hesitated, plainly unsure just where he was supposed to go on to. "And, well, that was it."

"And how often did you see him at the gym?"

"Pretty much every day," Rob said, as if it was the most normal thing in the world.

"Every day?"

"Yeah." Rob sounded defensive, picking up on Claire's tone though uncertain if it was disbelief or criticism. "Might take a Saturday or Sunday off but otherwise pretty much. It were Paul who got me working that hard. Up until then, I might only have gone in three or four times a week, but he was, like, full on, man."

"And did you ever socialise outside the gym?"

Rob's forehead furrowed. "What d'you mean?"

Claire elaborated. "Meet up? Go out together?"

"Go out together!"

"Yes. To the pub? Or clubbing? With other mates?"

"Paul? No way, man! I told you, he were full on. Didn't drink. Didn't smoke. Careful about what he ate. And we didn't go out. We were just mates, like. Gym mates. There were nowt queer about it."

"No need to be offensive, Mr. Taylor."

Rob's eyes widened. "I weren't..." he began.

"Did Paul use steroids, Rob?" Dave asked.

Rob's eyes shot back to Dave. "Were that...? Did that...?" He ground to a halt and stared down fixedly at the floor. It was what Dave thought of as the ostrich manoeuvre, pretty much what he'd seen Claire's son, Tony, try on his mum that morning. As a technique, it was about as successful for suspects as it was for the ostrich. "It's not illegal, is it?" Rob mumbled, still refusing to make eye contact.

"Actually..." Claire began.

"Broadly speaking, no," Dave interjected. "It's supply, not use, that can get you into trouble." He lowered his tone, trying to be less threatening. "It's Paul we want to know about, Rob, not you."

"I don't use 'em," he said. "Not...regularly. Haven't got the money, have I?" He looked up, straight into Claire's eyes. "Besides, they say they shrink your cock and balls, don't they?"

Claire didn't blink. "So we've been told."

"But Paul...?" Dave asked.

Rob's visible wrestling with his conscience gave them all the answer they needed. When he spoke, it was only to confirm what they'd already deduced. "Not at first. He were like me, couldn't afford 'em. Then, when he started getting some money, he started stacking. That's taking different types," he added quickly before Claire could ask. Rob's face momentarily lit up with a devotee's enthusiasm. "It were fuckin' amazing, man. He must have put on a stone of muscle in just over a couple of months." He found himself looking straight into Claire's unblinking blue eyes again. "Sorry," he mumbled and turned his attention groundward again.

"So, he had a job?" the inspector said carefully.

"He did odds and ends, like."

"Like what?"

"He did a bit of moving for a mate of ours, furniture and stuff, and some nights he worked the doors over at Pharos. You know it?"

"Oh yes," said Dave. He'd learned all about the Pharos nightclub on his first case at Foregate Street. "He get into any trouble on the doors?"

Rob snorted. "Guys'd take one look at Paul and back off. He only had to stare at 'em hard and they'd piss 'emselves."

Dave made a note of the Pharos club in his notepad and got the name of the guy Best would sometimes help out with moving. "And was there anyone else in the gym Paul would talk to or train with?"

Rob sat for a second or two in truculent silence then grudgingly gave a couple of names. Dave ticked them both off from the list Sue Green had already given them. "Only if they happened to be in, like, and I wasn't there," he added. "Otherwise it were me. We were training partners." He sat back for a minute, folding his arms across his chest, well aware of how much bigger the pose made his already huge biceps appear and unable to hold back a moment of pride. "There weren't many as could train as hard and long as me and Paul."

"Thank you, Mr. Taylor," Claire said shortly. "That'll be all."

Rob rose from his chair. He had the mildly bewildered air that Dave knew so well from all the other people he'd seen interviewed, the *is that it?* face. He gave the lad a small but friendly smile. Rob bobbed his head at both of them then shuffled to the door.

"Oh, just one thing before you go," Claire said, as Rob's hand was on the door handle. "The drugs that Paul was using."

"Steroids," Rob mumbled, as if the word was somehow less illegal than *drugs*.

"Yes. Them. Where did he get them? Who was his supplier?"

Rob hesitated. As intellectually challenged as he appeared to be, even he wasn't fooled by the apparently casual way Claire had framed her question. "Dunno." He stood with his hand on the door handle, obviously wanting both Dave and Claire to believe the truth of what he was saying. It was clear he was lying. But Dave had seen the direction his eyes had darted just before he had answered, and now had a pretty good idea just where Best's supplier was to be found. Rob had glanced out through the room's small window into the crowded gym of Heavy Metal.

"Thank you again, Mr. Taylor," Claire said. "You've been very helpful."

"YOU DIDN'T HAVE to do that, you know," Dave said as soon as the door had closed behind Rob. "Jump on him for his *we're not queer* crack."

"It was offensive," Claire said. "I'd have done the same if he'd made a joke about Jews or black people."

"I think it's 'people of colour' now, and I really don't think he was trying to be nasty. He just meant he and Best weren't...together. Sometimes these days, that's as far as people are thinking when they say something like that."

"You try to do the right thing! And anyway, you don't think maybe there was a bit of protesting too much going on there?"

"No."

"Nothing on the gaydar?"

"No."

Claire held her hands up in mock surrender. "I do not understand you at all."

"Is that you as in men or you as in gay men?"

"Both. And you as in you. I mean, c'mon. Guys who spend all their time obsessing about their muscles, comparing them with other guys' muscles. Most of them out there—" and she jerked a finger in the direction of the window "—have got to spend more time thinking about men's bodies than they do about women. Don't you think there's one whole lot of denial going on there? If it even is being denied."

"Not all gay men are into muscles."

"I've seen gay magazines, Dave. Not many beer bellies and man boobs in those. Gotcha," she concluded as Dave went to reply and realised he couldn't. Not sure herself anymore if she was making a valid point or going for a rise out of Dave, Claire went on, "So, you don't think there was a bit of a moment there?"

"What!"

"Well, he obviously preferred you to me."

"That's because you were being such a...police officer."

"And I saw that smile you gave him as he was leaving. C'mon. You telling me you weren't just a little turned on?"

"Were you?"

Claire blinked. Should she allow a question like that from a junior officer? But then should she have asked him that question in the first place? Would she have asked a straight colleague if he fancied a female suspect? *Oh, sod political correctness.* "It's different, isn't it?"

"Okay, so, assuming of course he's not actually a deranged, maniacal killer and putting aside for a moment the fact that we are in the process of a professional investigation..."

"For the moment."

"Do I fancy Robert Taylor?"

"Yes."

"No."

"Oh c'mon! I'd have thought a guy with a body like that would be literally a dream come true."

"He might have a body, but he's got precious little in the way of brains. And, believe it or not, I rather prefer someone I can talk to."

"But when guys do talk to you, you moan about them asking questions."

"Only the wrong questions. And there's basically only two of those."

"Are you sure you really want to meet anyone?" she asked.

"And are you sure you're here to investigate a murder or is it to cross-examine me on my love life?"

"I'm trying to find out if you've actually *got* a love life."

Dave was spared the need to answer by the door opening once more and Sue Green poking her head in again. "Ready for the next one?"

Claire sighed. "Thanks, Sue. Yes, wheel him in." With one stride she passed Dave and crossed the length of the office to Sue's miniature desk. "And this time, I'm bloody taking the chair."

IT WAS GETTING on for ten by the time Summerskill and Lyon had spoken to everyone on Sue Green's list. The gym owner had, they found, been very thorough. Claire leaned back as far as she dared in the cheap chair and rubbed her eyes. "You know what I would most like right now?"

"A solid lead?" Dave suggested dourly.

"A can of air freshener." After nearly three hours of guys sweaty from their training, the air in the confined space was heavy with sweat, muscle rub, and other scents neither of them wanted to think about too closely.

"Sorry about that," said a voice from the doorway, and Sue Green came in bearing two mugs. "Bottom drawer of the desk, right-hand side. I should have said. Help yourself. I use it myself, quite a lot."

Embarrassed at being caught out in her less-than-flattering remark, Claire began to deny it was that bad, but Sue waved her words aside with a smile. "I think noses and muscles are inversely proportional. Guys lose their sense of smell when they lift weights for too long." She handed the mugs over.

"Thanks, but I don't..." Claire stopped as the steam from the mug rose into her face.

"Camomile," Sue explained. "Didn't think you'd want caffeine this late in the evening."

Claire took a grateful sip. "Sometimes it's the only thing that keeps me going, but right now, you're right. This is great, thanks."

"So, any luck?"

Claire was about to answer when the door opened, as much as it could with the three of them in there, and a man stuck his head round. "My turn now, is it?"

With his back to the door and his face hidden from the new arrival, Dave winked at Claire over the rim of his mug and mouthed, "Your admirer."

Claire's heart sank. It was the older guy she'd seen that morning. The one with the tongue. "I'm sorry, Mr.—?"

"Bill," the new arrival said, forcing himself into the room. Dave pressed up against the wall to make more room for the shorter but much stockier man. Sue Green, he noticed, didn't budge an inch.

"I'm sorry, Bill," Claire said, trying to put as much formality into the single syllable of his name as she could. "Mr.—?"

"Kilby."

"I'm sorry, Mr. Kilby, but your name simply hasn't come up in connection with...the case we're investigating." Behind him, she saw Sue lean her head slightly in Kilby's direction and widen her eyes. The ends of her lips, Claire noticed, were twitching slightly, as if she were holding back a smile. Claire understood what the other woman was trying to communicate to her. *He fancies you.* She took a deep breath. "Perhaps my sergeant..."

Dave just had time to glare at her, suspecting, quite rightly, she was about to offload this sweaty individual off on him, but before either of them could do or say any more, Bill interrupted.

"I knew young Paul as well as most of 'em," he said.

Claire sighed in resignation, and Dave wearily pulled out the notebook he'd slipped back into his jacket pocket.

"I'll be out in the gym when you've finished," Sue said. She turned to face Bill and waited until he withdrew enough for her to leave the room without having to squeeze past him.

As soon as she was gone, Bill seemed to expand to fill the space made and took up a position directly in front of Claire with his broad back to Dave. "So, what do you want to know?"

Claire went through the by now extremely familiar list of questions she and Dave had been putting to the gym's clientele: the usual who, what, where, when, and why. In a very short time, Claire realised her assumptions had been right. Bill Kilby was a builder, had been training for nearly forty years now, had two ex-wives and a girlfriend who didn't understand him, and had practically nothing whatsoever to do with the case. He and Paul had trained at the same gym, had seen each other across the gym floor many times, but had hardly spoken on any of those occasions. And that was it.

"So, who do you think did it then?" Bill cheerily inquired as soon as he had given the officers all he had to give.

"I'm sorry?" said Claire, not quite believing she had heard such a crass question. She had been momentarily distracted by the way Bill, his arms folded across his barrel chest the way all the bodybuilders in this place seemed to, had been stroking his prominent pectoral muscle with one thumb all the time he was talking to her. Was it an unconscious thing? She thought back to the morning, to his cheery tongue out at her. Almost certainly not, she decided.

"Who's the killer?" Bill said with relish.

Me, if I have to spend much more time with you. "I'm sorry, Mr. Kilby. This is just the start of what may well be a lengthy process. We are nowhere near ready to start giving out names yet."

Bill shrugged his over-developed shoulders. "Fair enough. Guess that means I'll be seeing a lot more of you around here then?"

"I hope not," Claire said. She noted Dave's smile behind Kilby's back and knew he hadn't missed the ambiguity.

"I'll look forward to it," said Bill, who obviously had. He turned as if to leave but just as quickly turned back to face her. "You know who you should be talking to, though, don't you?"

Claire sat up. Against the odds, was this disgusting man about to say something useful?

"Danny. Dan Thompson."

Dave flicked through his notes to Sue's list before shaking his head.

"Who is Dan Thompson and why should we see him?"

"Trains here. Used to be the big thing. Mr. West Midlands three times in a row. Used to be Susie's favourite." Bill gave what he presumably thought was a smile, but which came across as more of a leer. "Then Paul comes along. Course, you could see straight away which of them was the better bodybuilder. Susie definitely knew. Wasn't any doubt either who was going to be taking the West Midlands title next year." He leaned in and winked to underline his point in case he had made it too subtly. "It was going to be Paul." He straightened. "Dan's usually here every night round about this time. Funny he isn't tonight."

Claire couldn't believe it, but the obnoxious prat then tapped the side of his nose with one finger and winked at her before giving a cheery, "See you around," and leaving, giving Dave a mock salute on his way out.

Claire watched Kilby through the window. She needed to see Sue Green to ask her about this Dan Thompson but wanted to make damn sure Kilby was well gone before she ventured out. She saw Sue at the far end of the gym in conversation with a man rather incongruously dressed in a suit, presumably a prospective client scoping the gym out. She watched as Kilby passed Sue, waving a goodbye to her too in that provoking way of his, before making his way out through the gym door.

"What do you think?" she asked Dave as she waited to be absolutely sure the man was gone and not coming back.

"I think it's a shame," Dave murmured. "I mean, to get to that age and still be acting like a kid when it comes to women." Dave closed his book and put it back in his pocket. "But then what do you expect, when you've got teenage acne? All across the back and shoulders."

Chapter Five

"YOU SKIPPED SCHOOL?"

"One lesson."

"It's still truancy."

"No one calls it that anymore."

"It doesn't matter what they call it, Tony. It's still against the law."

"Isn't that putting it a bit strongly, love?" Ian said mildly.

"No. No, it bloody well isn't!" Claire exploded.

Sam started crying.

It had been a very hard, very long day. Claire had been exhausted by the time Dave dropped her off back home, then annoyed to find both Sam and Tony were still up. But before she could remonstrate with her husband, Ian had broken the news to her. Tony had been caught bunking off school.

"But you like geography!" Claire yelled.

"Mr. North was away," Tony said, a bundle of teenage moodiness.

"Well, that doesn't make any difference. He left work for you, didn't he?"

"Yes. We had a cover. Mrs. Grant."

Claire searched her memory. Though she had a police officer's head for names and details connected to crime, it embarrassed her that she could hardly ever remember the names of Tony's teachers. True, barely any of them were criminals but, given that they were all her husband's colleagues, and some of them his friends too, it was pretty shameful. For the most part, however, she'd been able to fool both husband and son in the past that she knew the people they were talking about. Not tonight, though; not after several hours of sweaty bodybuilders and a murder investigation that appeared to be going precisely nowhere.

"Maths teacher?" she ventured hesitantly.

"Science," Tony said in an accusing tone. "I had her in Year Seven, remember?"

"Well it hardly matters, does it? Where did you go if you weren't in the lesson? You weren't off back of the bike sheds smoking, were you?"

"I don't smoke, Mum," Tony said witheringly. "None of my friends smoke. And no one goes *behind the bike sheds* anymore. They're plastic and see-through."

"So what *do* they do these days, eh? Where were you?"

Some of Tony's superiority dropped away. "In the boys' loos."

"In the boys'... For Pete's sake, why?"

"Let it go, love."

Claire blinked at her husband in surprise. "Let it go?"

"He'll do a detention and that will be that. We get a lot of kids bunking off lessons, especially if they've got a cover teacher and think they can get away with it. He just got caught because Angela is so thorough."

Tony gave a strangled sound, somewhere between a laugh and a cough, but kept his head down, his floppy fringe hiding his eyes from both of them.

"It's no big deal," Ian concluded.

Claire looked from one to the other of her husband and her son as if finding two strangers before her. "But you're the one who always goes on about him not doing his homework."

"And sometimes kids need to kick back against the rules a bit, make their own mistakes."

"No! No son of mine is making his own mistakes."

"So, you going to make them for me?" Tony muttered from under his fringe.

"And you can knock off the smart remarks now, my lad. I've seen too many dropout, dead-end kids to let mine go down the same route."

"Do you think," Ian suggested cautiously, "you might just be overreacting a little?"

"I'm going to bed." Tony stood.

"You are staying right where you are!" Claire ordered.

"Why? So you can yell at me some more and then send me to my room anyway?" And Tony stormed out of the room.

Claire went to follow him, but Ian put a hand gently on her arm. "Let him go, love. He'll calm down."

With reluctance, Claire held herself back. How? How could it be that she spent every working day dealing, for the most part successfully, with difficult colleagues and even more difficult, potentially even dangerous members of the public, and yet her own teenage son could reduce her to a state of seething impotence in just under five minutes?

"What has got into him, Ian? And what has got into you? How you can be so laid back about this?"

"We've been lucky," said Ian wearily. "He's been a good kid up until now. He *is* a good kid. One missed lesson isn't going to turn him into Al Capone. But he's fourteen now. Year Nine. They're all little shits at that age."

The main object of her anger having left the room, Claire found herself turning its heat on Ian. It wasn't fair, she knew it wasn't, but she couldn't help herself. "That is not the way parents should react when they're told their kid has truanted."

"He's not my kid, though, is he?" Ian said softly.

Claire felt stunned, almost as if she'd been physically slapped. "You're his dad."

"No, love, I'm not."

"THOUGHT YOU WEREN'T coming."

"Hard day at the office."

"You work in an office?"

Dave winced. Two seconds into what Claire would inevitably be calling another date and he and this new guy were already on to the first forbidden question. "Figure of speech. Drink?"

I shouldn't be here. I really shouldn't be here. I had five hours sleep last night and I'm right at the start of a messy murder investigation. I shouldn't be here.

But he was. And why?

Debs, that was why.

The discovery that Cortez had a girlfriend had nettled Dave. Not, he'd quickly told himself, because the revelation of a female love interest had finally and definitively marked the undeniably attractive Cortez as out of bounds. He didn't fancy the other sergeant. Not really. Not like that, anyway. Cortez was handsome and his workouts in whatever Birmingham gym he went to were certainly doing the job. No, it was more that Dave had assumed Cortez was like himself: married to the job, all his energies focused on fighting the forces of crime, or at least getting the paperwork in on time. Now it had turned out that at least half of Terry's energies were focused on this Debs, and no one had so much as mentioned it in the office. Not in front of Dave, anyway.

Then there had been Summerskill's cracks about his love life.

So when *Funguy 29 GSOH straight-acting WLTM similar* had popped up on his mobile hookup app even as he was leaving Heavy Metal, Dave had thought, *Why the bloody hell not?* and had fired off a reply.

"Let me," said the man in front of him, dragging Dave's thoughts back to the matter in hand. "What do you fancy...?" He waited for a name.

"Den," said Dave, in answer to Funguy's question. He had deleted *Lenny* from his profile the instant he had got back from his encounter with Duncan.

"As in Dirty Den? Dennis the Menace?"

Oh God. Next time I'm using my real name. It has got to be easier. "Just as in Dennis."

"Ah right. I'm Mushroom."

"What?"

"Mushroom. As in *fungi. Fun. Guy.*"

"Ah. Right." Dave forced a smile.

"No, but seriously, I'm Wally. As in *Where's?*"

Dave held onto the smile. It took an effort. That had to be a real name. Or this guy had a truly bad sense of humour.

"So, drink?" Wally hesitated for a fraction of a second. "Or do you want to come back to my place? I live just down the road."

Fast worker. Dave considered. Though nobody's idea of a model, Wally was quite easy on the eye. A bit chubbier than in his profile pic but who didn't use their most flattering pics? *God knows I could do with a happy ending to a shit day. But...* "I'll have a pint, please. First," and Dave pointed randomly at an advert for some local brew. "Cheers."

He thought he caught a flicker of disappointment on Wally's face, but the other man duly went to order their drinks, and while he stood at the bar, Dave stepped over to the only small table in the place, tucked right into the corner, and took a seat. He realised already that, just like the last time, he hated this hastily chosen venue. Funguy had recommended The Retired Airman in Malvern as a "quiet little pub" and Dave had been all for that. But "'little" turned out to mean "microscopic," not much more than a bar with a row of seats in front of it, most of which were occupied by overweight, middle-aged men in T-shirts and jeans who had probably been there since opening time that morning. In the polo shirt and slacks he had pulled on in his brief return to his flat, all it would have taken to make Dave feel completely out of place would be for a tinkling piano in the corner to have stopped playing as he walked in.

On the wall was a rack of well-thumbed papers and magazines, and Dave idly flicked through them as he waited. They had all the topicality and freshness of a dentist's waiting room selection. He settled on one of the free newspapers as something that could at least improve his local knowledge, pulled it out, saw that the front-page report was on a possible outbreak of some sheep disease he'd never heard of, and opened it in search of something less agricultural.

When he saw the picture of Paul Best grinning out at him from page five, his first thought was how on earth had a bog-standard rag like this got onto the story so quickly. A check of the date, though, showed the paper to be over three weeks old. He started to read the report below the picture.

"The great thing about this place is you never have to wait long to get served." Wally was back with their drinks.

"I can believe that." Reluctantly, Dave rolled the paper up and shoved it into his jacket pocket. He was too sleep-deprived anyway, with his head in too many places at once, to fully take in the implications, if any, of what he had just read. Besides, there was absolutely nothing he could do with it until tomorrow, while right now he had a guy, who had already invited him back to his flat, and was buying him a drink. He moved his chair to one side so Wally could squeeze in next to him, and took a grateful pull on his beer. "Cheers."

Wally took a sip of his own drink, put the glass down, turned to left and right to look around himself with all the subtlety of a pantomime actor, leaned in close to Dave and whispered in his ear.

Inwardly, Dave groaned. He'd cut straight to the second question.

Chapter Six

DAVE HAD EXPECTED to be able to tell Claire of his find on their drive into work the next morning, but when he got up and checked his phone, he found a text from her telling him she was already in work.

Didn't sleep. Don't ask! the text concluded.

So, he wasted no time breaking his news on walking into their office. "Paul Best and Susan Green were in the paper together..."

"Three weeks and two days ago," Claire said. "I know." She held up a photocopy of the picture and article from the newspaper Dave was waving in her face. "Snap."

"How'd you find that?"

Claire indicated Jenny Trent perched, again, on the edge of Cortez's desk.

"Longshot," Jenny said with affected modesty that didn't fool Dave for a minute. "Best was supposed to be this big competition winner. I thought there might be something about one of his wins in one of the local rags, maybe a quote from some jealous rival, y'know?" And she affected a deep, vaguely Germanic drawl which Dave assumed was meant to be an Arnold Schwarzenegger tribute. "I should haf vun the trophy, so now I vill kill this Paul Best." She dropped back into her normal voice. "No such luck. The only competition results I found were tiny articles, little more than lists and weight divisions. But I did find this." She indicated the photocopy Claire was holding.

"Good work, Jen." Claire took pity on her partner's discomfit. "You too, Sergeant." She indicated the paper Dave had let fall to his side. "Where did you find it? Bit of late-night research?"

"Local pub," Dave said shortly, throwing the paper onto his desk as he took his seat in front of his computer.

"Not like you to hit the bars that time of night." Claire leaned forward over her desk towards him. "Or were you on another *date?*" She smiled across at Jenny as she emphasised the last word, inviting her to join in with a little friendly banter. Jenny picked up the photocopy she'd provided and studied it as if she hadn't seen it before.

"Just a drink," said Dave, busying himself with his keyboard.

"Let me see if I can find any follow-up to this article," Jenny said, abruptly rising from the desk.

"Great. Thanks, Jen."

Jenny left. Across the office, Claire noted Rudge and Cortez were deep in conversation about some case of their own. No time for banter either. Course not. Except if they'd been ribbing Terry about the gorgeous Debs, or Jenny about her latest Mr. Right, or even if Claire had been moaning about one of Ian's latest blunders or male inadequacies. They'd all have been joining in then, sharing similar experiences, mercilessly mocking. But not with Dave. *My kids aren't this difficult!* Claire thought, but then remembered the previous night's row about Tony's truancy.

"So, why didn't Susan Green mention this?" Dave was tapping the newspaper article with a pen.

Claire looked again at her copy. *"Local gym owner joins MP's Fight for Fitness,"* proclaimed the headline. *"Former competitive bodybuilder Susie Green has joined forces with Worcester MP Sean Cullen to get our country fighting fit once more."*

She quickly read through the rest of the article about Sean Cullen's campaign to raise public awareness of getting and staying healthy through sport. A former university rower himself, Cullen had been working hard for the past couple of years, cajoling local clubs and businesses to sign up to his "Fitness First" initiative. Sandwiched midway through the piece was a photograph. It had obviously been taken in a gym, though the superior quality of the facilities made it clear this wasn't Heavy Metal. Paul Best was standing in the foreground in gym trousers and vest, grinning inanely at the camera, flexing one pumped arm. Standing next to him in a suit was Cullen, also wearing a broad smile, while managing at the same time, rather awkwardly, to shake hands with the last person in the group. This was Sue Green—Susie Green as the caption identified her—dressed in a tracksuit and as cool as ever, more confidently posed and altogether more photogenic than the men.

Claire leaned in to the picture to take in its details. It could just have been the odd combination of a man in a suit in a gym making her think this, but wasn't this the guy she and Dave had glimpsed last night in Heavy Metal talking to Green? "It's just another MP doing a bit of good to keep his name in the papers," she muttered, almost to herself.

"Cynical," said Dave. "The paper says his campaign's done a lot for young people, the less well-off, and the elderly."

"So, no votes there then? Pure altruism." Something was tickling the back of Claire's mind. By no means a political animal, unless the politics affected her own pay and conditions, she nevertheless thought she remembered something about Sean Cullen. She snapped her fingers. Of course. "He bats for your team, doesn't he?" she asked Dave.

"No. He's Tory."

From behind them, there was a small sound. It sounded like a snicker and Claire suspected it came from Jim who was supposedly still deep in conversation with his sergeant. She ignored it and went back to the newspaper. The gist of the piece was that Sue Green had been the latest to sign up to Cullen's Fitness First programme, and Claire was impressed to see she was indeed pledging to make all sorts of offers that would help the less well-off to pump as much iron as they wanted. "*So, this summer we can all be flexing our biceps as proudly as Sue and her customers down at the Venus and Adonis gym in the Shambles shopping area,*" the article concluded.

So it wasn't aimed at the Heavy Metal demographic. Probably because that lot didn't read.

She took one last look at the picture. She wished she had Sue's obvious ease at being photographed, doubtless a legacy of her posing during her bodybuilding competition days. There she was, smiling at the camera. Next to her stood Sean Cullen, whom Claire now thought she vaguely recognised from other newspaper pictures in the past. He was a strikingly tall man with thick blond hair, cut in a style that was fashionable but not so fashionable as to alarm the notoriously fickle "Worcester Woman" voter. From the article and the dates given for his sporting achievements at university she worked out he must have been in his early forties at least, though to give him, or the photographer, his due, he could have been a good decade younger. He was also smiling with rehearsed confidence. He and Green were shaking hands in the artificial way so beloved of newspaper photographers, eyes fixed on the camera rather than each other. And there was Paul, flexing and grinning like a loon. Apart from his name in the caption under the picture, there was no other mention of him. He seemed to be there just as window dressing.

"Bit surprising, don't you think?" Dave persisted, interrupting her train of thought. "That she didn't mention this last night."

"Hardly. I expect she does a lot of this kind of thing all the time. And Best's just there as eye candy. He could have just been training there and they dragged him into the shot."

"Yeah, except the Venus and Adonis isn't his gym, is it? He trains at Heavy Metal. And check out his vest. That's the Venus and Adonis logo."

Okay. Dave was right. But so what? "C'mon, Sergeant. Best was a good advert for what going to a gym can do for you, so Green shoved him in a vest and pulled him into the picture. After all, he was 'The Best'."

Dave, unconvinced, turned back to his computer. "Email from Francis," he announced almost immediately.

Claire laid the paper to one side. She'd fired off a query to the local drugs division late last night. Given their workload, it was impressive they'd got back to her so quickly. "What does she say?"

Dave scanned his screen and paraphrased. "They're aware of steroid use in the area." He made a wry face. "Nice when a department does its job. There's been a marked increase in recreational use across the country in recent years and Worcestershire's no exception. However, there's nothing unusually dirty out there and no indication that rival firms are fighting over distribution rights. Circulation in the city is pretty small scale, one-on-one stuff, and all the usual sanctions and preventative measures are fully in place." He chanted the last words as if reading them from an autocue.

"Which translated means, *we are too busy chasing Class As to worry about a bunch of muscleheads shooting up on pump juice.*"

"Basically yes. She says there are a couple of local gyms they know are distribution hotspots, but Heavy Metal isn't one of them. She has, however, passed on their names and addresses and gives us her blessing to go give them a shakedown if we want to."

"There's kind. Tell her thanks, but she can do her own housework." She leaned back in her chair and ran her fingers through her hair. "I don't get it. This stuff is bad for you, right? I mean, even apart from shrinking your tackle, giving you spots, and making your hair fall out."

"Wrecks your heart and liver too," Dave added.

"So why aren't we doing more about it?"

"Maybe if the people who use steroids *looked* as bad as people hooked on smack then we would. But apart from the spots and thinning hair, most of the guys using them look damn good. And everyone wants that these days."

"But some of us are just born that way," proclaimed a new voice. "Stand by your beds: the doctor is in the house."

Dave grimaced and Claire suppressed a groan as Dr. Aldridge strode jauntily into the office waving a manila folder in the air in a way Claire assumed was meant to be teasing. "Blood work on Paul Best," he announced.

Claire was grudgingly impressed and grateful. "Fast work. You didn't have to bring it over yourself though."

"My pleasure," Aldridge purred.

"No, you really shouldn't have," Dave muttered under his breath.

"Positive for steroids?"

"Oh boy, yes!" said Aldridge, pulling out the chair in front of Claire's desk and dropping into it uninvited. "Paulie was definitely into stacking the 'roids. Stacking is when..."

"Bodybuilders use lots of different drugs at the same time. We know." Claire found herself already growing irritated by the arcane vocabulary such a bloody simple pastime as lifting weights had gathered around itself.

"Yes, well, it's not quite so simple," Aldridge said, reluctant to concede superior knowledge. "Different steroids have different effects. Certain combinations work well, and others most definitely do not. And you have to work in a series of quite carefully calculated cycles. Some of these himbos become quite good amateur chemists—in a strictly limited field, of course."

"So what precisely was Paul Best taking?" Dave asked.

"Precisely, Sergeant?" Aldridge didn't bother to turn around to Lyon as he answered his question but sat still facing Claire. "Blood work showed evidence of testosterone-cypionate and trenbolone-acetate used for bulking, masteron-propionate for cutting, that's reducing the amount of water in the tissues to make muscle definition stand out, and fluoxymesterone which is your basic strength booster." He spoke over his shoulder at Dave. "Precise enough for you?" He turned back to Claire. "Best may have been on other stuff too, but it could have been metabolised before we got our hands on his blood. He'd almost certainly have been on other steroids long before these."

"How do you know that?"

"Because these aren't gateway steroids. Dianabol, Arimidex, these are your GCSE steroids, if you like. The shit Best was on is degree level."

"Hardcore," Dave murmured.

"And the side effects?" Claire asked.

"In point of fact," Aldridge admitted, "apart from the slight external features, the late acne, and the hair loss, which might have been genetic anyway, there don't seem to have been any. Heart and liver both checked out as fine. Of course, I can't say what use the old love muscle was." Claire winced at the ghastly euphemism but wisely held her tongue. "Reduced libido is often a side effect, as is sterility, though I don't imagine that was something bothering our young man just yet. Interestingly enough, that side effect did once lead to steroids being considered as a form of male contraceptive." He leaned his head to one side in Dave's direction. "Not something we have to worry about, though, eh Sergeant?"

"I'm sure it's of no concern to you, Doctor."

"Are any of these steroids...unusual?" Claire asked. "Dangerous even?"

"No. Nothing unusual, as such, about any of them," said Aldridge. "All well-known and fairly easily obtained, especially over the internet. And as for dangerous, well, paracetamol is dangerous if you misuse it. Young as he was, I'd say Best was a fairly experienced user. He wasn't making the mistakes some kids do when they start, typically shoving anything and everything down their necks or into their veins."

"And what about 'roid rage? Would this stuff have made Best aggressive, dangerous even?"

To Claire's surprise, Aldridge seemed faintly embarrassed. "Probably not," he said, almost reluctantly. "I know we talked about this when last we met and I know I may have suggested it as a possibility, but I've been doing a bit of research since then and there is evidence that might not be the case."

Claire had to give him credit, Aldridge was admitting he might have been wrong about something, or at least that he hadn't been the expert he usually claimed to be on every subject under the sun.

"So Best was a pussycat?" Dave said.

"I did not say that. Steroids may not make people prone to rage. But it may be that people prone to rage are more likely to turn to steroids. And there'd be a big difference facing up to an angry person built like Paul Best and an angry person built like, let's say, for example, you."

Claire thought of those brushes with the law back in Bristol they'd dug up, and knew Dave was thinking about them too. But that'd been small beer, nothing beyond what many a young lad might get involved in.

The phone on Claire's desk rang and she picked it up. "Summerskill." She listened then covered the phone with her hand to speak to Dave. "Sue Green." She took her hand away. "Put her through. Hi. Sue. DI Summerskill here. Yeah? Yeah, you're right. Okay, thanks. We'll be right over." She put the phone down, stood, and grabbed her coat. "C'mon you, back to the gym. Sue's given us the heads up. The guy who skipped his training session yesterday, Daniel Thompson. He's just turned up at Heavy Metal. Let's go see why his routine's up the spout, shall we? As ever, thank you so much, Dr. Aldridge."

"Always a pleasure, never a chore, Inspector," Aldridge said, rising from his chair as Claire swept out of the room. "Sergeant," he added, as Dave strode past.

"Doctor," Lyon replied.

Chapter Seven

SUE HADN'T BEEN there to meet them when they arrived at Heavy Metal, but Marc had obviously been briefed, and with his customary lack of grace he pointed to the guy they should interview.

"Can't imagine why Sue Green doesn't use him on publicity photos," Dave muttered, as they made their way across the gym floor.

"I doubt even a Photoshopped smile would stick on that face," Claire replied. "Hang on a minute." Abruptly, she stopped and pointed to one of the mirrored walls.

Dave looked, then looked again more closely. "Interesting. Shall we?"

"I think we shall."

The object of their attention saw them change direction and start heading towards him. He scanned quickly to left and right as if seeking an escape, but the only way out was through the advancing Summerskill and Lyon. He sank onto a bench and waited for the officers to reach him.

"Hello, Robert," said Claire. "Quite a black eye you've got there."

"Walked into a door," Rob said flatly.

"Careless," said Dave.

"I were pissed, weren't I?"

"Lot of sugar in alcohol, Robert," said Dave. "Not good for the body."

"Not good for the eyes," said Claire. "By the look of it."

"What do you want?"

"Just following up on some leads." Claire gave a small smile. "You'd be amazed how people remember things they forgot to tell us the first time round. Have you remembered anything you might want to tell us now, Robert?"

Robert shifted uncomfortably under Summerskill's level gaze. "No. Can I go now?"

"Of course you can. We're not here to arrest you." *Let's just put that thought out there.* "This isn't even a formal interview. But, Robert," she added, as the young man went to rise and walk away from them. "You will let us know if anything comes to mind, won't you? Anything that could help us find out how your friend died?"

"And you'll let us know if you have any more trouble with doors, yeah?" Dave added. "That last one gave you a right seeing-to."

Robert stalked off without another word into the changing rooms. "Do you believe him?" Dave asked Claire.

"Course not."

"Right. And..."

"Inspector!"

Claire turned and immediately wished she hadn't. "Oh bugger," she said under her breath. Dave grinned.

Bill Kilby was striding towards them, a thick towel wrapped around his neck and a big smile on his face.

"Mr. Kilby," she said out loud, then, "C'mon!" in a harsh whisper to Dave, turning and making it obvious she was about to move off. It was no use.

Kilby walked right up to them, closer than Claire would have liked. She noticed he was wearing the same exercise vest as last time. All the evidence suggested it hadn't seen the inside of a washing machine between then and now. "I see you've taken my advice," he said.

"I'm sorry?"

Kilby leaned in a little closer. Claire wished he hadn't. "You've come to have a word with Danny Thompson."

"We are...just tying up some loose ends after our last visit, Mr. Kilby. If you'll excuse us?"

"Of course," he said. He took one step back then stopped. "If you want me, I'll be on the bench by the water fountain."

Claire assured him they'd call him if they needed him and assured herself inwardly they never would.

When Summerskill and Lyon reached Daniel Thompson, he had finished the set of exercises he'd been working on and was sitting up on the end of his bench, swigging from a water bottle. He didn't seem surprised to see them. He didn't seem happy about it either. Claire noticed that whatever he was drinking was an odd purple colour. *Do bodybuilders drink meths?*

"Mr. Thompson?" Claire held out her police ID card. Dave, one step behind, mirrored her action. "My name is Detective Inspector Summerskill. This is Detective..."

"Yeah, yeah, police, I know. You want to ask me about Paul Best, right?"

"Sergeant Lyon," Claire concluded. She pocketed her card. "That is correct."

"He was a cocky little git and probably got what he deserved."

Refreshingly honest. "Are you aware of the manner of Mr. Best's death, Mr. Thompson?" *And do you think anyone deserves that?*

Thompson nodded once and stopped just shy of shrugging. Claire briefly considered taking him into Sue Green's office. There was no one in earshot, though, and she'd had enough of being in confined spaces with sweaty weightlifters. She looked pointedly at the bench Thompson was sitting on. Grudgingly, he shifted along to one edge and Claire sat down next to him. Dave remained standing, pen poised over his notepad.

"Let's not beat about the bush, Danny," she began.

"Dan," he said firmly.

"Dan. You obviously didn't like Paul Best. Fair enough. We can't all like everybody. But *why* did you dislike him?"

"He was...," Thompson began, then stopped, obviously forcing himself to choose his words with care. "He was full of himself."

Claire nodded as if agreeing or, at the very least, as if thinking about what he had just said. "But, don't you have to be? Confident. Assertive even. If you're competing, I mean." She gestured to Thompson's built frame. "I don't imagine you get far in your game if you're a shrinking violet."

Thompson gave a grunt. It might have been agreement.

"Can I ask where you were on the evening of the nineteenth?"

Thompson's eyes hardened. "What, so you're thinking I might have done it?"

"Just routine questions, Dan."

"I was at home. All night."

"Alone?"

"Yes."

"So, forgive me, no one to corroborate that?"

"No."

"Right. Some of the people we've interviewed have suggested there was...some bad feeling between you and Paul Best." *Like you hadn't made that clear enough yourself.* As she asked the question, Claire watched Thompson closely. She was aware of Bill Kilby across the gym, none too subtly also watching what was going on. She wanted to see if Thompson gave any sign he knew Kilby was her source. "Was that true?"

Thompson took another swig from his bottle of oddly coloured water but when he raised his head again it was to look at her, not at Kilby. "Best was a thieving little shit, and he didn't care who knew it."

"Thieving? You're saying he stole things from you?"

"Cheating then. He was on the juice, wasn't he? Steroids. You don't get as big as quick as he did without getting a ton of shit down your neck."

"Okay, but he can't have been the only one, can he, Dan?" said Dave. "I mean, from what we've heard, most bodybuilders these days are using some kind of...chemical help." They waited, alert for some kind of response: anger, denial? Dan just sat there, staring at the ground between his trainers. "But you don't?" he pressed, taking in the man's swollen arm muscles, pumped chest, and frankly unbelievable thighs.

"It's not like that," Thompson muttered.

"I'm sorry, Mr. Thompson," Claire said. "This is a whole new world to us. You're going to have to explain."

Thompson took a deep breath. "People outside the sport don't get it, but bodybuilding is literally about being the best you can. About pushing yourself as hard and as far as you can. And yeah, okay, if you can get a little help along the way..."

"Steroids," Dave interjected.

"Then you go for it," Thompson continued, darting an angry glare at Dave but otherwise ignoring his comment. "But the work has to come first. You earn your successes, you don't buy them. You get it?"

Claire didn't get it. She doubted Dave did either. The one thing she did know was that the man's obvious double standards were making her feel distinctly queasy. "And by successes you mean..." Dave mouthed the words *West Midlands* at her. "Mr. West Midlands? That was you, I believe?" Dave held up three fingers. "Three times running?"

Her opinion of Dan Thompson sank another notch as he visibly brightened under her blatant flattery. "Yeah," he said.

"Though the smart money was on Best taking the title this year." She caught Dave rolling his eyes but was unrepentant. She wanted to see how Thompson reacted to the goad. And she hadn't been able to resist puncturing the vain gorilla's swollen ego.

"I'll get there," he said, in a tone that was practically a snarl. "I'm training harder, smarter, and for longer. Best was big, was moving the weights, but it's about more than size and weights. There's conditioning and performance. Most competitions are won just in the last week through diet. And now that he's not in it..." Thompson ground to an abrupt halt, suddenly aware of what he had been about to say.

"Now that Paul Best is not in the competition, you're the favourite to win it again, aren't you, Mr. Thompson?"

Suddenly, this muscular inflation of a man was like a rabbit finding itself trapped in headlights, and Claire couldn't deny it made a welcome contrast to the Charles Atlas bombast she'd just had to sit through.

"Aw c'mon!" he exploded. "You're not saying I killed him just so's I could take the trophy again? That's mad. I mean, it's big, yeah, it's important, but it's not...!"

"A matter of life or death?" Dave suggested.

"I can't help thinking, Mr. Thompson, that when a man focuses as hard on a goal as you've told us you have to focus, when you push yourself for as long and as hard as you say you have, then maybe, just maybe you could...lose your sense of perspective?" She paused to give him a tight smile. "When I say you, I mean any man...in your position."

Thompson was now visibly squirming, and Claire couldn't deny an indecent pleasure from watching him. "What? I mean... I didn't say... I mean... Aw, c'mon! You can't really believe...."

No, Claire reluctantly admitted to herself. *I don't. But I've shaken you up, haven't I? So let's see what falls out.* "Do you know where Paul Best got these steroids you say he was taking?"

Thompson hesitated. Summerskill and Lyon waited. "No," he said finally.

Damn! He was lying. They both knew it. But Claire could sense something else too and had no doubt Dave could also. Thompson was over six feet tall, well over two hundred pounds, and built like the proverbial. But he was lying because he was shit scared of something. She could practically smell it. Even over Heavy Metal's polluted atmosphere.

"Thank you, Mr. Thompson." Claire stood, fighting the urge not to wipe off her trousers whatever was making them stick slightly to the cheap plastic of the bench. "We'll be in touch."

"More detailed background check?" Dave asked as they made their way back across the gym floor to the exit.

"Definitely."

Just before they reached the desk and the miserable Marc, the gym door opened, and Sue Green came in, bearing a tray and followed by a familiar man. "Glad I caught you before you left," she said brightly. She gestured to the man following her. "There's someone I thought you might like to meet. Inspector Summerskill. Sergeant Lyon. This is Sean Cullen."

THE NEW ARRIVAL stepped forward, hand outstretched. "Pleased to meet you." He smiled diffidently. "I'm..."

"Our local MP," Claire said taking his hand. "Yes, I do know."

Cullen laughed. "You'd be amazed how many people don't know who their local MP is. Or depressed."

I'd have been hard-pushed to pick you out in a lineup too, if I hadn't just seen your face in that paper, Dave thought. He took the MP's hand when it was offered. *Firm. Very firm.*

"As I said before," Sue Green went on breezily, "I can't offer you much in the way of decent coffee here, so I took the liberty of popping down to the coffee shop on the corner to pick something up. Sean here was on his way to talk about the Fitness First programme, so I've got one for him too." She gestured to a small table set up to one side of the reception desk and the two battered sofas on either side of it.

"I'm afraid..." Dave began.

"Very kind. Thank you, Sue," Claire said, and she sat down on one of the sofas. Silently, after the smallest of pauses, Dave joined her.

"You know about the Fitness First programme, I hope?" Cullen asked as he took his seat facing them.

"Of course," Claire said.

For all of two hours, Dave thought.

"Great." Cullen grinned. "It's a terrific cause and one I genuinely believe in. But it's a bit of a relief not to have to evangelise all of the time."

She said she'd heard of it. She didn't say she wanted to sign up to it. Dave watched as inspector and politician engaged in small talk. Was she actually warming to him? Maybe it was just the contrast with the largely monosyllabic bunch they'd met so far in this gym. Maybe it was the charming, rather boyish smile. *Professional politician. Take it with a pinch of salt!* Or maybe it was the good looks. Dave had the sudden feeling someone was watching him. Sue Green was suddenly busying herself with the tray of cardboard cups she had brought. But he could see she was smiling. "You didn't tell us you were working with Mr. Cullen," he said to her.

"Sean, please," said Cullen, but Dave kept his eyes on Sue.

Sue paused in the act of removing the coffee cups from their cardboard tray. "I don't think I did," she said, "but then it doesn't really have anything to do with...why you're here, does it?"

"Your picture was in the paper with Mr. Cullen—Sean—and with Paul Best. Only about three weeks ago."

"Oh that. D'you know, I'd completely forgotten about that. Poor Paul," she said softly. "The local paper had sent their girl around to interview Sean and me about Fitness First and to take a couple of pictures. I think she saw Paul and quite fell for him so the next thing we knew, she'd dragged him into the frame and told him to stand there in the background flexing his guns while she took shots of Sean and me."

"Not that Paul needed much encouragement to show off a bit, did he?" Cullen added.

"You sound like you knew him quite well," Dave said.

"It's just what I saw on that occasion. Not to speak ill of... Well, let's just say the boy was a bit of a peacock."

"But then I suppose that's what bodybuilding is all about, isn't it?" said Claire. Dave could tell she was irritated by the lead he'd been taking and the directions he'd been steering them. "Showing off, I mean," she explained. "That is," she added, realising too late just who she was talking to.

Sue Green laughed. "You're not wrong," she said, clearly not offended at all. "That's one of the reasons I got out of competition. Showing off's excusable in the young, but sooner or later it's something we should all grow out of."

"You'd be no good as a politician then," Cullen said.

Green laughed again. "Now, I've taken the liberty of guessing what kind of coffees people would like. So it's skinny lattes for you and me, Claire—" and she handed over a steaming paper cup to the inspector "—and I thought you and our member of parliament here would both be cappuccino types." She smiled at Claire in what Dave sourly assumed was an attempt at girlish confidence. "Strong and dark."

"Well, half right," Cullen said. He gestured to his decidedly Nordic features. "I'm not dark."

There was an awkward silence.

"Do you have any sugar?" Claire said. "Or is that like asking for rare steak in a vegan restaurant?" With a reproving tut, Sue asked Marc to go and find some sugar for them. He returned with an opened bag which he left with little ceremony in the centre of the table.

"Was Paul involved in any other publicity work with you or Mr. Cullen?" Dave asked, well aware of Claire's glare and choosing to ignore it.

"No. No, I don't think he was." Sue looked to Cullen who considered and shook his head.

"How long have you been with Foregate Street, Sergeant?" Cullen asked.

Dave was mildly surprised to have a question asked of him. "Getting on for two months now." He only just held himself back from ending the answer with a *sir*.

"And before you came here?"

"Redditch."

Cullen nodded. "Chief Superintendent...Jones," he said, after the briefest pause for thought.

Now Dave definitely was surprised. "You know him?"

"I have to mix with all manner of the great and good," Cullen said, raising his cup. "Hence my association with Sue here."

"Which brings us back to part of the reason we're all sitting here," Sue said. "Sean's Fitness First programme and the real benefits I think getting Foregate Street police station to sign up for it would have for the whole of our community."

"You really are a businesswoman, aren't you, Sue?" Dave said.

Sue gave him a broad smile. "Most of the time."

"YOU REALLY ARE an ungrateful cuss, aren't you?" Claire said as she and Lyon walked back to their car.

"What?"

"You were being fixed up back there."

"Fixed up or set up?"

"*Set up?* My God, you're ungrateful *and* paranoid."

"And you're dead set on pairing me off with everyone involved with this case."

Claire considered. "Okay, so the lad..."

"Robert Taylor."

"Was just a bit of banter. But Sean Cullen's an MP. So, he must have some kind of brain. And he's gorgeous."

"And he's a Tory."

"Gorgeous?"

"Tory. And definitely not my type."

"I'm definitely beginning to wonder if you've even got a type."

They got into their car. "You really think Sue Green was trying to set me up with him?"

"I think that may have been part of it, yes."

Dave turned the car key viciously in the ignition. "Bloody cow!"

"What? What is it with you and her?"

"Maybe it's that I'm not up for a spot of matchmaking during a murder investigation."

"*Matchmaking?* I thought gays were supposed to be cool. No one calls it matchmaking anymore."

"So, you'd have been okay with it, would you, if she'd tried to fix you up with someone?"

"I'm married."

"And does she know I'm not?"

"It's a fairly safe bet..." Claire stopped too late as she realised the misstep she'd just taken.

"A fairly safe bet that a gay man under fifty probably isn't married or even if he is he'll be up for a little bit of fun with some random guy he's never met before."

"Not *random*. Successful. Handsome. Quite probably well off." But even as she listed Cullen's supposed attributes, Claire knew she was defending a losing argument.

They drove on in silence for a few minutes.

"I'm wondering if you're just a bit intimidated by a strong woman," Claire said finally, feeling it was an unworthy crack even as she said it, but hating not to have the last word.

"I'm not intimidated by you."

"Well. You bloody well should be."

Chapter Eight

SUE GREEN STOOD, hands on hips, and surveyed the gym floor at Heavy Metal. It could have been worse. The news about Paul had been out in the media now for nearly a week, even the details of the gruesome nature of his death, along with much speculation as to what the actual cause might have been. She'd feared that might be bad for business, that it would drive people away. Then she'd briefly considered the opposite possibility, that Heavy Metal might have become a focus for sensation-seeking rubberneckers.

She needn't have worried. Heavy Metal had only been mentioned in passing once in all the reports she had seen and read. If there were any crime tourists, they were presumably getting their kicks around Shrub Hill station where the body had been found. As far as she could tell, after the brief stir caused by Summerskill and Lyon's visits, business was pretty normal. All the usual clients she'd expect at this time of day were in and working out as per. She paused, taking in one particular workbench. A new client, though obviously not a gym virgin judging by the build of him. Fit. In every sense of the word.

Casually, Sue wandered over, passing the odd word with some of the regulars on the way. When she got to his bench, she stood politely to one side, waiting until he had finished his set of inclined dumbbell presses. Quite impressive weights, and when he finished, he laid the dumbbells back on the floor, not letting them drop to the ground in the showy way some of the other guys did. She liked that. She stepped round so she was standing in front of him and extended her hand.

"Hi. I'm Sue Green, the owner. You're new here, aren't you?"

The man on the bench hurriedly wiped his hand with a towel and returned the handshake. "Yeah. I'm Terry. Terry Cortez."

IT'D HAD BEEN Dave's idea, and Terry hadn't liked it one bit. Which kind of pleased Dave.

A background check on Robert Taylor had told them he'd been excluded from two high schools as a lad and had completed his education at a local pupil referral unit. After that there had been a string of petty offences, mostly drink-related, culminating in a shoplifting conviction. "Two bottles of bargain basement cider," Dave read out from his conviction report.

"Classy," Claire remarked.

The judge had decided enough was enough and Robert had received a two-month custodial sentence. According to his probation worker, this had been a turning point.

"Short sharp shock worked, did it?" Claire asked.

"Not exactly. He made a discovery while he was banged up. Weight-training." He read on. "His probation worker said his new interest in bodybuilding gave him a real focus, attainable goals that he wanted to achieve. Her main worry was that, on the outside, he just wouldn't be able to afford to keep it up. Interesting. Guess who came to the rescue. Sean Cullen. Well, indirectly. Robert Taylor was one of the first disadvantaged kids to benefit from the Fitness First Initiative Sue Green is trying to sign us up to." He put down the papers he had been reading from. "The man's a regular Samaritan."

Claire groaned. "Life would have been a damn sight easier if we'd turned up a conviction for axe murder. All right. Time to take stock. What have we got?"

Dave checked his notebook but, given the little they had to go on, didn't need to refer to it. "One dead guy, almost certainly murdered. Possible manslaughter but definite attempt to conceal the circumstances and to obstruct the course of justice. Bit of a lad, not universally liked, but, so far as we can tell, nobody so pissed off by him that they had enough of a motive for murder."

"Unless they're mad."

"There is always that happy possibility." Dave tapped the report on Taylor with his notebook pencil. "I think this guy is our best bet."

"More than Thompson, the jealous rival?"

"Bill Kilby said Best was *going* to take Thompson's title from him. The time to get jealous is *after* the event, not before. And even then, to get murderous over a poxy local competition?"

"Mr. West Midlands," Claire reminded him.

"Yeah. Right."

"You don't think Kilby did it, do you?"

"That's just wishful thinking on your part."

"You're right. I'd so like to see him stick his tongue out at me from behind bars." She picked up the report on Dave's desk. "So, Taylor you say. His mate."

"Yeah. And that's why. They were mates. But what if they had fallen out over something? Or what if Best had simply got tired of Taylor? Taylor clearly wasn't in his league when it came to bodybuilding. He's only a kid. And he's obviously not bright. Some kids can't handle it. They argue. They fight..."

"And Robert nearly pulls his head off?"

"It's a theory. I haven't worked out all the bugs yet."

"No. I don't see it." She sighed. "You're right about kids and friendships breaking down, though."

"Sorry?"

"Oh, it's nothing. It's Tony. He was put on report yesterday at school. For fighting."

Dave thought about the young lad he'd got to know over the last month or so. Quiet. A little shy at first. But friendly enough for a teenager, especially when they had discovered their mutual love of science fiction at his first excruciating dinner party at Claire's. "I wouldn't have expected that."

"Me neither! Right out of the blue."

"What kind of fight? Schools sometimes exaggerate."

"Not much more than a scuffle really, but the thing is, it was with his best mate, Brett." Claire hesitated. "Or Barney. Something beginning with B. Anyway, ordinarily, parents would have been called in—I think the other lad's parents were—but Ian being on site, he dealt with our side of it." She sighed. "With the result that Tony is now being a little shit with Ian because Ian got cast as the bad cop..."

"Ironic."

"Only because I didn't have time to get into school because of this mess of a case."

"Sam okay?" Dave asked, not sure how or even if he should comment any further on this domestic.

"No, he's being a right little shit too." Claire leaned back on her chair again and ran her fingers through her hair. "Actually, that's a bit unfair, I suppose. He's just being clingy and whiny, probably because we're all at each other's throats."

Dave nodded slowly as if he understood. He didn't. There were times when he wondered how different his life might have been if he'd been straight, if there'd been a family waiting for him at home at the end of every long day. They weren't frequent, though, and he rarely imagined a wife and string of little Daves would really make life better. The picture Claire was painting only confirmed that. "So, what was the fight over?"

"Name-calling. Stupid boy stuff. I tell you, I wish I'd had girls."

"Boys are more affectionate."

"You would say that."

"I mean, as children," Dave said patiently. "That's what my mum always said anyway."

"And she had two boys, right?" Dave nodded. "Then she was only making the best of a bad situation, trust me."

"So, you were never a minute's trouble to your parents then?"

Claire ignored that one. "I guess I should have expected this. He's fourteen now, going on fifteen. That means I've had two okay teenage years out of, what is it, seven? I should count myself lucky. I just don't understand why he's changed so much in such a short space of time. He'd never been a minute's trouble at school until now. Is it a boy thing?" She carried on before Dave even had a chance to consider how to respond. "I've asked Ian if he was like that, but he was just bloody perfect at school. According to his mum and dad too," she added under her breath.

In-laws. Dave added them to his list of a straight life's downsides. "So, you're saying girls don't change in adolescence. Didn't you?"

"We don't *change.* We *mature.* I didn't have time to fight other girls. I was into...things."

"Other boys?"

"Like you? Or did you go off the rails too?"

"Not exactly off the rails," Dave said slowly, "but definitely off the straight and narrow."

Claire leaned forward, clearly happy for a moment to put the case and her home life on hold in the light of these fascinating glimpses into Dave's early life. "So, did you start kicking off? Truanting? Fighting?"

"Actually," Dave admitted, "I overcompensated. Threw myself into schoolwork. I think Mum and Dad could hardly believe their luck. I was the apple of Dad's eye—for a while."

"God, I am surrounded by boring men!"

"I made up for it later."

Claire was unconvinced. "Did you? Because you're not making up for it now. How's the boyfriend hunt going?"

"Which brings us back to the case in hand," Dave said, none too subtly.

"Why don't you ever want to...?"

"Madden."

The reminder of their Chief Superintendent, waiting for some kind of result, focused Claire's mind wonderfully. "All right, all right. One dead body. And only two real suspects, neither of whom, when all's said and done, are that suspicious. And, as far as we can see, only one thing in common."

"The Heavy Metal gym."

"I was referring to the giant, overdeveloped elephant in the gym."

"Steroids?"

"I want to know where they are coming from. I know," she said in the face of Dave's obvious doubt, "but there's nothing else to go on. God!" She jammed both elbows onto her desk, threw her head into her hands, and massaged her temples. "Why couldn't this have come up when I still had a family at home, not a zoo?"

Dave opened one of the drawers in his desk, took out a bottle of paracetamol, and chucked it to his boss.

"Thanks," said Claire, "and could you...?"

"Already on it."

Dave headed for the office percolator and poured out two mugs. As he put Claire's mug down in front of her, he pointed to the writing on its side. The wobbly letters spelled out, *Worlds' Best Mum.* "Something to remember when things get tough," he said.

"That was Sam, with a lot of help from his teacher."

"Shame she couldn't help him with his apostrophes."

Claire knocked back two tablets and washed them down with the coffee. "I'd send you in undercover to that fleapit of a gym if I thought we could get away with it."

"I'm pretty sure I'd be recognised now."

"I meant, if we could get away with convincing people you'd want to be a bodybuilder."

"Thanks. Can I have my bottle back?"

"What we need," said Claire, narrowing her eyes and staring into the steam from her mug, "is someone who could pass as a gym rat and sniff around a bit, find out where the stuff they're all using is coming from and what, if anything, it had to do with Best's murder."

Dave grinned, for the most part good-humouredly. "And you really can't think of anyone?"

"IS THIS YOUR first day in the gym?" Sue Green asked Cortez.

"Second," he replied.

"I hope Marc gave you the grand tour."

Terry thought back to the previous day's introduction. *These are the legs machines. These are the abs machines. This is a free weights area. You got any questions?* "Yes. He did, thank you. Very...thorough."

Sue Green laughed. "I know, I know. Not the most articulate member of staff but if you want someone reliable to spot for you just give him a whistle and he'll do the job." She leaned back a little on the bench, the better to take in all of Terry. "And I'm guessing you know your way around a gym anyway. Am I right?"

"I try to stay in shape."

Sue nodded appreciatively. "Well, you're doing a good job of it." She leaned in closer and, even over the gym's signature smells, Terry caught the scent of her perfume, a heavy, musky scent, nothing like the flowery stuff Debs used. "Although," she said, glancing around herself to check they were unobserved, and lowering her voice, "I find myself wondering why you're here."

"I'm sorry?" Inwardly, Terry swore. Just for a second, he'd thought perhaps this woman was coming on to him. Now he feared she had already rumbled him as an undercover cop after only having spoken to him for a few seconds. *Damn Summerskill for talking me into this. "Just for a week. Maybe two. Just to sniff around for a bit. You look the part."* Yeah, that'd been the hook, hadn't it? *She played me like a pro and now I'm going to end up looking like a prat. Couldn't have got her own sergeant to do it, could she? Yeah right. Like that would have worked. Neither of them are going to let me live this down.*

"Don't get me wrong," Sue Green went on. "Heavy Metal is a great gym, and if it's what you're looking for, then we're happy to help. But I do have other gyms, you know. Another one less than a mile away in the city centre, the Venus and Adonis." She reached out and lightly touched the designer label on Terry's vest, her eyes turning briefly to the matching label on his shorts. "It caters for...a slightly different kind of clientele."

Terry shifted slightly on the bench. He felt its plastic surface, slick next to the bare skin of his thighs. Moving one of his feet, he felt the stickiness of the worn carpet underneath. Yeah, he was definitely used to a better training environment than this, and he could well imagine the upmarket Venus and Adonis was more in his style. "Nah," he said, smiling back at the attractive woman sitting so close to him, "this is exactly where I want to be at the moment."

"I'm happy to hear that."

There was a slight pause. "I was thinking new gym, new start," Terry said to fill the silence. "Time to get down to what I want to do, y'know?"

Sue sat down next to him. The bench was short and narrow. She was very close to him. "And what might that be?"

Their eyes now on the same level, Terry noticed how striking they were. Quite stunningly green. "Get big," he said. "I mean, I definitely want to bulk up, y'know? I heard this was the place to go. If you want to make gains."

Sue put her hands behind her and leaned back on the bench.

Okay, she's older than my normal type, but she has got a fabulous figure. Better than Debs? No, no, no. Don't go there.

"Well, we can certainly do that for you," she said. "Yes, you have definitely come to the right place." Abruptly, she stood up, unselfconsciously readjusting the perfect cut of her training top as she did. "Let me draw up a training schedule for you. There's normally a small fee, but you can have the first one on the house. It'll be ready for you next time you come in and I'll get Marc to take you through it and spot for you." She leaned down again slightly, and Terry caught another hint of heavy scent. "Or I could take you through it myself. I am fully qualified."

"I know. I mean, you're obviously very...fit." *Debs would kill me if she was here.*

Sue straightened up and laughed. "Thank you. I'll see you tomorrow then, same time?"

Terry nodded, and Sue walked off to another part of the gym, leaving him to try to work out exactly what had just happened. *She was coming onto me, wasn't she? Was I coming onto her? Well, I'm only human. But would it count as entrapment if I did find anything out? More importantly, would Debs see it as all just in a day's work? Shit! I'm not cut out for this kind of stuff. But she is...*

"A cracker, isn't she?"

A squat man in ill-matching vest and shorts had come over to stand by him and was grinning at him and holding out a hand. "You're new, aren't you? I'm Bill Kilby."

"CAN I HELP you, sir?"

Dave turned around to find a petite young woman in a rather smart white polo shirt smiling at him from behind the reception desk. He smiled warmly back at her. "I hope so, thank you. I was just passing through and I thought I'd come and have a look-see. I've heard a lot about you."

The girl smiled even more, her teeth quite dazzlingly white. "That's always nice to hear. Well, welcome to the Venus and Adonis. My name's Maia." She stepped out from behind the reception desk and shook Dave's hand. "Let me show you around."

This place even smells nicer than the other one, Dave thought, as Maia walked him through the different areas of the gym, showing him the extensive range of machines, the free weight areas with their variety of coloured kettle weights as well as more traditional dumbbells and barbells, and the warm-up and cool-down matted areas. Everything was bright, colourful, coordinated, and apparently new, and none of the weights even approached the frankly insane size of the largest weights at Heavy Metal. Dave was assured that, as well as being able to use all of their cutting-edge equipment, if he took up membership of the Venus and Adonis, he could also sign up for any number of classes to help him stretch, tone, reduce or increase any part of his body he cared to identify. As Maia chatted on, Dave discreetly took note of the people working out. Far fewer tattoos and much better kit. Less swearing too. Instead of the crash of weights bouncing off the floor and colourful expletives, the air was filled with soft Muzak and the gentle chink of significantly lighter and less stressful weights and machines.

"And should you ever feel like a little pampering at the end of a heavy workout," Maia was saying, "Alys here is our latest recruit."

Maia ushered forward another, even younger woman from a small room where she had been hanging back, peeking out at the new arrival. She too was wearing the white polo shirt Maia had on, bearing the gym's logo, a stylised V and A embroidered in purple silk, but over it, she wore a salt-white coat like a doctor or dentist. She gave the smallest of smiles and nodded rather than shook hands. Dave caught the briefest flash of disapproval from Maia at the girl before she went on with an unflagging level of enthusiasm.

"Alys has just joined us from one of our other branches. She's training to be a masseuse and beauty therapist. And don't you go telling me," she added, wagging a playful finger at Dave, "that you men don't make a fuss over your appearance. My boyfriend's had more facials and waxings than I have, if you can believe it."

Dave said he could and wondered if he should have said he couldn't. "From one of your other branches," he said, as much as anything to change the subject. "Heavy Metal by any chance?"

He couldn't imagine the rather mousy Alys fitting in there. He knew competitive bodybuilders had their body hair removed for competitions so perhaps she had been at Heavy Metal for that, but from what he'd seen of the guys there, he wouldn't have been shocked if they'd just scraped off superfluous hair with broken glass.

Maia gave another of her small laughs which were, Dave realised, beginning to grate on his nerves. "No, no. Heavy Metal and Venus and Adonis are just two of the five run by our owner, Susan Green. You might have heard of her?"

Dave made an ambiguous sound which Maia chose to take as a no, using the opportunity to launch into a fulsome eulogy of her boss, detailing not just her successes in bodybuilding but her achievements as the owner of a small but growing chain of gyms, her work for charity, and her generosity as an employer.

And when does she come up with a cure for cancer and the common cold?

"So, at the moment," Maia said, coming to the end of what Dave was internally labelling as her *spiel,* "Sue Green runs five gyms. This one, Heavy Metal down on the Blackpole trading estate." Maia dropped her voice conspiratorially while scanning the gym. "Different clientele," she whispered. *You can say that again.* "Two others in the south-east and south-west, and she's currently completing a deal that will lead to another opening in the north. Manchester." Her tone of voice suggested she herself was rather in awe of that.

Dave gave the whistle of mild surprise which Maia seemed to expect from the idea of a gym so far away.

"And she's got plans to open at least two more in the next year or so." Maia lowered her voice again. "Though don't ask me where. Trade secret."

Dave promised her he wouldn't ask.

"And the great thing is, membership of one is membership of all."

Catchy.

The telephone back on the reception desk began to ring. A ripple of irritation crossed Maia's carefully made-up features. He could read the conflict in her face: the professional pull to answer the phone, and the angler's reluctance to let go of this catch of a new member before she had landed him.

"Please," he said, gesturing towards the phone.

Maia hesitated but then surrendered to her professional instincts. "I won't be a minute," she said, dashing off towards the reception desk. "Alys. Why don't you show Mr. Lyon our photo wall?" And she was gone.

Dave turned to Alys who was standing there with a face like a startled mouse, obviously unhappy at finding herself the sudden focus of his attention. For a moment, he even wondered whether she might bolt back to her massage parlour, beauty room, or whatever she called it. In the end, she simply ducked her head, the better to avoid his eyes, and gestured to a part of the gym they hadn't visited. Dave stepped back so she could lead the way and followed.

Alys took him to a wall with a water cooler and a pair of sofas, far plusher and more comfortable than the ones he and Claire had squashed up on back at Heavy Metal.

"These are pictures of Mrs. Green," Alys said, rather unnecessarily, pointing at the many photos fixed to the wall. Her words were heavily accented. Dave guessed she was Polish, early twenties, if that, and her youth plus the slightly stilted way in which she spoke suggested reasons for why she had been reluctant to take over Maia's sales pitch. She was simply not as fluent as her supremely slick colleague.

Dave moved closer to the wall to inspect the pictures.

They came in all sizes, landscape and portrait, mostly colour though some were black and white. A few were printouts, some came from newspapers and magazines, but most were best quality photographs. They featured a host of different people, but all contained Sue Green.

"This is Mrs. Green with actor Richard Grey. This is Mrs. Green with footballer Ricardo Colombus. This is Mrs. Green on set of *The Huntress* where she trained the leading lady. This is Mrs. Green with leading lady from *Return of the Huntress.*"

Alys droned on and Dave pretended to listen. In his opinion there was impressive, there was publicity, and there was plain showing off. This was definitely showing off. But then that was the recurring mantra, wasn't it: bodybuilding was all about showing off?

"Isn't there a Mr. Green?" he asked, as much to stop the tedious repetition of *Mrs. Green, Mrs. Green, Mrs. Green* as to receive an answer.

Alys's features twitched, as if the unexpected question threatened to throw her practised recitation. "No," she said. "This is Mrs. Green with leading lady from *The Huntress 3*. This..."

"What's she like to work for?"

"She is a good woman," Alys said immediately.

That was quick. Dave waited for some elaboration.

"She is a *very* good woman."

"Some people say she can be a little...pushy?" *I bloody well think she is.*

"Is not true!" said Alys, and Dave blinked at her sudden vehemence. Alys collected herself again. "Mrs. Green is a very good woman. Very kind. She has a hard life, but she works hard, makes something of herself. And now she helps others. She always helps others. She helped me. She gave me this job. She look after me. She look after all the people who work for her." Alys stopped as suddenly as she had begun.

"Er, right. Okay." Dave turned back to the picture wall. "And who is that?" he said, pointing randomly at the pictures.

"Marcus Oldman, Olympian." Alys's face was once again stonily neutral, her voice flat. She picked up her recital of names from where she had left off before, working her way mechanically down the pictures, from top left to bottom right.

Dave let Alys's words wash over him as he thought about what she'd just told him. He'd expected her to be positive about Green, to flannel him with corporate speak. He'd definitely not expected such energetic sincerity, and he was forced to ask himself, was Claire right? Was he misjudging Sue Green? And why? Had Claire been right? Did he find strong women...difficult? He'd only ever been on the receiving end of prejudice before. The thought that he might now be dishing out some of his own made him feel distinctly uneasy.

His uncomfortable train of thought was brought to a halt as his eye fell on a small photograph in the bottom left-hand corner. He leaned down to get closer to it. "Who's this?" he said, dragging Alys away from her relentlessly methodical progress through the pictures.

"Surely you know who that is, Sergeant," said a voice behind him. "You had coffee with him just the other day." Dave whirled round. Sue Green was standing behind him, her hands on her hips, a knowing smile on her lips.

"That's our local MP, Sean Cullen. I can't believe you've forgotten someone so...striking already. It's all right, Alys. I'll take over from here."

The girl gave Dave a glare, partway between surprise and anger and scurried back to her room.

"I hope my girls have been giving you the full tour, Sergeant. And answered all your questions. I'm sorry, is it Sergeant or Dave? I suppose it depends whether you're here officially or not."

"They did, thank you," said Dave, sidestepping the question.

"You should have let me know you were coming," Sue went on. "I could have arranged for one of my boys to show you around." She smiled again. "Some men prefer that. Having another man show them the ropes."

"I don't have any problem with women."

"Of course you don't. I don't see any kit, so I assume you haven't come for a trial workout."

"Ah no, thank you."

"We could lend you some kit if you'd like. Normally there's a charge but for you, free for a first session. I'll even take you through it myself."

"Thank you but no. This was just...a look around. Very impressive. This too." He gestured to the wall of photos. "You're right, of course. I should have recognised Sean Cullen. I suppose I was a bit thrown because the picture wasn't taken here, was it?"

"No."

Dave leaned down as if to peer more closely at the picture. "It's Heavy Metal, isn't it?" He went on, not waiting for an answer, "And the person with him?" The picture showed Sue Green, Sean Cullen, and one other. Green was standing to one side, smiling into the camera with the confident ease she showed in all of the photos. Cullen was staring directly into the camera, his mouth a round O of pantomimic surprise. Next to him, in training vest and shorts, a tall bodybuilder was also mugging for the photographer, one arm flexed to make the massive biceps bulge, much as Best had posed for the local paper. Cullen was pointing to the swollen muscle with one hand while squeezing it with the other. Sue Green leaned closer. "So many pictures," she murmured. "I can't remember...Ah yes. Dan."

"Dan Thompson," Dave confirmed. "So this must have been taken before that other photo with Paul Best? I mean, if it had been more recent I'm sure you would have remembered it."

Sue straightened. "Yes," she said carelessly. "It was some time ago. In fact, I think it was the first time Sean got in touch with me about his Fitness First project and I invited him to come down to Heavy Metal. We took a number of photos that day. This was the one I liked. It made me smile. Sean is like me: he works hard, but he likes to have fun too." She straightened up and regarded Dave. "You'd really like him if you got to know him."

"Perhaps I will arrange to meet him again, sometime soon. For a chat."

Sue held out her hand and Dave took it. "And I'll dig out the rest of the pictures we took that first time at Heavy Metal if you like. You might like to see them. And I genuinely do want to help. In any way I can."

Back outside in the Shambles shopping area, Dave took a moment to try and process what he'd just learned. But had he learned *anything?* What had he been *trying* to learn? He doubted Summerskill was going to be happy with his unsolicited poking around at the Venus and Adonis.

Moodily, he made his way back to the car park, so absorbed in his own musings he nearly didn't see the figure so obviously trying to avoid him. It was the figure's abrupt dodging behind a pillar as he approached that first made him aware. Had someone followed him from the gym? Dave suddenly shifted to one side, to see around the pillar, and there, half angry and half embarrassed at having been discovered, was...

"Tony?"

"SO, TO SUM up, everyone likes him." Jenny spread her hands. "Sorry, boss, but I couldn't find any dirt on Robert Taylor."

Claire swore under her breath. "Local?"

"Local. Workplace. Neighbours. I've done the lot, though it's sad really how small a social circle lads like Taylor have. He lives with his mum, works at the supermarket down the road from there, and drinks, occasionally, at the pub round the corner. And if he's not doing any of the above, then he's working out at Heavy Metal. His supermarket boss says he gets on and does his work humping heavy boxes around all day, so he's in hog heaven, and most of the girls on the tills think he's fit, though one of them thinks he might be gay because of the tight T-shirts he always wears." She gave a short laugh. "You should send Lyon round to have few quiet words with him."

"Sergeant Lyon has more important things to do, thank you."

Jenny sobered though she didn't look repentant. "Right. Seriously, though, if I was to ask anyone any more questions, I think Taylor would have a case for harassment. There's nothing going on there. In every sense of the word."

"Damn it!" They were going around in circles and the circles were getting smaller. When the phone on her desk rang she snatched it up angrily. "Summerskill!" She listened to the voice at the other end. "Put him on." She covered the receiver with her hand. "It's Ian."

"Trouble?" Jenny mouthed.

Before she could answer, Claire's husband was put through. "Ian? What's up?" Jenny watched Claire's face darken as Ian spoke on the other end of the phone. "When...? How did he manage that...? Where is he now...? Well why, for God's sake...? Have you tried his mobile...? All right... No, I'll not be sending out bobbies to hunt for him. Don't be daft. Like as not, he'll have gone home. I'll try his mobile and then I'll call there... I'm not worried, Ian, I'm bloody furious... All right. I'll call you if I hear anything." She slammed the phone back down. "It's Tony," Claire said, answering Jenny's mute question. "He's truanted again. I'll bloody kill him when I get my hands on him."

"YOU KNOW YOUR mum will kill you when she finds out."

Tony grunted, his head bent over the cup of coffee Dave had just bought him, his fringe flopping down over his eyes.

"And, on top of everything else today, she'll probably kill me too."

Tony raised his head and Dave could finally see the boy's eyes properly. They were suspiciously red. "What, for buying me a coffee?"

"For taking you to a café rather than giving you a quick clip round the ear and taking you straight back to school, yes."

Tony turned his attention back to his coffee. "Isn't that police brutality? Couldn't I, like, sue and make a lot of money?"

God, kids learn quickly these days. Dave sat back and took a sip of his cappuccino. His first instinct had, indeed, been to take Tony straight back to school, though without the physical assault. But when he'd seen the lad's obvious distress, despite Tony's every effort to conceal it, he'd thought it would be a good idea to take just a little time out first, to let him collect himself, before he had to go back to face the inevitable music. He recalled what Claire had told him about Tony's recent troubles at school. Perhaps he could do a bit of good here, after the cock-up he'd made of his impromptu trip to the Venus and Adonis. It couldn't hurt with

Summerskill. And besides, he genuinely liked Tony who always came across as a decent enough kid. So, he waited—standard interrogation technique—sipping on his coffee, and giving the suspect enough time until he felt he had to fill the silence with something. Of course, it tended to work better when the subject wasn't someone you frequently drove to school in the morning and who was therefore generally quite comfortable in your presence. And when he wasn't the son of your immediate boss. Dave suddenly realised it was he who was feeling uncomfortable and keen to fill in the silence.

"So, what were you planning to do?" he said when the boy showed no sign of cracking under this ruthless interrogation. "Where were you going?"

Tony shrugged. "Dunno. I just walked out of school and a bus pulled up right next to me. Like a sign. So I just got on and found myself in the centre. Suppose I could have gone along to the library."

"I thought truants went off into the woods for a fag and cider, not into the library for a little extra learning?"

Tony sighed. "I don't smoke."

"I didn't mean... Never mind." Dave put his cup down and leaned across the table. "Seriously, Tony. What were you thinking? You know your mum's going to be worried when she hears about this."

This time Dave saw the genuine sorrow in Tony's eyes. "Is she?"

"Of course she is. Didn't you realise?" *No, you didn't, did you? Kids are so thick sometimes.*

"I can't win. I just can't win." Tony buried his head in his hands, and for one awful moment, Dave thought he was going to cry. Much to his relief, however, that wasn't the case. Tony was just trying to blot everything out of sight. Dave waited again. After what seemed like an eternity Tony slowly lowered his hands. "You're gay, right?" he said eventually, in a small voice.

"Yes," Dave said cautiously. *Oh shit!*

"I'm sorry. I mean, it's not like meant to be a secret or anything is it?"

Dave gave a dry laugh. "No, of course not. It's just, I mean, I wasn't expecting to be talking about my...about that, here and now." *With a kid. With my boss's kid. Who is about to tell me something that is going to make my boss very unhappy. I think.*

"I only ask 'cause I guess it was kind of hard. Telling your parents, I mean. Coming out, yeah? It must have been hugely difficult all those years ago."

Yeah. What with the Plague and Black Death and all the other bad things going on at the time. Dave bit down on the response he could have made. *All kids think adults come from the Stone Age.* "Yes," he said carefully. "It wasn't easy."

"Cause it like changes everything, doesn't it? When you let something like that out of the bag, things can never be the same again."

Dave couldn't deny it: he remembered the feeling all too well. "Yes," he said. "But change is part of growing up, Tony." *Oh my God! Even gay people turn into parent clichés when talking to kids!* "Sorry. That's such a boring adult sort of thing to say."

Tony gave a small, forgiving smile. "It's all right. I kind of don't think of you like an adult." Dave felt unexpectedly touched. "I mean," Tony went on, "it's probably 'cause you work for my mum, y'know? It's like you have to do what she says the same way I do."

Dave's fuzzy, warm feeling cooled a little. "We're practically brothers," he said. "Just kidding." The boy relapsed into staring at his coffee cup. Dave realised he had brought himself to a critical moment, and this wasn't the time for jokes or an in-depth discussion of the real dynamic of his working relationship with Claire Summerskill which, in any case, as far as he was concerned, was still a work in progress. "Tony. Tell me what's the matter."

"HOW MUCH LONGER have I got to keep this up?" Terry Cortez demanded as he stalked into the office at Foregate Street, throwing his kit bag to the floor by his desk.

Mobile phone to her ear, Summerskill gave Cortez a none-too-sympathetic shrug. "Heavy Metal too heavy for you, Terry?"

"The place is a flea pit," Terry snarled. "I could feel my trainers sticking to the mats. And some git even went and stole one of my towels while I was in the showers."

"My heart bleeds," Claire said. "Damn it!" She slammed her phone down onto the desk. "Why is it you can't get a kid off a mobile right until the point you're trying to call him?" She refocused on Cortez. "So, did you learn anything? And where have you been?"

This last was directed at Dave who had entered the office right behind Cortez. He was saved from having to reply immediately by Cortez's answer to Claire's question. "Yeah. Not to wear kit I don't want to burn as soon as this little favour of yours is done."

"I meant anything that might help with our murder investigation, *Sergeant*."

With an obvious effort, Cortez reined in his bad temper. "No, *ma'am*. I've met a couple of the guys on the list you gave me. Decent enough. Pretty focused, I'll give them that."

"Hardcore," Dave murmured. "Sorry, go on."

"Yeah well, I've seen Taylor working out both times I've been there. He trained with the same couple of lads each time."

"Did you speak with him? Join in?"

"It's not like skipping in the schoolyard, Claire. You can't just waltz up and say, 'Can I be in your gang?'"

"And I guess they'd have been lifting some pretty serious weights," Dave said. "Not that you weren't too, of course," he added quickly.

"I saw Thompson just the once," Cortez went on, ignoring or unaware of the jibe. "He was training with another couple of guys too, serious competition stuff. And no, there was no way I could have just sidled up and suggested I spot for him." He paused. "Spotting's when…"

"We know!" Claire snapped.

"Apart from that, the longest conversation I had with anyone in the place was with the gorilla on the desk…"

"Marc," Dave said automatically. "With a C."

"And Sue Green."

There was a slight pause.

"Give you the sales pitch, did she?" Claire said.

"And what was she selling?" Dave asked.

"She…was friendly," Terry admitted. "Professionally." Summerskill and Lyon waited. "She offered to take me through a routine." Summerskill and Lyon exchanged a look. "And that was it. Oh, apart from some older guy, pain in the neck, who wanted to bend my ear about all sorts of crap. More interested in finding out about me than letting me find out anything from him."

"Your boyfriend," said Dave to Claire.

"Bill Kilby?" she asked. Terry nodded. "So, nothing concrete yet? No sign of any steroid use?"

Cortez laughed. "Shit yeah! You don't get as big as some of the guys there that young without a ton of chemical help. But I don't think it's much of a problem."

"It's illegal, Sergeant."

"And so's parking on double yellow lines."

"We're talking about drugs."

"We're talking about steroids, not heroin," Terry insisted. "I mean, where do you draw the line between a performance-enhancing drug and a vitamin supplement?"

"I don't have to," Claire said. "The law has already done it for me. Now—" She turned to Dave. "—where have you been?"

Again Dave went to answer. The phone on Claire's desk rang. She picked up, signalling for Dave to wait. "Summerskill. Put him through. Mr. Steward? Yes, this is Mrs. Summerskill. He has? When? And he's okay? Good. Thank you. Yes, of course, I completely agree. I'll be sanctioning him myself when I get back home. A lot! Thank you for letting me know. Yes. Goodbye." She put the phone down. "Tony's Head of Year. Tony went walkabout, but he's turned up again. What? It's not that unusual."

Dave tried to cover a small smile. "It's not that, it's just... I never think of you as *Mrs. Summerskill*. It sounds so..."

"Mumsy?" Claire said dangerously. "Well, that's what I bloody am, God help me. And if you think that's an easier job than leading a murder investigation, then you bloody well try it. Now, for the last time, will you tell me where the...?"

"Visitor," said Jenny Trent at the office doorway.

"Tell him to wait!"

"Can't," said Jenny tersely. "It's a she, and she won't." To their surprise, her next comment was directed across the room at Terry. "And I think you might want to get out of sight too. It's Susan Green."

"What?"

"Shit!" exclaimed Cortez.

"Okay." Claire thought quickly then gestured to Terry. "Get yourself into Interview Room One. It's free, yeah?" Jenny nodded. "All right. I'll give you the all clear when she's gone."

"He could always hide under my desk," Dave suggested.

"What?"

"Sorry, but if this has become a French farce, I thought we might as well go all the way."

"I'm so glad this is amusing you," Claire said. "But we are on the verge of having an undercover operation that is part of a murder investigation blown out of the water."

"Yeah. And I'm on the verge of ending up looking a right dick," Cortez muttered angrily as he stormed past them out to his hiding place.

"Don't we have to let accounting know if we're launching an *undercover operation?*" Dave asked. "Just wondering."

"Okay, Jenny. Send her in. And you," she said to Lyon, "I haven't finished with you yet."

Within a minute, Susan Green was being shown into the office. "Mrs. Green. Sue." Claire smiled and held out a hand.

"Claire," said Sue, taking the hand and also smiling. She nodded in Dave's direction. "Sergeant."

"Please, take a seat. Coffee?"

Sue took in the suspiciously antique percolator in the room that Claire indicated. "Thanks, no. I'd love a glass of water though." And she looked to Dave hopefully.

Dave didn't move.

"Sergeant," Claire said, "could you fetch Mrs. Green a glass of water, please?"

Without a word, Dave got up from his desk and left the room.

"Now, Sue. What can I do for you?"

"Well, it's a couple of things really." Green crossed her legs, settling herself before she spoke. Claire wondered how someone who had pumped the kind of weights Sue must have could still manage to be so elegant. "First, of course, if you don't mind my asking, how are things going? With finding out about...what happened to Paul, I mean."

Claire took a deep breath. "It's...an on-going investigation," she said carefully. "I'm sure you'll appreciate we can't say much at this moment. But we are following up on some promising leads."

Sue nodded gravely. "Of course. Oh, thank you, Sergeant."

Dave had returned with a glass of water which he put in front of her on Summerskill's desk. "It's tap water," he said.

Sue smiled. "Absolutely fine." She made no move to pick the glass up. She turned back to Claire. "The second thing I wanted to talk about, and I hope you don't mind this, is a little bit of shameless promotion." She slipped off the shoulder bag she was carrying, opened it, and took out a small sheaf of papers. "I know you said you've got a gym on the premises..."

"Well, it's more of a..."

"But when Sergeant Lyon came round to the Venus and Adonis today, I thought perhaps that was because you were thinking of taking staff fitness a little bit more seriously."

"Sergeant Lyon was at your gym today?" Claire said. She looked across at Dave who nodded once, a touch too defiantly, Claire thought.

"So," Sue continued, "I've taken the liberty of drawing up some schemes under which your officers could have access at discounted terms." She paused. "Sorry. Sales speak. I mean I can cut you a deal for group membership, so you end up paying less. And if you sign up for Sean Cullen's Fitness First programme you can save even more."

"Er, yes. Thanks, Sue. Thank you very much." More preoccupied with the news of her sergeant's impromptu investigations than with staff fitness, Claire took the papers the other woman was holding out to her. There were several glossy pictures of people smiling far more than she would have ever thought possible in a gym. *Mind you, if I could look that good in Lycra then maybe I'd grin like a crazy person too.* "I will definitely...give it some thought."

Sue smiled. "Great." She made as if to get up then stopped and reached once more into her bag. "I nearly forgot. The other reason I came here." She pulled out a lime green towel, neatly washed and folded. "I thought I'd return this. It's Sergeant Cortez's."

Blushing, and furious at herself for blushing, Claire took the towel. "Thank you," she said. Denial was clearly out of the question, but she literally had no idea what else to say.

"I thought he might have been here for me to hand it back to him myself, but...I see he isn't."

"Sue..." Claire began.

Sue Green held up a hand. "You don't have to say anything, Claire. I understand. You're investigating a suspicious death. You have to do what you have to do. I'm fine with Sergeant Cortez—Terry—working out at Heavy Metal and asking his questions, though it makes me sick to my stomach you think there might be a link between what happened to Paul and my gym. It's just—" she hesitated. "I think you could have asked me first. You'd have had my full support. You do know you have my full support?"

Inwardly, Claire gave a sigh of relief. That could have been a lot stickier. Although technically there wasn't much Sue Green could have done about a perfectly legitimate police operation, Claire didn't want to antagonise the woman when there was no need. "Thank you, Sue. It's obviously nothing personal. I asked Sergeant Cortez to...drop by because..." She could practically feel Dave willing her not to say any more. *Well perhaps he needs a reminder of who is in charge of this investigation.*

"Best was a steroid user. We wanted to see if his supplier was someone from Heavy Metal." Her words had been for Sue, but as she spoke, Claire's eyes were on Dave. His jaw tightened, and she watched him deliberately turn away from her. He was angry. She turned her attention back to Sue.

The gym owner was silent, staring down at her hands in her lap as if considering something. When she finally lifted her head, she spoke quietly but clearly. "Claire, I've been involved in bodybuilding for more years now than I care to admit. I've seen it from all sides. As a competitor, trainer and gym owner." She took a deep breath. "And I'd be lying if I said there was no drugs use. Anyone who said that would be. But I will tell you this. I see the guys, and the women, at my gyms who are obviously on steroids, but they don't get them from me. And, at the end of the day, it's their choice. You can't understand what it's like to want to be..." She stopped.

"The best?" Dave said.

Sue went on. "And the thing is, they're just...people. Not druggies. Not addicts. Steroids don't make people...murder."

She hesitated over the word and Claire regarded her closely. She was sure the woman genuinely believed what she was saying. She nodded once. "I'll take Sergeant Cortez off the operation immediately."

Sue smiled in gratitude. "Thank you, Claire." She gathered her bag to her again and stood.

"One thing though," Claire said, unable to resist a professional reaction to what had just happened. "How did you know Cortez was police?"

Sue laughed. "He's got a good body. He's a looker, and I'm sure he's a great policeman. But he's no spy, is he? Seriously though, like I told you before, and as you yourself remarked, Sergeant," she added, addressing Dave directly for the first time, "I am a businesswoman, and that means I have to be able to read people." She gave a small smile, almost to herself. "Let's just say he didn't react the way I would have expected." She collected herself again. "And now I must go. Good to see you again, Claire. Please do think about the gym deal. It would be good for Foregate Street station, and for my gyms if you joined. And don't forget Sean's initiative. It can save you even more money. Bye."

"Goodbye, Sue."

"Goodbye, Sergeant," Sue called over her shoulder and she strode from the office.

Claire waited ten seconds before she spoke. "You were at the Venus and Adonis today?" she said to Dave with deceptive calmness.

"Just trying to root out a fresh lead."

"And are you going to go around all the gyms in the city? There are about half a dozen, I think."

"Not unless there are connections to our case. Which there are here."

"Yes." Claire gestured to the door Sue Green had just gone through. "And that connection couldn't be more cooperative."

"Thanks for letting me know it was okay to show my face again," Terry said sarcastically as he walked back into the office.

Claire picked up the towel Sue had left and threw it at him. "You've been rumbled."

"What? How?"

"Because you're a shit spy."

"She was playing with you," Dave said. "Playing with us."

Claire gave an exasperated sigh. "And what do you mean by that?"

"She's mad at us for planting Terry in her gym, yeah? But she leaves it until the end of her visit before she mentions it?"

"She wasn't mad. She was disappointed."

"She was laughing at us the whole time."

"Well, good for her. We were pretty damn laughable."

"And don't give me that, *It's because I'm a businesswoman* crap. How did she really find out about Terry?"

"Because Terry is no James Bond!"

"I..." Cortez began.

"So, why didn't she say something to him as soon as she'd bust his cover rather than come here to play the big scene?"

The office door opened again before Claire could answer, and Jenny Trent stuck her head in. "Madden wants to see you, ma'am."

Discomfited as much by Jenny's formality as by a summons from the station's Chief Superintendent, Claire swore quietly to herself, stood, straightened her skirt, and automatically ran her fingers through her hair. "You two try and sort something worthwhile out of this mess," was her parting shot.

"SHE DOES REMEMBER I'm working on cases with Rudge, doesn't she?" asked Cortez.

"Do you think she cares?" Dave said. "So, Heavy Metal was a bust?"

"Course it was." Cortez threw himself into his chair and leaned back with his hands behind his head. "The place is a dive but, to be fair, it's meant for people who really want to work out and build muscle, not just spend ten minutes on a cross-trainer before having a latte and natter with their mates."

"And what about Sue Green?"

"What about her? You're not suggesting she murdered Best, are you?"

"I'm not saying she had to have done it herself, but I'm not ruling out that she might have been implicated in some way. I'm not ruling anyone out. Isn't that what we're not supposed to do?" Dave came to an uncertain stop, as uncertain about the double negatives as about seeming to be unfairly on Sue Green's case.

"You just don't like her because she's a strong woman." Cortez sat up and leaned forward towards his own computer. "Or just because she's a woman," he added quietly.

He should have let it go. Cortez's body language was making it clear that, as far as he was concerned, the topic was closed. They could both have pretended those last few words weren't meant for Dave. *I should let it go,* Dave thought. "What's that supposed to mean?" he said out loud.

Cortez turned back to his computer screen. "You tell me." He started typing.

WHEN CLAIRE RETURNED to the office fifteen minutes later, her mood was far too foul for her to notice the frosty silence between Cortez and Lyon. "Terry, you can tell Jim he can stop bitching about the couple of hours you were giving me on the Heavy Metal operation. As of right now, it's off."

"Madden's overruled it?" Dave asked. Claire nodded once, as if not trusting herself to speak. "I don't get it. The only person likely to put in an official complaint would be Sue Green, but she wouldn't have had time to get one in so quickly after leaving here. And complaining before she came just wouldn't make sense."

"Do you have any idea how senior management works, Sergeant?"

"I'm guessing, sometimes not," he said uncertainly.

"Well, maybe if you did, you'd be an inspector now yourself and you'd be taking shit from on high like I've just had to."

Across the room, Cortez smirked. Dave went to retort but before he could speak the office door opened and Jenny reappeared. It was clear from her face she was not bringing good news.

"What now?" Claire demanded. "Has the old bastard found some more rules and regulations he can crucify me with?"

"No," said Jenny. "There's been another killing."

Chapter Nine

DAN THOMPSON'S FLAT was so small, Summerskill and Lyon had to wait virtually on the landing outside his front door while the various members of the SOCO team, in their full-body plastic suits, boots, and gloves, took their pictures and secured the scene. Even when the preliminary work had been done and the SOCO men and woman stepped back to let Claire and Dave see the corpse, the two officers could only lean into the room containing the body, over the yellow tape stretched across the doorway. Any further and they would have been walking through the blood and brain still soaking into the carpet.

"No doubt how this one was done," Dave said grimly. Next to the remains of Thompson's head was a sizeable dumbbell, the companion to another they could see stacked neatly up against the far wall.

Claire steeled herself to take it all in: the single sofa, the pictures on the wall, the small collection of books, the television and stack of DVDs, and Thompson's powerful but mutilated body sprawled on the carpet, taking up almost all of the free floor space. She nodded once before stepping back into the narrow hallway to take a deep breath. It was always the smell that got to her. "Okay," she said to Dave who had taken her place in the living room doorway and was making his own survey of the scene. "What are you thinking?"

"Vicious. His head's been pulped. Someone hit him several times." He stepped back. "But Thompson must have been dead or at least unconscious from the first blow. Small room like this, if a big man like him had had a chance to fight back there'd have been a lot more damage—telly knocked over, DVDs scattered." He gestured to the room, the macabre contrast of the neatly organised contents, and the brutally broken remains of a human being on the floor.

"Which means..."

"Either he was surprised..."

"And how could anyone sneak into a room this small and not be noticed?"

"Or it was someone he knew."

"Isn't it usually?" Claire said, almost to herself. With a nod of her head, she indicated to the waiting SOCO officers that they could return to their work, taking the samples they required while waiting for Aldridge to arrive. She and Dave took a look around the rest of the cramped flat. A bedroom, bathroom, and a kitchen so small it should have been called a galley, all told the same story. Firstly, there were the pictures, on every wall. Bodybuilders. In gyms, on competition stages, in studios, outdoors and even, in one bizarre picture, on an iceberg. Many were in frames, generally the cheap, discount store kind, though some in the kitchen were carefully clipped from magazines and precisely Blu-tacked to the wall. When a man was wearing only a tiny posing pouch there weren't the usual fashion hints to help a viewer work out when a picture had been taken, but from the varying hairstyles and the fact that some of the pictures were black and white, Claire guessed they were of famous bodybuilders shot over a period of many decades. "Inspirational?"

"Something like that," Dave murmured.

The second thing that stood out about the rooms was their neatness. The entire flat, with the now obvious exception of the living room, was spotless, and it was clear everything had its place and there was a place for everything. The bed was made with military precision, bathroom items were arranged with an orderliness that smacked of obsessive compulsion, and all of the beefcake pictures might have been hung using a set square. Everything was spotless.

"God, I wish I could keep my kitchen like this," Claire muttered as she opened cupboards carefully with a pen to avoid smudging possible prints and took in the neat rows of cans and packets. "I bet yours is, isn't it?"

Dave considered the troughs and bins of fresh fruit and vegetables. "Pot noodles are easy to stack," he admitted.

Claire peered into the fridge. "There's more meat here than I get in to feed my family for a fortnight. And I've never seen so many eggs in one place outside of a supermarket."

"Takes a lot to fuel and maintain a body like his," Dave said. He turned to face her holding up a large plastic canister with a picture of a luridly coloured and highly pumped biceps under the words "Protein Plus!". He gestured to the worktop to one side of the fridge. There were more canisters like the one he was holding, neatly stacked, of course, their different colours presumably indicating their different flavours. Next to them were the much smaller white boxes. These had no pictures or garish logos. The only identifying features on them were labels that Claire guessed Dan had written himself.

Dave opened one of the packets and tipped out a blister pack of capsules. He peered closely at the writing on them and opened and flicked through his notebook, nodding with satisfaction when he found what he was looking for. "This is one of the steroids Aldridge told us Paul Best had in his blood." He indicated the rest of the cache of boxes. "I'm guessing the rest aren't headache pills and tummy tablets."

"More's the pity." An industrial size box of aspirin was exactly what Claire felt the need for right then.

IT'S WRONG, CLAIRE thought, as she read again through the pages and pages of information they had begun amassing on Dan Thompson. *Why should you only try to get to know a person, get a real understanding of a person, when he's dead?* She studied the incident board she and Dave had set up in their office. Next to the details on Best, there was now the beginnings of another set of information about Thompson. It was depressingly thin.

"Spartan," said Dave, coming to stand next to her at the board. "If he'd been a wrestler or a gladiator, that could have been his nickname."

"There's already a gladiator called Spartan, isn't there?" Claire said vaguely. "What do you mean, anyway?"

"No frills. No luxuries. Everything about the man was focused on the one thing: bodybuilding."

"No luxuries?" Claire flipped through her papers and held up one sheet for Dave's inspection. "Did you see the price tag on his steroid stash?"

"True," Dave had to concede. "But I don't think Thompson would have seen that as a luxury. More a necessity."

"Whatever." Claire replaced the paper in its folder. "But, the man's only job as far as we can tell was driving a delivery van for a sportswear company on a zero hours contract. How was he able to pay the rent on his flat and build up a pile of drugs the local chemists would have been jealous of on just that? And that's not even taking into account his food bill."

"At the moment it literally doesn't add up," Dave agreed. "He lived on his own, no one to help with the bills. Mum's in a home somewhere up in Scotland with practically no contact. No other family or close friends we can see yet who might be subsidising him. Bank account's just a way of paying the essential bills: money goes in and straight out again. All very hand to mouth."

"But someone's got to be putting something into his hands."

"Or his mouth."

"Meaning?"

Dave rubbed his hands over his face wearily. "Nothing. Too soon to be making wild accusations."

Claire grunted. "What are we getting from the neighbours?"

"Nothing. Old dear downstairs said he'd helped her move a cupboard once. The young couple on the same floor only moved in last week and thought he was a bit odd but hadn't even spoken to him yet. Nobody saw or heard anything at the time of the murder."

"Bloody English," Claire muttered. "If this had been in one of the valleys they'd all have been able to tell us his mam's maiden name and his mam's mam's national insurance number. And what did they mean by odd?"

"As far as I can tell, they just meant big. Guys like him do tend to stand out, even if they're just, y'know, ordinary." Dave hesitated. "They also thought he was gay."

"Yeah, well, fill your flat with pictures of practically naked men and people might think that."

"Could have been role models?"

"I'm an inspector. I don't have pictures of Sherlock Holmes plastered over my walls."

"Miss Marple?" Dave suggested.

"Careful!"

"Yes, mum. And it was the DVDs that clinched it for me."

"What DVDs?" Claire turned again to her papers but could see nothing there she had missed.

"The ones by his telly. I saw some of them when we were at the door."

"Saw them?"

"Okay, recognised them."

"Right." Claire closed her folder again. "So, we get out into the local gay bars and clubs, see if he was known, see if he had any jealous boyfriends."

"Yeah, because, as a gay man he must have been out practically every night and associating with emotionally unstable potential killers."

"Because I can't think of a bloody better way in at the moment. Feel free to help me with other ideas if you can, Sergeant. And unbunch your knickers while you're at it." Claire couldn't help herself. "Y'know, this would be a damn sight easier if you were on the scene yourself."

"Maybe I would be if you ever gave me the time."

"I'm beginning to doubt it. Anyway, now you've got a legitimate excuse to go and shake your booty down at The Pharos and wherever else you think Thompson might have been shaking his."

"You're the boss."

"So I have to remind you."

"But..."

"Why did I not think that was coming?"

"I don't think that's necessarily the best use of our time at this point."

Claire leaned back in her chair. "And why, pray tell?" There was a distinctly dangerous edge to her voice.

"Paul Best was as straight as they come. No pun intended. I don't think we're going to find any links to their murderer on the gay scene."

Claire nodded slowly as if agreeing, though her eyes made it perfectly clear she was not. "So, what do you suggest?"

"We go back to Heavy Metal. Best and Thompson might have slept on different sides of the bed, but they were both bodybuilders and they both used that gym."

"We've already done Heavy Metal."

"When we thought it was only indirectly connected. Now the link is clearer. And we were only asking questions last time. Maybe this time we need to be a bit more...proactive. Shake it hard and sees what falls out of the lockers."

Claire considered. Sometimes, like now, Dave was a know-it-all, pain in the arse. But, she reluctantly admitted to herself, sometimes he was also right. And she knew talk of shaking lockers wasn't just metaphorical. "I can't see Madden okaying a search warrant application when neither crime was committed on the premises."

"Okay, so maybe you get your new friend to agree to a voluntary search."

"*Friend* is pushing it at the moment, don't you think?" She pushed her chair back and stood up. "All right. Heavy Metal it is again." She went to go for her coat but stopped, turned back to her desk, and reached for the bottom drawer.

Dave watched as she took out a small spray bottle and applied sizeable bursts of perfume to her wrists and neck. "Hoping to win over some of the guys?"

"Hoping to block out the smell." Claire slipped the bottle into her pocket. "Okay. Let's go."

"I WANT TO help, Claire, I think you know that. And of course I'm sorry about what has happened to Dan. But do you think this is really going to help?"

Claire regarded Sue Green as they stood by Heavy Metal's entrance desk while, in the gym itself, all the plain clothes and uniforms she'd been able to scrape together from Acquisitions, led by Dave Lyon, were once again questioning the men and women working out. She mentally shut her eyes to the questions Madden was going to raise when he saw the balance sheet for this piece of work. "I know, Sue, and I'm sorry, but we have no choice. We know there was no love lost between Best and Thompson, but was there anyone who disliked them both? Someone they'd both upset? Another competition rival, maybe?"

Sue cast her eyes around her gym. "I find it hard enough to believe *anyone* would want to kill someone, let alone for that person to be someone I know."

Dave appeared at their side. "I'd like the names and addresses of everyone who has been here in the past two weeks or so at least. I assume you have some kind of signing-in system?"

Sue nodded distractedly. "There's a book." She gestured to the desk by the entrance.

"So, members sign in when they enter." Sue nodded again. "But they don't have to. I mean, nothing happens if they don't?"

"They're asked to," Sue said with slight irritation in her voice. "There's usually someone on the desk, and if there isn't, there's a big sign saying, *Please Sign In*. Nobody has ever refused point blank. But," she concluded grudgingly, "there is nothing to stop someone forgetting to if the desk isn't manned."

"Seems a little careless. The Venus and Adonis uses a swipe card system, doesn't it?"

"This isn't the Venus and Adonis. And we weren't expecting to be at the centre of a murder investigation." Sue took a deep breath. "I'm sorry. I am intending to update Heavy Metal's facilities, bring it in line with my other gyms. I just haven't had time to get round to it yet. We do, however, have contact details of everyone who has ever been to the gym. They are, of course, yours if you want them."

"Thank you." Dave checked the entrance desk to see if Marc was there. He was, and he wasn't alone. It took a second or two for his brain to catch up with what he was seeing and put a name to the face, and in that time Sue Green caught him looking at the young woman by Marc's side. "Yes, Sergeant," she said softly. "I'm afraid Marc does have a girlfriend."

"I know." Dave's tone was cold. "That is, I know the girl. I didn't know she and Marc were an item. That's Alys," he said for Claire's benefit. "She's a beautician who works for Mrs. Green."

"Wouldn't have thought you'd have had much need of a beautician at Heavy Metal, Sue," Claire said.

Sue pulled a face. "Have you seen some of the guys here? No, Alys works at the Venus and Adonis. And she's a *trainee* beautician, Sergeant. But she's also Marc's girlfriend. I think they first met on a night out on the town I organised for my Worcester staff a while back. Marc sometimes helps with the maintenance of the equipment down at the V and A so they met again." She spread her hands. "Love grew. It happens. I think it's sweet, don't you?"

"Sweet" wasn't a word Dave would have considered in any union involving Marc, and catching the black looks Alys was shooting him, he certainly wasn't feeling the love.

"She's not happy," Claire remarked.

Sue Green turned back to the inspector. "She's worried, Claire. A lot of them are."

"Them? Who are they? And worried about what?"

"Do you have to ask? Two bodybuilders have been killed. Marc, in case you hadn't noticed, as well as working at this gym, is a bodybuilder. Alys is worried he might be next. A lot of the other guys are worrying they might be next."

"I don't think..." began Dave.

"They're worried it's the work of a serial killer."

THE HOURS CRAWLED by and the pile of statements Dave was collecting and collating grew ever thicker. Claire had done her best to deflect Sue Green's sensationalist thoughts about serial killers and though she sounded unconvinced, Sue had been as helpful as before, providing records, introducing her gym members to the interviewing officers, and keeping everyone supplied with tea and coffee. Bill Kilby, as ever, hung around like a bad smell, making a show of curling a massive pair of dumbbells, though he was obviously more interested in watching the police at their work than training. Robert Taylor came in, grudgingly answered the few cursory questions Dave put to him, and scowled at everyone during his workout. And Alys sat behind the desk with Marc, both glowering at Dave. *I didn't lie to you, love,* Dave thought. *Get over it.*

It was nearing nine when Claire's mobile went off. A few terse exchanges later and she was reaching for her coat. "You're going to have to finish off here," she said to Dave. "I've got to go home."

"Trouble?"

Claire grimaced. "Yes and no. Sam's had a fall. Nothing major," she said quickly, "but he's shook up and Tony can't get him to settle."

"What about Ian?" The glint in Claire's eye made it clear he shouldn't have asked that question.

"At another one of his bloody meetings, apparently."

"Could be worse. Could be at another bloody interview session." Claire's expression made it clear to Dave he shouldn't have said that either.

"You're lucky," said Sue Green, who had walked over to stand by them. "Having a family, I mean."

"It's...a mixed blessing," Claire said. "No kids then?"

"Didn't happen. But hey, you find other things to do. Start up a nation-conquering gym empire, for example."

"Conquering a country or bringing up two boys? You don't know how easy you've got it." Claire turned to Dave. "When the reports are in, file them then head home yourself. We'll start on them first thing tomorrow."

"I can make a start on them tonight when I get back to the station."

"Go home," Claire said forcefully. "And I'll see you in the morning. Good night, Sue, and thanks again for all your help."

With Claire gone, Dave carried on sorting out the reports being handed to him, dismissing his officers one by one. The flood of statements turned to a stream then a merciful trickle, as the gym's cohort of physical perfectionists completed their workouts then took themselves off home to collapse. Boxing up the reports, Dave became aware of Sue Green standing quietly to one side of him.

"No one waiting back home for you either, Sergeant?" she asked.

"Not at the moment." He took a pad from a WPC and signed her off for the night.

"What a shame."

And none of your bloody business. Dave focused on his paperwork.

"Still, sometimes the seeking is more fun than the finding, isn't it? The hunt more exciting than the capture."

"I've no time for hunting, Mrs. Green. Or fishing." And it was at then, with damnable irony, that Dave's phone played the distinctive and frustratingly unchangeable xylophone tones that indicated he had a message from his dating app.

"If you say so, Sergeant," Sue said, but as she turned away and headed for her tiny office, he caught the hint of a smile on her face and guessed she had recognised the sound. Swearing to himself, Dave pulled the mobile out of his pocket and scanned the message that had just arrived.

U Look HOT.

Dave deleted it with a savage jab of his finger. *And you, you desperate sod, need to check that the guys you're trying to pull have actually posted a picture!*

"Can't live with 'em. Can't live without 'em, eh?"

Dave jerked his head up. Bill Kilby was heading towards him, grubby towel round his neck, leering at him. "What?"

Kilby pointed at Dave's mobile. "Phones."

"Ah right. Yes." *Okay, so maybe you're not leering. Maybe that's what your face does when you're just trying to be friendly. Now piss off.*

"My money's on Gav," Kilby said.

Dave struggled to work out Kilby's meaning. He failed. "What?" he said again.

Kilby jerked his thumb in the direction of a bench not too far from them where another of the die-hard bodybuilders was still working out. "Gav Hall. He was training here Paul's last session. And Danny's."

"I'm sorry, Mr. Kilby..."

"Bill."

"Mr. Kilby. But are you suggesting that Mr. Hall is in any way connected with the murders of Paul Best and Dan Thompson?"

Kilby snickered. "That twat? No! I'm suggesting he could be the next one to be offed."

Rendered almost speechless by the man's crassness, Dave could only stare at Kilby's hugely amused round face for a moment before asking, "Why?"

"He's a gay boy, isn't he? Like Thompson."

Involuntarily, Dave checked out the man Kilby was referring to. *Is he? My gaydar is utter shit!* He turned back to Kilby. "So, you're claiming," he said out loud and choosing his words carefully, "that Dan Thompson's murder was a homophobic hate crime?"

"If that's how you want to put it, yeah."

Dave nodded as though agreeing with the man while all the time struggling with a real desire to bang him up then and there for wasting police time. Or loitering with intent. Anything, to wipe the smug self-satisfaction off the brainless little wanker's face. "But Paul Best, who was killed first, wasn't gay," he said, his face deceptively expressionless.

Kilby was unfazed. "Doesn't matter sometimes, does it?"

In the face of such staggering illogic, Dave was rendered speechless, and could only watch in stunned silence as Kilby tapped his nose, threw his kit bag over his shoulder, and wandered off through the gym exit.

Then his dating app went off again.

Swearing, aloud this time, at his own stupidity at still not having put the bloody thing on silent, Dave yanked the phone back out of his pocket and prepared to delete the new message as immediately as the last one.

But then he read the text.

CLAIRE'S FIRST THOUGHT when her phone went off in the car and she heard Sue's voice was that she must have left something behind in the gym. It quickly became clear that wasn't why Sue had called. "Can I talk to you?"

"Of course. Go ahead."

"No, I mean, can I talk to you properly. I know I've only just seen you but…"

"Isn't Sergeant Lyon still there? Anything you have to say to me you can just as easily say to him."

There was a silence on the other end of the line. When Sue spoke again, it sounded like she was trying to be tactful. "I don't think I can talk to him as easily as I can to you."

True, Claire thought. *Dammit, Dave.* She'd reached home and would ordinarily have pulled into the drive. Now, though, she parked by the kerb as she spoke to Sue. "I could come round the gym first thing tomorrow and…"

"I've found something," Sue said. "I think you'll want to see."

Claire looked at her house. The upstairs lights were all out. That could be a good sign, suggesting Tony had finally got Sam off to sleep. She had to know. "All right. I've just got to check on my kids, okay, and then I can be back at the gym in about fifteen minutes."

"Where do you live?" Sue asked. Claire told her. "Come to my place. It's closer."

With reluctance, Claire agreed, entering Green's address into her satnav as she gave it to her. "I'll be with you in about ten minutes. Providing my kids are both still alive."

"Thanks, Claire. See you then."

Claire got out of the car and headed up her garden path. If Dave hadn't got such a stick up his arse about Sue Green, then she could have talked to him. He might not like the woman, but that shouldn't get in the way of his ability to do his job. Mind you, Claire thought, recalling what he had said about Sue Green's visit to Foregate Street station, perhaps he had been right when he suggested Sue enjoyed playing up the drama of any given situation. What the hell could she have found that warranted this degree of fuss?

THERE'S NO WAY either Paul Best or Dan Thompson would have been seen dead in a place like this. Dave took another pull from his pint of artisan beer as he pretended to scan a menu of tapas while really scanning the people sitting and standing around him. *And given the choice, neither would I.*

Piano lounge music was playing under the sound of quiet talk and soft laughter. Men with men. Women with women. *Sometimes, a rainbow flag in your window is just redundant.* He took in the brass, walnut, and velvet surrounds. Not that Gallery 48 would have stooped to anything so crass. *Then again, is this any worse than The Halfway House or The Retired Airman?*

Dave was distracted from his morose thoughts by a man coming up to the bar he was standing at and positioning himself, with studied casualness, right next to him. He stood there for a moment, as if waiting for the bartender to come and ask him what he wanted. The bartender, at the other end of the bar, saw him but made no move. They all three knew the game being played.

"Oh, hi," said the new guy, as if suddenly becoming aware of the man he was standing next to.

Dave turned to face him. *Good teeth. Good hair. Trying a bit too hard with the open-necked shirt in this weather.* "Hi."

"Not seen you here before."

"First time."

"Right." The man stood, openly eying Dave up now, from his haircut to choice of shoes. He smiled and nodded with an open approval Dave found so condescending he wanted to bust him for something there and then. "Waiting for anyone in particular?" he asked.

"Yes," Dave said bluntly. *And it's not you.* His copper's instincts were telling him this was not the man who had sent him the app message. Every other instinct was telling him this man was a tosser.

"Oh. Right. Shame. Later." And without another word, the man was off.

Not if I see you first. Dave watched as open-necked shirt guy drifted, again with studied casualness, over to another part of the bar where another solitary man was nursing a drink. *Poor sod,* Dave thought. Then he saw the guy give the new arrival exactly the same up and down inspection he was being subjected to and watched both of them smile like cats who had been given saucers of cream. Dave withdrew all sympathy immediately, turned back to the drink he'd already been making last for twenty minutes past its natural life expectancy, and waited.

Men and women came and went. None stayed long, and the feeling grew in Dave that if he left alone, he'd be the only one who did that night. Open-necked shirt guy left ten minutes later with his new friend in tow. Dave followed them with his eyes, wondering whether the guy who'd hit on him would look back. A *shame-it's-not-you* face would have been some consolation. A *this-could-have-been-you* face was probably more likely. In the end, he didn't get either. *Probably forgotten I even exist.*

Dave stared into the depths of his now empty beer glass. It was well over an hour past the time specified in the app message and whoever had sent it had not shown. An hour he could have used going through the results of the Heavy Metal trawl, and that he'd now have to claw back from somewhere. *Sod it.* He pushed the glass to one side and turned to go.

"Hello, Sergeant," said the man in front of him. "What a pleasant surprise."

Dave blinked, also surprised, though not pleasantly. "Hello, Mr. Cullen," he said.

"Please," said the Worcester MP, smiling warmly, "like I said before, call me Sean."

CLAIRE HAD IMAGINED Sue Green owning a flat, something chic, modern and minimalist, perhaps even one of those trendy new loft apartments built in the city centre with a fantastic view of the cricket ground and race course and of the river that now flooded both of them every summer. She'd formed a mental picture of something open-plan, quite possibly with a training bench and weights in one corner, the sort of place young people in adverts lived in. But then Sue wasn't so young, was she, and in fact, she lived in a small chocolate-box-type cottage in Powick, technically a village on the outskirts of Worcester, though if you blinked as you drove through it, you were quite liable never even to have known it was there.

Sue opened the door to Claire dressed in T-shirt and jeans. *But she still looks better than I do after hours of preening.* She showed her into a small lounge. "Tea? Coffee? Something stronger? You aren't officially on duty, I'm guessing?"

Settling into a large and wonderfully comfortable armchair, Claire thought wistfully of the bottle of beer waiting in the fridge back home for her. "A cup of tea, please."

"Any particular kind?" Sue called back as she headed into the kitchen.

"Builder's will be fine. If you've got any," Claire added, taking in the tasteful elegance of the room she was in. She was relieved to see the framed photographs on the mantelpiece were not of scantily clad bodybuilders, male or female. She peered at them. Young men, as far as she could tell, smiling happily for the camera.

"My nephews," Sue said, coming back in with a tray. "I'm very proud of them." She set the tray down, walked across to the photos, and picked them up, bringing them back to Claire for her to see them properly. "My sister's boys. Artie's working in America now and Geoff is at uni. Philosophy, would you believe, so God knows what he's going to do when he leaves."

Claire made a vague murmuring sound suggestive of *What indeed?* What she really wanted was for Sue to get to the reason she'd called her here.

"Child substitutes, if I'm honest," Sue said with a small laugh, taking the pictures back and replacing them.

"You're not married, then? Is Mrs. Green a business thing?"

"In a way. You'll never guess how many doors closed to me when I was starting out as Miss or even Ms. But yes, there was a Mr. Green, and no, we're not married any longer. Not for a long while." Sue shrugged her shoulders. "It didn't work out." She poured out the tea. "And now I find life a lot easier telling the men what to do." She handed Claire a cup. "Don't you?"

Clare stirred her tea and thought of Dave Lyon. "Sometimes." She sipped at her drink, wishing it was that beer. "Sue, why did you ask me to come here?"

"MAY I BUY you a drink?" Cullen asked. "Or are you expecting someone?"

"I...have been waiting for someone."

Cullen nodded. "I thought so." He coughed slightly. "I know so, actually. I've been watching you. From over there." He gestured to a distant part of the room where a table was partly obscured by a hideous plastic cheese plant.

"I didn't notice you," Dave said. "Behind that."

"Yes. It does feel a bit like sitting in the set for a cheap jungle movie, but it's quite handy sometimes. For watching without being seen. Which I expect you know all about."

"I'm sorry?"

"Surveillance. Stake-outs. Isn't that what they call it?"

"Ah. Yes. Though I rarely take a large plastic plant with me."

Cullen laughed. "I recognised you as soon as you came in." He looked down momentarily, as if embarrassed. "To be honest, I nearly came over straight away, but then I thought that could have been a little awkward. You know. If you were...meeting someone. I saw Freddie get the cold shoulder, so I thought there was definitely someone else in the frame, but when you finished your drink and seemed ready to leave, I thought, either he's been stood up or he's just not found what he's looking for. So maybe..." He looked up again. "So here I am."

"Freddie?"

"The guy who came up and offered to buy you a drink. At least I assume that's what he offered you. Freddie isn't one for beating around the bush ordinarily. To use an unfortunate metaphor."

"I can imagine. You know him?"

"We've...met. So, yes, I do know Freddie." Cullen contrived faint embarrassment. "In fact, I think I know practically everyone in this bar. Though not," he added with a smile, "in the same way. You come here as long as I've been coming here, you get to know pretty much everyone. Time was, this was the only gay-friendly pub in the city. It used to draw in guys from all three counties. I remember the first time I came here, not much more than a teenager. I thought this must have been what speakeasies felt like in Prohibition America. You know? Not exactly illegal, of course, but *illicit.*"

Dave nodded. He remembered all too clearly the first gay bar he'd gone to: carefully chosen, a long way from home and from anyone who might know him. Since that time, he'd been on dawn raids, arrested several violent thugs and, on one occasion, been involved in a street riot. None of it had been as scary as that first gay pub on his own.

"I'm astonished I've not seen you here before," Cullen was saying. "Or have I just missed you?"

"I'm not on the scene much."

Cullen nodded as if he understood all too well. "Too busy, I guess. I don't get much chance myself these days. But, well, here we both are now. And you, Sergeant, unless I miss my guess, have been stood up. So, can I buy you a drink?"

Dave took a closer look at the man who was making him the most tempting offer he'd received in a long time. He hadn't forgotten how indignant he'd been when Sue Green had first tried to fix him up with Cullen like some fag hag matchmaker. And he hadn't forgotten he'd gone to Gallery 48 to follow a possible lead. Or that Cullen was connected to the case, albeit extremely tangentially. But Cullen was very handsome, with a roguish charm and truly stunning blue eyes.

And he was almost convincing.

"You sent me that text, didn't you?" said Dave.

"Ah," Sean Cullen spoke like a man who'd been caught out. "Yes. Yes, I'm afraid I did."

"WHAT DO YOU think of gay men?"

Claire took a second to make sure she had heard Sue properly. "I'm sorry?"

"I mean, I find them a lot easier to deal with than straight men. Don't you?"

Claire thought again about Dave, but this time said nothing.

"I suppose it's because I don't feel any of that battle of the sexes bullshit with them. Straight men always see themselves as the leaders, the dominant ones, don't they? Gay men, the sorted ones anyway, don't care about it. It's liberating, really." Sue sipped from her tea.

Claire caught the odour of it. She couldn't tell her Oolong from her Lapsang, but she could tell Sue wasn't drinking the builder's she had asked for. In spite of herself, she thought about what Sue had said. Dave was a fairly sorted gay man, wasn't he? Did that mean he fully accepted her as his dominant superior? She doubted it. She thought of his record. He could have been an inspector now, probably even should have been. And if he had been, or even if he was promoted in the next couple of years, he'd have got there sooner in his career than she had. But it didn't seem likely, did it? She wondered briefly: should she be worrying about Dave angling for her job, or using her as a rung on his way up the promotional ladder? God knows he had a habit of striking out on his own. Take that business at the Venus and Adonis, for instance.

No. Claire took a swig of her tea and pushed those thoughts to the back of her mind. She didn't think Dave was that type of guy. And not just because he was gay, but because...he wasn't that type of guy. And she hadn't come here to talk about station politics with a gym owner.

"But then you've got rank, haven't you?" Sue went on. "All those uniforms and stripes and things. It helps to keep people in their places, I suppose, men and women. Me? I've got to do it all on my own."

And a good job you're doing of it too, Claire thought, wondering how much easier her job would be if she had the other woman's looks, style, and, of course, body. And then it struck her, the answer to why any woman would take physical development to the extreme level Sue had. "Is that why you got into bodybuilding?" she asked. "To keep the men in line?"

"You're good, Claire. I knew you'd understand. Yes, I've got this." Sue patted one biceps in at least semi-ironic fashion. "Not as much as I used to, of course, but then you make up for it with other things as you...mature. And maybe I don't need to be as built as I used to be. But my God, did it help when I was starting out."

"So, did you always know you wanted to make a career of bodybuilding," Claire asked, the detective in her instinctively wanting to better understand this woman and her motivations, "or did you just start working out one day and it all grew from there?"

"Actually, neither," Sue said, and for a second her brisk self-confidence was replaced by something else. Something sadder, more reflective. "I was...hurt. Quite early on. By a man. He treated me quite badly. Very badly, in fact." She paused for a second, but then went on as if pushing herself past unhappy memories. "But I moved on. I decided I wasn't going to be hurt again and set about literally remaking myself so it could never happen. And I found I liked it and was really quite good at it." She raised her teacup in mock salute.

And just how badly would you have to be hurt, Claire wondered, even as she raised her own cup in return, *to go through all that pain and denial to remake yourself in a new image of your own choosing, gruelling workout after gruelling workout, for weeks, months, years even. What happened to you, Sue?* "And is that why the men do it too?" she asked, unable to ask the question she really wanted to.

Sue laughed outright. "Good lord, no! With most of them, it's pure ego. And yes," she said, catching the doubt Claire had been unable to hide, "I know that's pot calling the kettle weight black. You know—" She put down her cup. "I'm glad we've finally had a chance to have a good talk together, just you and me, away from all the others. I'm going to be honest, I rarely meet other strong women. And I don't mean physically, no offence meant."

"Absolutely none taken." She hesitated but knew there was no way she could leave this conversation without asking what, to her police training, seemed the obvious question. "So, do you mind me asking but was the man who hurt you your husband?"

Sue shook her head sadly. "No. I fought my way back up from a dark place after that first relationship, made myself strong, physically and emotionally, and then, almost inevitably I suppose, I fell for a gorgeous bodybuilder. And he was a bastard too, and found a whole new set of ways to mess me about. Stupid or what?"

"So, you moved on again. And up?"

Sue nodded. "Always up."

Claire sipped her tea as she tried to decide what exactly she felt about this woman. She knew from first-hand experience the pain of a failed relationship, the damage it could inflict on all parties, and she couldn't deny now a feeling of something almost like camaraderie with Sue. Certainly of respect for the way this woman had taken charge of her life and staked her claim to happiness and success. But wasn't there something just a bit too...aggressive about Sue? She made her relationships sound like battles. But then, maybe that was just her nature, and given her nature maybe she couldn't have turned out to be anything other than who and what she was: a competition winner in one of the most demanding of sporting disciplines, and the owner of a growing business empire with a lovely home and great taste in clothes. *And at least two failed relationships behind her.* Claire was aware of the unworthiness of the thought but needed to bear it in mind to prevent being completely overwhelmed by jealousy.

"Which kind of brings us back to the gays and why I like them," Sue said. "I know a lot of it has to do with them not being interested in me for sex, but I also think they're more honest overall, about what they want, about relationships. It's only sad when they feel they have to hide or suppress what they really are. Don't you think?"

"I...don't think about it much." She was not really sure why they were coming back to this topic.

"Your Sergeant Lyon, for instance."

Claire stiffened. "I'm sorry, Sue, but it is not at all appropriate for me to comment on one of my officers."

"Of course," Sue said hurriedly. "Of course. I'm sorry, I understand completely. I'd feel the same if someone asked me about someone who worked for me."

It's not the same at all, Claire thought, but let it pass, for the moment.

"It was just, seeing you with your sergeant, it was like another point of similarity between you and me." She saw Claire's bemusement. "You've got him, and I've got Sean Cullen."

Sergeant Lyon is not my friend. And... Claire shifted in her armchair which wasn't as comfortable now as it had up till then. The empathy she'd begun to feel for Sue didn't, she found, extend to this particular parallel. And she was beginning again to wonder just why Sue had called her and asked her to come over. "Sue..." she began.

Sue reached down to one side of the armchair she was sitting in and pulled up an A4 envelope that had been waiting on the floor there. She placed it on her lap and rested her hands on it. "What do *you* think, though, about Sean?"

GALLERY 48 10:00 for info on Danny Thompson.

Dave held up his phone for Cullen to see the message he had been sent.

Cullen had the grace, or the nerve, depending on how you saw it, to appear slightly abashed. "I don't need to see it again, Dave. Like I said, I did send it." He spread his hands and smiled. "It's a fair cop."

"Are you taking... Are you treating this like some kind of joke, Mr. Cullen?"

"Please, it's Sean, and..."

"Because I can assure you, wasting police time is taken seriously. Something I would have expected you as an MP to know very well."

Cullen sighed. "Actually, the clue was kind of in the username."

"What?"

Cullen pointed to the phone Dave was still holding in his face. "My username on that app. *Empy*. M. P. I did think, as a detective, you might have worked it out."

Dave shoved the phone back into his pocket in disgust. Bloody tricksy fake names. He was sick to death of them. "Have you, or have you not, any new information on the investigation into the murder of Dan Thompson, or Paul Best for that matter?"

Cullen looked down at his hands which were folded in his lap. "That's...not why I texted you."

Dave stood. "Then I've got a bloody good mind to take you back to the station right now and book you for..."

"I'm sorry," Cullen said.

Dave hesitated. He'd been quite genuine about his threat of marching Cullen back to Foregate Street and, at the least, tying him up in administrative red tape that would keep him there until the small hours of the morning. But then he considered the report he would have to write. *I responded to a message sent to a gay dating app designed primarily for the purpose of providing quick shags to those in need.* It would not look good. And besides, something about this still wasn't adding up.

"How did you know it was me on the app?" he snapped. "I haven't posted a picture." *And even I would have trouble recognising me from the written description I gave.*

Cullen cleared his throat. "Leo?" he said. "I'm not a detective, but even I could work that one out, Sergeant Lyon."

"No, no, no. That's way too much of a longshot for anyone to take a chance on."

Cullen shrugged. "True," he admitted. "But then if I had reeled in a Leo other than the one I was hoping for, I did at least have the opportunity to check him out from my hidden vantage point. And if he hadn't been you, but had been at least as handsome..." He shrugged his shoulders. "Win-win."

"Flattering," Dave said coldly.

Cullen's smile faltered just a little. "Sorry, that did sound rather crass. I think maybe this place brings out the hidden shallows in everyone. No, I knew you were Leo. The app has a proximity function, remember? I happened to be thirty metres from Heavy Metal when you were in there. You and Gavin."

"Gavin?" *Oh right. Gav. The guy Kilby had pegged as victim three. Everyone has Gav sussed, except me.*

"So there you go," Cullen concluded. His smile returned, as confident and charming as before. "Elementary, you might say."

Not quite. Dave ran Cullen's account through his head. There was still something that didn't... He snapped his fingers. His app going off in the gym. Bill Kilby had heard it. Him and...

"Sue Green!" Her comment. Her running off to her little office. Her bloody smile! Now it made sense. She'd called Cullen, told him Dave was there in the gym, without Summerskill, and he'd come running—with his proximity function.

"Now that is good detective work, Sergeant. Yes, Sue's a good friend."

"She's also now an accessory to wasting police time."

"Sue likes to see people happy, and she honestly thought we could...be good for each other."

"The last thing I need is for a woman to be organising my...my private life."

"Don't you like women?"

"Yes, I like women!" Dave stopped, aware that, in his anger, he had spoken too loudly.

A couple of men to one side of the bar stopped their conversation and turned towards them. He glared back at them and they turned away again quickly, but Dave heard the muttered comment one of them made and the laugh that followed.

Cullen was making a poor attempt to conceal how amusing he found the situation. "Personally, I find the friendship and support of strong women like Sue Green a blessing," he said. "One of the decided advantages of our...lifestyle. I had thought perhaps you enjoyed a similar relationship with your detective inspector."

Really? Really? Dave tried to imagine Claire Summerskill fixing him up with dates. The idea was ludicrous. Then he remembered their recent conversations, her asking him about his dates, about Rob. *"I'm trying to find out if you've actually got a love life."* He shook his head. No. DI Summerskill was absolutely nothing like Susan Green. Not at all. Really.

"I'm sorry, Sergeant," Cullen said smoothly, "if you've taken our little subterfuge the wrong way. I really had hoped we could get to know each other a little better. To the mutual advantage of both of us, as they say. But I think perhaps maybe it's best I left now." He hesitated. "But, if you should happen to change your mind—" He tapped the mobile in his breast pocket. "You know my app name. Good night."

Dave sat, fuming as the MP sauntered from the bar, waving at a guy across the room as he went. The last thing Dave wanted to do was waste any more time in this chichi palace, but he definitely didn't want it to look as if he was following Cullen or run the risk of bumping into him again outside. So he sat and waited, brooding furiously on what had just happened.

The friendship and support of strong women. A similar relationship with your detective inspector. *Ha! She's my boss, you pompous queen. And are you so vain you think you can pull a juvenile, insulting trick like this and I'll just laugh and fall into bed with you because you're good-looking and successful and well-off and...*

"Stood you up, has he?"

It was the barman who had walked over to Dave's end of the counter and was standing with an air of vague amusement as he wiped a glass with a cloth.

Glad to be pulled from the furious direction his thoughts had been taking, Dave was nevertheless reluctant to appear the blown off loser. "Not exactly."

The barman shrugged, obviously not believing Dave but willing to give him the benefit of the doubt if it would help his self-respect. "I shouldn't let it get to you. You're not exactly his type anyway."

"You know him, then?"

"I know them all here." The barman stopped wiping his glass, set it down, and leaned over towards Dave, resting his elbows on the bar top. "I don't know you, though. New in town?"

Three come-ons in one night? Dave thought in surprise. *No. Two. Cullen's con trick doesn't count. Even so, that's a better hit rate than the app gives. Maybe Claire's right. Maybe I should play the scene more.* "Kind of," he said.

The barman smiled. *Nice teeth.* "What do you do?"

Dave didn't blink. "Quantity surveyor."

"Cool. I get off in ten minutes. You still be here?"

"Yeah, I guess I could be."

The barman smiled again. *Really, those are film star teeth.* "Cool." He straightened, and Dave recognised the moment, the pivotal point where two guys had to decide. Casual? Or something more serious.

Dave considered. *The guy. Those teeth. The time. A drink? Two? His place? Mine? The next morning. Work? The double murder investigation I am supposed to be working on.*

He sighed. "Look..." He waited for the other guy to give him his name but the barman didn't; he just stood there, waiting. "I'm sorry, but on consideration, could we maybe postpone? I mean. I'd love to...have a drink with you but I really have got a lot on my plate at the moment and I don't think..."

"Sure. Whatever," the barman said, his gorgeous smile not even wavering. "See you around." And he was off, up the other end of the bar, still polishing his glass and still smiling.

You could at least have faked some disappointment, Dave thought morosely as he left the bar. *What is it with some gay men? Would it have killed you to have acted more like a human being and less like a sex worker?* He pushed his way moodily through the exit doors into the street outside. At least there was no sign of Cullen there. *And that's a good thing, right? Yeah.*

Dave made his way back to the car park. *Maybe life would have been easier if I'd grown up to be straight. Or a real quantity surveyor.*

Chapter Ten

DAVE'S FIRST SURPRISE of the next morning was being beaten to the office by Claire for the second day in a row. His second surprise was her first words to him. "We're bringing Sean Cullen in."

"What?" *Bloody hell, she is good. I haven't even told her about last night yet. But much as I'd like to wipe the smile off the slimy git's face, I don't think...*

Claire threw an A4 envelope across the desk to him. "Cop a load of these."

Dave tipped the envelope up and half a dozen photos slid out. He took one and held it up, first one way up then another. "Oh my." He picked up another, then another. "My, my, my."

"Enjoying yourself?"

"Not half as much as Cullen clearly was. But where did these come from?"

"Sue Green found them in a locker at Heavy Metal. Or rather, one of her staff did."

"Marc the Mirthless?"

"Possibly. Anyway, it's a routine thing. Once every two weeks, they do a sweep of the lockers, clearing them of things people have left behind. She says it's amazing what you find."

"Certainly is," Dave said, slowly turning the photo he was studying through three hundred and sixty degrees, the better to appreciate it from all angles.

Claire's desk phone rang out. "Summerskill?" A few terse comments later, Claire put the phone down, the enthusiastic anticipation of a minute earlier completely gone. "It's Robert Taylor. He's been assaulted. He's in Ronkswood Hospital."

"Is it serious? Did he say who did it?"

"He's unconscious. They don't know yet how serious it is. He's taken a beating, but it looks like whoever did it just used his fists and feet, not a dumbbell this time." Claire reached for her desk phone again and punched in an internal connection. "Jenny? I want you to get down to Ronkswood Hospital, ward ten. Robert Taylor's in intensive there. Find out everything you can from the doctors. And if Taylor comes round, call me immediately." She hung up. "Come on, you. Let's go and get Cullen."

"Wait. Hold on a minute." Dave was thinking of Paul Best and his mashed throat; Dan Thompson and his caved-in head; and now Robert Taylor, punched and kicked into unconsciousness. He ran his finger over the photos Claire had spread out in front of him like a pack of smutty postcards. "Okay, we've got these somehow. And Cullen's a greasy toe rag—more on that later—but a violent killer? I'm not sure..."

"If all killers acted like Dick Dastardly our job would be a lot easier. But until then..."

The office door opened, and a uniform put his head round. "Visitor for you, ma'am."

"He'll have to wait. We're off. Get WPC Trent to..."

"It's the local MP, ma'am." Summerskill and Lyon stopped dead in their tracks. "Sean Cullen."

"BLACKMAILED?"

Sean Cullen nodded calmly. "Yes, Inspector. I am being blackmailed."

Claire leaned in across the small table in the interview room. "Who by, Mr. Cullen?"

Cullen shifted slightly. "William Kilby."

"William...? *Bill* Kilby?"

"If we're being informal, yes."

Dave wrote the name down in his notepad even though every word any of them spoke was being recorded by the machine set up between them.

"And what was the nature of the blackmail, Mr. Cullen?" Claire asked.

The officers waited. Dave examined the man in front of them, not as he had last night but now with the licence of an interviewing police officer. He was still handsome, of course. What was perhaps surprising was that he seemed almost as at ease here in Interview Room Number One as he had at Gallery 48. Not quite, though. Dave saw the pulse beating quickly in his throat, over the cut of the expensive silk shirt, saw his Adam's apple move as he swallowed again, noted the way his one hand went to play with the simple gold band on the ring finger of the other hand, and the way he folded both hands and placed them in his lap when he saw Dave noting them. *Smooth. Or is it slippery?*

"Mr. Kilby is an unpleasant man," Cullen began.

We know.

"That is an opinion, Mr. Cullen. But…"

"There are photographs, Inspector. Embarrassing photographs."

We know that too.

"Of you?"

"Yes. Of me." And was that just a hint of testiness, of exasperation at the dim-wittedness of socially inferior police officers? Dave thought it was, and he hoped Claire had noted it too. He couldn't think of anyone more likely and able to—what was it?—tear an arrogant MP a new one.

"And may we ask the nature of these photographs, Mr. Cullen?"

Dave waited for a response to the question, the tip of his pen over his pad. He knew *what* the pictures were of. His chief curiosity was *how* Cullen was going to describe them.

"They were of me with other men, Inspector."

"Were they of a sexual nature?"

"That depends on how you define sex."

"I can define it very graphically, Mr. Cullen. But, as a mature adult, I was assuming you'd have a pretty good idea yourself."

Dave saw the corner of Cullen's lip twitch, almost as if he was trying not to smile. "Then I suppose, Inspector, yes, they were of a sexual nature. At least they were once I was alone and had them…to hand."

"Mr. Cullen…!"

Cullen held his hands up. "I'm sorry, Inspector. I don't mean to make light of a serious situation. But I am determined not to let this get blown out of proportion. The photographs in question are…embarrassing, I can't deny. But they are not at all what I would call *incriminating*. They are of men, usually on their own but sometimes with me. And only ever one at a time."

"Of a sexual nature?" Claire repeated slowly.

Cullen gave a sigh. "The pictures were of young men in…a state of undress. Not *that* young, I hasten to add. We are not talking twinks here." He glanced at Dave as if expecting the sergeant to acknowledge his understanding of the gay term for boys in their late teens. Dave kept his face expressionless. "I have never made a secret of the fact that I prefer the company of men. Real men. Muscular men."

Dave recalled the words of the barman the previous night. *You're not exactly his type anyway.* He watched Cullen now calmly outlining his preferences. *So why were you coming on to me last night?*

"Men like Paul Best and Dan Thompson?" Claire asked.

"Yes."

If someone had taken a picture of Cullen now, it would have shown a man completely composed and relaxed, engaged in nothing more than a normal conversation with two police officers. But Dave wondered what was really going on under his polished exterior. How much was this costing him? He hoped it was a lot, with an intensity that irked him.

"I enjoy the company of muscular men. I respect their dedication and I find their physical perfection aesthetically pleasing."

"They turn you on?"

Cullen made a fleeting moue of distaste. "I like looking at them. I have a collection of bodybuilding magazines the size of which would possibly surprise you." He took in Claire's face. "Or possibly not. None of them go beyond anything you might easily buy in any high street shop. But sometimes, I like something a little more...private. A little more up-front, you might say. And there are more than enough men who are perfectly happy to oblige."

Claire raised her eyes to the ceiling and gave a deliberate sigh of exasperation. "Mr. Cullen, please stop wasting my time. Are you telling us that you paid men to undress for you and have their photographs taken for you and with you?"

"Yes, Inspector. I did. But not just *men*. Competitive bodybuilders," Cullen said. "And it's what they do: undress and show off their bodies."

"Not usually *all* of their bodies, Mr. Cullen. Did you pay them to take off *all* of their clothes?"

"Does it make a difference?" Claire waited. "Yes. Sometimes I did."

"Sometimes?"

Cullen's demeanour hardened slightly into something approaching defiance. "Often."

"And did you pose with them?"

"Sometimes. Yes."

"And did you...?"

"And that is all." Cullen leaned forward. *Still in control,* Dave thought. *He's bloody good. But the cracks are starting to show.* "I say again, these are embarrassing pictures, Inspector, not incriminating. And not illegal. There was no recording of any sexual act between myself and the men I was photographing. Most of the men, as far as I know, have been straight. But, it might surprise you to know, that doesn't matter. They like showing off their bodies, I like seeing them show off their bodies, and they like the money I am happy to pay them for showing off their bodies. Satisfaction on all sides."

"I'm sure," Claire said tightly. "And did these men include Paul Best and Dan Thompson?"

There was the briefest of pauses, a sense of Cullen gathering himself for a difficult moment. "Yes."

"And what did Mr. Kilby have to do with this?"

"Absolutely nothing."

"Then how...?"

"Did he come to have copies of some of the photographs? I...have my suspicions, but the important thing is, he did have them. And two days ago, he said he was going to send them to the local papers if I didn't pay him a certain sum of money. A quite ridiculously substantial amount of money. Though the amount is irrelevant as I have no intention of paying the repulsive little lowlife anything."

Dave made a point of recording *repulsive little lowlife* in his notebook. He thought Claire would especially enjoy hearing that again. He also wrote down and underlined *two days ago*. That meant Cullen had received Kilby's blackmail communication before last night's meeting with Dave. He had come to Gallery 48 knowing he was a potential blackmail victim. Cullen's parting words came back to him: *to the mutual advantage of both of us.* The potential advantage for Cullen was suddenly a lot clearer.

"I am sure," Cullen continued, "you are even more aware than I am that there is nothing to stop a blackmailer coming back again and again for money once the first payment has been made. I have no intention of becoming a perpetual source of funding for Mr. Kilby. I am not a victim, Inspector."

"But Paul Best and Dan Thompson have been, Mr. Cullen," Claire said smoothly.

Dave saw the vein in Cullen's neck pulse again.

"And while I appreciate the strength of character your resistance to blackmail suggests, we have to admit the...exposure would not have done your political career much good."

"Probably not," he admitted. "Although I'm sure you're aware just how big my majority is. Do you remember one of the key demographics identified by the poll analysts a few years back? *Worcester Woman.* The voting pattern of Worcester Woman was said to be an indicator of who would win elections. Worcester Woman has put me where I am today. And she does hate political change. I think some of them might even like the *frisson* of a little sexual scandal. No, Inspector. Today's scandal is tomorrow's fish and chip paper, a metaphor largely lost on the youth of today but an image of a political truth still. My parliamentary career might stumble, but I honestly do not think it will come to an end because of this." He paused. "But my Fitness First programme is another matter. That, I do think, might suffer. And, believe it or not, that programme does matter to me, very much."

"That's as may be, Mr. Cullen," said Claire, "but what is a *frisson* for you is a murder case for us. Double murder. Possibly even triple now."

Dave noted Cullen's puzzled reaction. "Triple?" Both police officers remained silent. "I...don't know what you mean. I had nothing to do with the deaths of Paul and Dan. And who...?"

"Did Robert Taylor ever pose for you, Mr. Cullen?"

"Robert? No. Never."

"You're very emphatic about that."

Cullen gave a half smile. "While my...dalliance with built young man has been primarily physical in nature I do appreciate at least a partial meeting of minds. There has to be something to talk about..."

"Between exposures?"

"Quite. And when it comes to Robert's mind... Well, there's not a great deal in it, to be honest, is there? And I doubt he would ever have the flexibility to allow him to put his inhibitions and prejudices to one side, even for a bit of harmless amusement."

Dave thought back to their first interview with Robert. *"Nowt queer about it."* No, he didn't think Robert would have stripped to a posing pouch or less for a gay man either. But did he know that Paul, his best mate, had done? How had he felt about it?

"Paul certainly had no inhibitions in the face of decent remuneration. And Dan..." He stopped. "But you said there might be a third death. Would that be Robert?"

"It's not appropriate for us to comment at this time," said Claire. "In the meantime, we will need the names and details of all the men you have photographed. Or *had* photographed. Did you take the photographs yourself, Mr. Cullen, or was there a third person with you?"

"Just me, Inspector." *But had that been just the fraction of a hesitation before he answered?* "And is that truly necessary? Believe it or not, I'm not thinking of myself here. As I said, nothing illegal was happening. These were just lads making a bit of easy money. It could really embarrass them at the least; at worst cause all sorts of havoc to their private lives. For what? Just to make sure I haven't chopped them up and buried them under the Elgar statue outside the Cathedral?"

"Yes," said Claire.

Cullen winced. "I see. Then might I suggest you go along to Heavy Metal most any day of the week and I can guarantee you'll see them all still very much alive and pumping."

"With a couple of exceptions."

"Have all of your...contacts come from Heavy Metal, sir?" asked Dave. And he saw it again: a fraction of a hesitation. But was it simply surprise at Dave's first contribution to the interview? "Or did you frequent any of the other gyms in the city or thereabouts? The Venus and Adonis, for example."

"While passing over for a moment the pejorative associations of that word *frequent,* yes, Sergeant. The men who have agreed to be photographed with me have been drawn from the Heavy Metal gym. But then that is because Heavy Metal is a serious gym for serious bodybuilders. And that is the kind of man that, for the most part, I like."

"Your type?" Dave asked. He could tell from Claire's puzzled frown that she realised there was something going on she wasn't fully party to. He didn't look forward to explaining it to her.

Claire took a second now to think through what Cullen had told them so far. "How did Bill Kilby make contact with you about the photographs?" she asked.

Cullen pulled a face as if even the memory was distasteful. "At Heavy Metal. I was there on Fitness First business. I'd spoken to him several times before, of course. It was hard not to. He had a rather loathsome habit of sidling up to you, and before you knew it, he was talking to you as if he'd known you for ages."

Tell us about it!

"And then, two days ago, he came up to me and said he'd got some photographs I'd probably be interested in. I didn't know what he was talking about at first, was only listening with half an ear, like I did most of the time he buttonholed me. But then he pretty quickly made it clear exactly what he meant."

Dave flipped back a page in his notes. "You said you had an idea of how he had got hold of these pictures?"

"Yes." Cullen sighed regretfully. "I think it was Dan Thompson."

"Why him?" Claire asked.

Not for the first time, Dave had a strong sense of Cullen's choosing his words precisely. *Or is he just being careful to remember the story he has rehearsed?* "There are two reasons. I've said that most of the lads who posed for me were straight. Credits to our modern, metrosexual age: perfectly comfortable in their own sexuality and not bothered by mine. Or so interested in money they couldn't care one way or the other. Anyway, Dan...was not."

"We know he was gay."

Cullen nodded. "And in retrospect, I think that was a mistake I made. Dan mistook my interest for more than it was. It sounds hard in the circumstances, but I did just admire his body. There could never have been anything more. But I think he took it hard when..."

"When you ditched him in favour of Paul Best?" Dave said. *Bingo!* he thought at the flash of anger in Cullen's eye.

"*Ditching* implies we were in some kind of relationship. I can assure you, we were not. There were no scenes, no promises. Very little said at all at any time, but I could tell Dan was hurt, angry even. I thought he'd get over it."

"But then Paul was killed."

"I didn't think for a second Dan had anything to do with that!"

Interesting, Dave thought. *And I actually think you mean it.*

"Why not?" Claire asked.

"Because, Inspector, you may not believe it for someone as physically well-developed as Dan, but he was a very gentle man. He could never have done something like that."

"But he could have handed over *embarrassing* photos to drop you in it?" *Which explained why there were only pictures of Thompson and Cullen in the pile of photos Claire had.*

"Sadly, yes. And..."

"And Mr. Cullen?"

"Dan needed the money."

"What for?" Claire thought back to Thompson's flat: the piles and piles of white boxes. She knew why he had needed the money. Did Cullen?

"Steroids. I'm afraid Dan wasn't beyond artificial assistance in his bodybuilding endeavours. You'd be mad not to, really, in today's competition culture. Although," Cullen concluded, "I suppose if it was he who gave the pictures to Kilby, the money was all rather academic."

"What do you mean?"

"Oh, come on, officers. All this time spent at Heavy Metal and you haven't found out yet? Bill Kilby is *the* man to go to for steroids. He's a one-man drug warehouse!"

"THOUGHTS?" ASKED CLAIRE after the interview had concluded and Cullen had been allowed to leave the station but strongly advised not to go anywhere too far away in the immediate future.

"He's a slimy, two-faced, untrustworthy, pompous bastard."

"He's a politician."

"But..."

"But?"

"I don't think he's our killer."

"And do we have any reasons for that assumption, other than that he looks great in a suit?"

Dave didn't rise to the bait. "Why would Thompson have copies of the pictures? Come to that, why does anyone have pictures anymore? I thought all porn was computer-based these days. But that aside, Cullen would have been a fool to let Thompson have copies."

"Unless our member for parliament was being economical with the truth when he said these were all selfies."

"A third person?"

"Who kept copies."

Dave considered this. "So, are we saying the third person gave, or sold, the pictures to Thompson who then passed them on to Kilby, or that he passed them straight on to Kilby, cutting out the middleman?"

"More likely the first."

"So...?"

"So, we have ample reason to be highly suspicious of the tale our duly elected representative has just spun us, which should make us all the more suspicious of his involvement in two, possibly three murders."

"Yes and no, boss."

Summerskill and Lyon looked up from their discussion to see Jenny standing in the door of the interview room. "I thought I told you to get on to Taylor in Ronkswood?" Claire said sharply.

"And I did," Jenny replied, with more asperity than Dave would have accepted from a WPC. "But I thought you'd want to hear as soon as possible that he's conscious and talking again."

"At last!" Claire punched the air. "Good news at last. Has he said anything useful? Did he say who attacked him?"

Jenny hesitated, and Dave wondered briefly if it was because she was still smarting from Summerskill's sharpness. *Suck it up, girlfriend.*

"Yes," Jenny said. "It was Bill Kilby."

"Why did I ever doubt it?" Claire rose from her seat. "Right, Sergeant, get a team together. This time of day he's likely to be down at Heavy Metal. Get that new uniform. The big one from Durham, what's his name?"

"Gareth," said Dave immediately. "PC Evans."

On a high at the change of fortune, Claire chuckled. "Thought you'd know. Yes, get him. He looks like he could handle himself in a barney, and Kilby is just stupid enough to try it on. At least, I'm hoping he is. Jenny, get me his address from the file. If he's not at the gym, we'll..."

"Thirty-seven Blackwell Street," Jenny said. "And he's there."

Claire stopped mid-flow. "Impressive work, WPC Trent. But aren't we getting just a bit ahead of ourselves? You could at least wait for the officers in charge of the investigation to issue some instructions."

Dave saw clearly the ambivalence in Claire's words, part jest, part seriousness; saw Jenny redden and heard the coldness in her voice when she replied. "I suppose I could have, ma'am. But then I thought you might like the news I've just been given. Bill Kilby is at home. But he's dead."

Chapter Eleven

"HE NEARLY MADE it," Aldridge said, matter-of-factly.

Bill Kilby's bloated, discoloured face stared up sightlessly at Summerskill and Lyon as they stood over his corpse. Around the man's bull neck someone had coiled a length of thick twine and pulled it so tight it dug deep into the flesh, almost hidden from sight in places. Lengths of it hung down from either side of his neck, ending in wooden handles of some kind. They saw the tears in the skin where the dying man had clawed at the makeshift garrotte that had choked the life out of him. They saw the tongue, protruding, purple, a ghastly parody of that first encounter and the grotesque way he had tried to impress himself on Summerskill. It was that thought, Claire decided, that strangely enough was the most upsetting of this awful tableau.

"What do you mean?" she said, forcing the juxtaposed images out of her mind for a moment.

Aldridge bent to the level of his autopsy table, took a probe, and jammed it into the cold flesh of Kilby's neck, pressing it upwards hard to expose part of the rope biting into his throat. "This is plastic. Strong, but if you look here and here—" he indicated sections of the plastic where it was noticeably thinner, the blue colour paler than elsewhere "—you can see where it was stretching under the strain. Much more and it would have snapped." He withdrew the probe and stepped back. Kilby's grey flesh closed over the plastic again. "But it didn't."

Reluctantly, but determined not to show any of that reluctance to either Aldridge or Lyon, Claire reached out and fingered part of the length of plastic that hung to one side. It was thick and tough. "It would take a strong man to pull it so hard," she murmured. She saw the same question in Dave's eyes. *Was Cullen that strong?*

"Well obviously," Aldridge said. "But then it would also have taken a strong man to overpower this chap in the first place. I mean...." Aldridge waved his hand over the corpse as objectively as a butcher describing a cut of meat. "Past his prime, no doubt, but still packing some serious muscle.

Oh, and you noticed these, of course." Aldridge stooped and raised one end of the plastic line and the handle that dangled from it. There was another at the other end. "Both dusted," he said before Dave could interject. "Clean. I don't think the killer even used them."

"Yes, we noticed," Claire said. How could they fail to have seen and recognised them? Kilby had been throttled with a skipping rope. The kind you found in gyms.

Aldridge let the line slip through his fingers and the wooden pommel at the end swing free again. "Y'know, time was when the serial killers went after helpless young women. Now they're taking out bodybuilders. It's an upside down, topsy-turvy world we're living in nowadays. Isn't it, Sergeant?"

"If the murderer came up on him from behind," Dave said, pointedly ignoring Aldridge's comment, "then relative strength wouldn't have been such an issue. A couple of quick twists then let torque do the rest."

The coroner gave a scornful laugh. "He's not likely to have stood quietly while someone came at him from the front, now, is he? And you can see he put up one hell of a struggle. No, this man was killed by another man. A strong man."

"You'd be surprised what some women can manage," Claire murmured.

Aldridge's attitude was part pity, part condescension. Mostly condescension. "Oh, and you'll have noticed this," he added, indicating the thickset shoulders of the body.

Summerskill and Lyon nodded at the spray of acne there. "Test his blood," said Claire. "I think we all know what you'll find in it."

KILBY'S BODY HAD been found outside the back door to his home, a surprisingly pleasant and utterly conventional semi-detached in a bland and unexceptional housing estate. From the police point of view, the position of Kilby's house, at the end of a row of similar box-like residences, with its annoyingly tall leylandii hedges around the small patch of back garden, meant that the murderer had had ample opportunity to drive up close to the rear gate, enter, kill Kilby and leave, quickly and with little chance of being seen. *Thank you, Neighbourhood bloody Watch!* Claire thought, taking in the number of posters in house windows proclaiming the area to be under constant civilian surveillance. *Give me one good CCTV camera any day of the week.*

They left SOCO doing their work in the immediate crime scene outside the house and stepped into the house to see if there was anything that might help, though Claire had a fatalistic sense they'd find nothing. The locked door and the key they'd found lying next to the body had made it clear Kilby had been killed before he could even get indoors. What they did find was confirmation of what Kilby's acne had led them to suspect. Dave whistled. "It's like Thompson's flat."

"Writ large," Claire agreed. "Very large."

Like Dan Thompson, Kilby had his piles of white boxes in his kitchen, next, of course, to the huge canisters of protein powder. Unlike Thompson, he also had boxes of steroids in his bedroom, living room and garage. Many, many boxes. "He was a dealer," Dave said.

"Either that or he was stockpiling enough of the shit to keep him going for the next couple of hundred years."

"Not the only thing he was stockpiling either." Dave had had a cursory flick through one of the piles of magazines on a garage workbench. "Porn."

"Gay?" Claire asked, already guessing the answer from the wrinkle of distaste on her sergeant's face.

"Not in the slightest," Dave said emphatically. "Sorry."

"Damn. A couple of piles of *Hot Hunks* or *Big Beef* might have given us some kind of link with Cullen and Thompson."

"If they existed. Though full marks for imaginative naming, ma'am."

Claire swore under her breath. "So, the only link we have between the three dead men is still that they were all bodybuilders who used steroids."

"And the Heavy Metal gym."

SUE GREEN LOOKED at the plastic bag Claire Summerskill was holding out with bemusement. Dave noticed she had automatically gone to take it from the inspector but had withdrawn her hand when she saw what was inside. *Now why was that?* But then he took in his boss's grim expression. That in itself might have been enough to give the gym owner pause. "Yes, I recognise it. That is, I think I do." She leaned down and peered a little closer then drew back sharply. The cord had been drawn deep into Kilby's neck. There had been blood. "It's a skipping rope," she said slowly. "But is that...?"

"Are you missing any of your ropes, Mrs. Green?"

Sue Green tore her eyes away from the bag Claire was still holding up to meet Dave's. "No. That is... I don't think so."

"Can you check for us, please?"

Some of the confusion left Sue's eyes replaced by a sudden hardness. "Sergeant. I have no idea how many skipping ropes this gym has. They're just...skipping ropes, for God's sake. I buy them ten or twenty at a time, share them out around my gyms. They wear out, we replace them." She came to a halt, her eyes drawn back almost as if against her volition, to the coiled rope in the bag Claire was still holding up. "Why...?"

Claire handed the bag back to Dave who put it to one side, for the moment. "Bill Kilby is dead," she said bluntly.

Dave watched Sue working through the implications of what she had been told—and shown. "And you think...?" she said slowly, then stopped. "What do you think?"

"He was strangled with that rope."

Dave watched as Sue Green swallowed, taking in the implications of what Summerskill was telling her with calculated bluntness. He knew Summerskill was watching as closely as he was for how exactly Sue Green was going to react.

"Okay," she said, nodding slowly. "I'll check as best I can to see if the rope is one of ours, but Claire, you've got to know, there's nothing special about it. I use ropes like that here, in Venus and Adonis, and in my other gyms. And I dare say you'd find them in any of the other gyms in the city."

"But Kilby used this gym," Dave said quietly. "As did Dan Thompson and Paul Best."

Sue Green turned to him. Her face was pale, but her voice, when she spoke, was calm and level. "Then find who killed them, Sergeant. Find him and stop him. Before any more of my clients end up dead."

"HE WAS A right bastard." Robert Taylor stopped, his heavily bruised eyes registering sudden panic at his possible mistake. "You gonna use that as evidence against me?"

Like a shot, Claire thought, *if I believed you could have murdered Kilby from your hospital bed.* "No, Robert," she said out loud. "You have not been arrested. This is not..."

"Course I've not been arrested," Taylor protested. "I'm the one that's been bloody assaulted. I'm the one that's..." He gasped, winced, and fell back onto his hospital bed.

Claire steadied the drip by the bedside that had been shaken by the violence of the lad's surge upwards. On television, these were always accompanied by machines that blinked and beeped then, at moments like this, stopped beeping and gave out nerve-shredding single notes that brought teams of po-faced medics with electric paddles. Fortunately, there were no machines by Robert's hospital bed, just a cheap get-well card and a floaty balloon shaped like a teddy bear in shocking colours which she assumed were from his admirers at the supermarket where he worked. The balloon was already losing its floatiness. No teams of medics came running. She and Dave were left in peace to conduct their interview with the young man lying between them.

"And why did Bill Kilby assault you, Robert?"

She watched as a procession of thoughts ran through his head and made their presence known on his all too easily readable face: sullen resentment at being unable to avoid more questioning; anger at what Kilby had done to him; some lingering vestige of schoolboy honour; then a bleak realisation he was in deep shit and had no choice in the matter whatsoever.

"He was worried I was going to grass him up."

"About what?"

Taylor squirmed in his bed. "Juice," he said finally. "Steroids. He was dealing. He's been dealing for years. He was worried you were going to bust him."

Claire and Dave waited some more. "Is that all?" Dave said at last.

Taylor frowned. "Yeah."

"Did he try to extort money out of you?" Taylor looked baffled. "Did he ever try to blackmail you?" Claire clarified.

"No. What could he blackmail me about?"

"Did you think Bill Kilby murdered Paul Best?"

Taylor turned his head on his pillow to face Dave. "Course not," he said scornfully. "Kilby could never have laid a finger on Paul."

Claire thought of the gruesome method of Paul's death. *Not in a fair fight, maybe.* "He did a good job on you, Robert."

Taylor winced, as if the reminder probed his all too obvious wounds. "Yeah. Well..."

Claire rolled her eyes. She had less time for his wounded pride than she did for his wounded body. "So why, Robert, did he try to kill you?"

Taylor gave a dry, rasping laugh. "He weren't trying to kill me."

Claire gestured to the hospital bed. "Could have fooled me."

"I was...upset, like," Taylor went on.

"About Paul?" Dave offered.

"Yeah. The only thing I knew he'd done that were, like, dodgy, were the drugs. I didn't think it could be that, but I said so to Bill and he..."

"Didn't agree." Claire thought back to their second meeting with Robert in Heavy Metal—his black eye.

"Yeah. But then when Dan Thompson was done too, I got really worried."

"You spoke to Bill again and he got worried you'd give him away to us?" Taylor nodded. "So, he tried to...persuade you otherwise?" He nodded again, miserably.

Claire swore softly under her breath. Yes, Kilby had been a bastard. But not, or so it seemed, the killer of Paul Best and Dan Thompson.

DAVE HAD TO pick up his pace to keep up with Claire as she stormed out of the hospital. "No motive," she raged. "Still not one bloody clear motive for three bloody killings."

"But a clear link between all of them."

"Links aren't motives. Links...don't make sense!"

He finally caught up with her at the car where she had to stop and wait for him to open it. "Sometimes links don't have to make sense. Sometimes...they're just links."

"No."

"I know you don't want to accept it, but it is looking increasingly likely..."

"No!" Claire's eyes blazed at her sergeant across the roof of his car. *"This is not a bloody serial killer!"*

Chapter Twelve

"THE MUSCLEMAN MURDERER." Chief Superintendent Madden tapped the paper lying on the desk between him and Claire. "Catchy."

Claire grit her teeth. When she'd been a sergeant working under Rudge, she'd seen him verbally eviscerate officers. She'd been on the receiving end too. But, unlike most, she'd been able to give as good as she got, and she'd survived. More than that, she'd earned the respect and eventual friendship of DI Rudge. But CS Madden's deceptively quiet "briefings" always left her feeling as baffled and beaten as she had been when she'd been an empty-headed teenager back in Pontypridd Comp raging against the world and its restrictions. The man was like a Zen master of urbane demolition. She wondered if it was something you learned or something you got given when they stuck a silver spoon up your arse.

"Of course, this one—" Madden tapped the other paper on his desk "—calls him *The Bodybuilder Butcher.*" He shrugged. "Hard to tell at the moment which one will stick."

"It's not..." Claire stopped and collected herself. "They're trying to make out it's a serial killer. I don't... We don't know yet whether it is."

"I see." Madden sat back in his chair, his hands in front of him, fingers interlinked, his face thoughtful as if he was considering a challenging crossword. *The Times* crossword perhaps. "Three dead men?" he said.

"Yes."

"With little in common except..."

"They were bodybuilders. Yes."

"And went to the same gym?"

"Yes."

"But you are saying that, in your opinion, this is not the work of a serial killer."

Claire tried to swallow. She couldn't. Her mouth was arid. "Yes."

Madden nodded as if a particularly cryptic clue was approaching solution. "I see." Abruptly he unclasped his hands and leaned forward across his desk. "My question for you then, Inspector, is this: Why won't you *let* it be a serial killer?"

"Because..." She stopped. "Because..." She tried again, with no more success. *Let me go, you bastard! Let me get out of this office and do my job!* But Madden waited, inscrutable as ever. "Because it doesn't make sense," she finally blurted out.

"Sometimes, things don't make sense," Madden said evenly.

Just what Dave said. Is that something they teach you at university? She felt a familiar anger growing within her. *Well I didn't go to some fancy English school and university, did I? I went to a bog-standard Welsh comp. So how do you expect me to put it into words someone like you can understand?* "I *need* them to make sense," she said fiercely. She bit her lip so hard she thought she tasted blood, but she had to stop herself from saying anything else. More, and she doubted she'd be able to control her pent-up rage. She already feared she'd let too much of it show.

Madden showed no reaction to her words, even though they had been practically shouted into his face. He remained, leaning forward, as if searching her face. Then, as abruptly as before, he sat back. "Good."

"I'm sorry?" Claire resisted the luxury of relief, all too familiar with her superior's tactic of letting her settle on a rug before yanking it out from under her feet.

"That's what makes you a good officer. I hope it's what will make you a good inspector. Now, have you come to ask for a bigger team? I warn you now, DI Rudge is already raising merry hell about the money you're taking from his good causes."

"I... Yes. Yes, sir, that would be...very helpful." *Damn it! Why can't I talk?*

"Very well." Madden reached for his laptop and began entering the information that would translate into more officers, more resources, for Summerskill and Lyon in their investigation. Weirdly, Claire found herself thinking of her son, Tony, when he played his computer games. There was the same fixity of attention on the screen as information was input that made the characters jump. Was that all she and Dave were to people like Madden?

"Sean Cullen," Madden said.

What? Claire snapped out of her disturbing dislocation. *Here it comes. The carpet pull.* "Sir?"

"I understand you've interviewed with Sean Cullen. Yes? Presumably in connection with this case."

Claire nodded dumbly as her mind whirled. How had he known? As ever, she was behind with her paperwork and hadn't had time to submit the report on that interview yet.

"Mr. Cullen, *Sean*, had been to see me before then. He wanted to express his concern that a friend of his was being...well, harassed is too strong a word, but certainly unfairly treated. He asked if I could possibly do anything about it."

Sean? Claire had caught the way Madden had deliberately placed and inflected the name. There was a message there. She knew she had to be careful in the next few minutes to read that message correctly. She forced herself to be calm, to think logically. Then the realisation hit her. "He told you to pull Cortez out of Heavy Metal, didn't he?" she blurted out.

"No," Madden said calmly. "Sean Cullen is not in a position to tell me to do anything. The instruction to pull Cortez out of the operation came from me and was mine alone. And I gave it because planting DS Cortez in the gym in that way was a bloody stupid idea. It was a waste of time and money and ham-fisted to boot. Please don't do anything so stupid again, Inspector."

Claire Summerskill had come a long way from the bolshie sixteen-year-old who had known it all and whose slanging matches with teachers, tutors, deputies, and even, on one memorable occasion, the Head back in Ponty had passed into the stuff of the school's legends. But sometimes the hot-headed madam in her soul who knew it all still raised her head and would not be told to shut up.

"So, was Cullen talking to you as an MP or as a friend?" *Could he fire me for that? It was just a question. But he knew what I was implying. So, could he fire me? Or bust me back to uniform?*

"Sean Cullen," Madden said smoothly, "is indeed our city's MP. As such he is in a position to help us or hinder us. A lot. And, so far, he has only helped us. He is, in point of fact, a friend, a very good friend. To us." Again, he leaned towards her over the desk and it took every ounce of self-control she had for Claire not to draw back or give any indication whatsoever of how very, very nervous she felt right then. "I make no apologies for that, Inspector. If you ever rise to such an exalted position as myself, you will quickly discover the need for friends like Sean Cullen. And of the need for making compromises. If—" and he cocked his head slightly as if asking a question "—you haven't already."

Claire sat and digested. What had she been expecting? Madden's confession to some sort of Masonic conspiracy? Yes, actually. But as her anger ebbed, she felt a depressing sense of her own stupidity rising to take its place.

"But," Madden said, intruding on her slide into despond, "on this occasion, I may have gone too far."

Stunned into silence, Claire waited. How many times could a carpet be pulled from under you? Was it even possible to do it more than once?

"Cullen didn't come into my office complaining about Cortez and demanding his withdrawal. The matter came up in the course of a longer conversation, a meeting about police welfare and charities. He expressed concern for...a friend, and when he outlined what was going on, I agreed he might have a case. It didn't seem that important to him." Madden leaned back in his chair. "But the facts unearthed by your investigation do now suggest otherwise, don't they?"

Claire sat up slightly. "Yes, sir."

Madden nodded. "Do you think he's your killer?"

It would be so easy to say yes. Life could be so much simpler. "No, sir," she said.

"And what does your sergeant think?"

What the hell does it matter what my sergeant thinks? "He agrees with me, sir," she said stiffly.

"Good." Madden turned to his computer again, entered more data that would turn itself into money and then men, women, and time. When he spoke again, his voice had a meditative tone to it. "At the moment this is tabloid titillation. They're creating a bogeyman and people are enjoying feeling scared, especially because, unless they happen to be blessed with muscles the size of bowling balls, they can feel safe at the same time."

Claire thought back to her last meeting with Sue Green. "Some of the men at Heavy Metal are starting to feel scared, sir."

"I doubt the public can empathise with men built like tanks. But if these victims had been women..."

Claire thought of the female victims of crime, of the hateful suggestion almost always there, unspoken but corrosive: *they must have been doing something to deserve it.* No one was going to suggest that about Best, Thompson, and Bill Kilby, were they?

"Your head would be on the line for having let it get this far. Simple fact, Inspector."

Yes, Claire thought. *You're probably right. And I have no idea how I feel about that right now.*

Madden nodded and turned fully to face his computer, and knowing that at last, after what felt like an eternity, she had been dismissed, Claire rose to leave. Then one last insight struck her.

"The friend Cullen talked about, sir, the one who was being upset by my operation. It was Susan Green, wasn't it?"

"BIT LATE FOR your usual, Sergeant."

Dave looked up from his gloomy inspection of a tomato sauce bottle. The canteen manager, Eileen, was wheeling a trolley of dirty plates and cutlery past and smiling at him with that peculiar mix of the maternal and the something less than maternal that made Claire laugh every time she saw it. "Just waiting for the boss, Eileen."

"Ah," said Eileen and she nodded with an understanding that twenty-two years of work in the station canteen had given her. "She'll be all right, love. Do you want me to fix you a bacon sandwich while you're waiting?"

"D'you know, that would be great. Thanks."

"White or brown? Buttered or unbuttered?"

"White, please. And easy on the butter. One side only, if you wouldn't mind?"

"Watching the waistline, eh? Keeping trim for someone special?"

Dave thought about his recent dates. It was rarely the size of his waist that guys were interested in. He made a non-committal noise.

Eileen patted him on the shoulder then hastily wiped off the crumbs the act had left on his jacket. "Trust me, you've got no need to worry on that score. Now, you hang on here and I'll be right back. Shan't be a mo." With a conspiratorial wink and a much more energetic push of the trolley than she had hitherto given it, Eileen hurried back behind the counter to work her culinary magic.

"Y'know, I've waited over an hour before now for a curled-up ham sandwich and a rock-hard tomato. And that was when the canteen was actually officially open."

DI Rudge was standing behind Dave. This was unexpected. As Rudge had made clear, the canteen was officially closed for meals, though often used by officers on the scrounge or as an unofficial waiting room. More to the point, the packed lunches Rudge's wife prepared for him daily were things of beauty and much admired by all—apart from Eileen, for commercial reasons.

It was also unexpected for Dave to be addressed at all by Rudge on anything other than official business anywhere than in their office.

"Guess she doesn't feel threatened by you."

"I generally try not to threaten canteen staff. You get better service that way."

Rudge grunted. "Mind if I join you?" Before Dave could respond, Rudge pulled up the chair on the opposite side of the table and sat down facing him. "Was that your idea?" he said without further preamble. "Putting Cortez in that gym, undercover?"

Dave recognised the famed Rudge interrogation technique: straight in, no nonsense. Claire had spoken admiringly of it. He could see how she had tried to adapt it to her own style. She was, he thought, better at it. "Partly," he said, knowing that was true but hating the way it sounded defensive. "DI Summerskill came up with the idea and I suggested DS Cortez as the most likely candidate."

"Bloody stupid."

"It didn't work."

"Because it was bloody stupid."

Dave's dad had given his youngest son precious little advice as he grew up. Much of the crumbs he had doled out had been about girls and what and what not to do with them, information which, as it turned out, had been largely wasted. But one bit of advice his policeman father had given him was when a senior officer was being an arse and there was nothing to be gained by shooting your mouth off, you kept your mouth shut. Dave hadn't always been able to follow that advice. He was hoping he could now.

"That's why she's in there now being chewed over by Madden."

"Eileen thinks she'll be all right."

"And that's why Eileen's in there making you a bacon butty and not out on the streets in a patrol car. So, what are you doing, apart from sitting on your arse waiting for a late breakfast?"

Caught between, on the one hand, his dislike of Rudge in general and of his bullying manner now in particular, and, on the other, the constraints of rank and his father's good advice, Dave gave a clipped account of his and DI Summerskill's investigation so far. The leads, the dead ends, the suspects. Delivered so tersely, even Dave had to admit it sounded threadbare.

Rudge sat like a stone and listened. When Dave had finished, he grunted a second time. "And again, what are *you* doing?"

Dave took a deep breath. His father's words were beginning to feel like something he'd heard a long time ago, a long way away. There'd been times during his previous posting, at the Redditch station, that he'd felt like this. He sometimes suspected those times were the reason he was no longer at the Redditch station.

"I'm not sure I understand what you're getting at, sir," he said, in much the tone of voice he would have used giving evidence to a hostile barrister in court.

"Who's your money on? What's your gut telling you? You have got a gut, haven't you? Apart from the one Eileen's making for you?"

Dave grit his teeth. "It's...too soon to say."

"Too soon? How many more gym bunnies do you want to see dead? You've had Cullen in. Why haven't you charged him?"

"I... We don't think it's him."

"Why? Cause you fancy him?"

Dave coloured dangerously. Now he couldn't hear his father's words at all through the singing of the blood in his ears. "No, *sir,* it is not. I am not attracted to Sean Cullen in any way."

"Right. Does Claire fancy him?"

"No!"

"Good. Then don't let Madden pull the old school tie on you. If Cullen is bent, and don't get PC with me over words, then you need to nail him. And not in a good way."

Dave nodded tersely, jaws clenched so tight he could feel the muscles in his cheeks bunching. He'd lost track of who, if anyone, was being insulted.

Rudge picked up the salt cellar from the table and toyed with it for a moment as if it was just some casual distraction. Slowly he closed his hand on it tightly, holding it in a fist in front of him. Then he looked over it at Dave. "Claire Summerskill is good, right? Better than she thinks, and better than idiots like Madden know. She might even be better than me one day. But that doesn't mean she doesn't make stupid bloody mistakes. When she was under me, nine times out of ten, she didn't listen to me, which was fine because I was in charge and I don't get it wrong. But now she's in charge, at least for the moment, and nine times out of ten she still won't listen to people. So bloody well make her if you've got something to offer or—" he banged the salt cellar down hard on the table "—sod off and let someone else do the job."

"And do you think Jenny Trent would have done a better job than me at keeping DI Summerskill in line?" Dave said. *And where the hell did that come from?* The words were out of his mouth before he'd consciously thought them through. But they were out there now. "That was the plan, wasn't it," he pressed on, abandoning himself to the impetus of his anger, "before I came along? Summerskill and Trent, moving up the ladder together?"

Dave was mortified to see Rudge was almost laughing. The old bastard actually thought his outburst was funny!

"If we're talking career reviews here, sergeant," he said, "then, just between you and me, I happen to think WPC Trent is exactly where she belongs at the moment. I also happen to think DI Summerskill, if pushed, would agree with me. Whether WPC Trent would agree with either of us is another matter altogether." Rudge pushed his chair back with an ear-piercing scrape of its legs on the floor and stood up. "You want to know what I think? I think Claire Summerskill needs a man as a partner. And how much of a dinosaur does that make me, eh?"

A man? Or a straight *man?* Had Rudge just endorsed him or made it clear why he disliked him? Under the table, Dave's hands curled into fists. He looked into Rudge's craggy, bigoted features and knew exactly what he wanted to say and do.

Then, probably for the best all round, two things happened.

Firstly, a decidedly cheery Eileen reappeared with a trilled, "Here you go," and a plate of bacon sandwiches complete with rolled-up lettuce leaf garnish.

Secondly, a decidedly uncheery Claire Summerskill stormed into the canteen with a snarled, "We're off!" She stopped, momentarily nonplussed by the sight of Lyon and Rudge together at one table. "What's up?"

Rudge smiled. It was like a fissure in a cliff face. "Nothing, darlin'," he said easily. "Just comparing notes."

Claire looked to Dave for confirmation, but he just sat there, glaring at Rudge. "C'mon, you," she said to Dave. "I need your magic fingers."

"Massage or paperwork?"

"Neither. Computer. I want you to do some cyber-digging for me."

Rudge grinned. "Still don't know your Bing from your Yahoo, girl?"

"Can't all have grandchildren to tell us the difference, Jim. You can bring your sandwich with you," she added to Dave.

"No thanks," Dave said, rising to join her. "I've lost my appetite."

RUDGE WATCHED AS the two officers left the room. When they'd gone, he transferred his attention to the bacon sandwich left cooling on its plate. He shrugged, reached down, and picked it up.

"Any brown sauce, Eileen?" he called out.

"SO, WHAT DID Jim want?" asked Claire.

"He was...just checking how the investigation was going," said Dave.

"Right."

"What did Madden want?"

"The same."

"Right."

Each was well aware the other was glossing over the truth. Time enough for details later.

"Right," said Claire briskly. "I want everything you can find for me on Susan Green."

"But we've done the routine background checks."

"I know. But unless her name was anywhere on a computer right next to the word 'criminal' that wasn't going to tell us anything really, was it? I want you to get busy and find out *exactly* who she is and what she's been doing with her life up to and including starting that damn gym."

"And why this sudden interest?" Dave asked, even as he began his computer search. Claire told him what Madden had confirmed. That Cullen had spoken to him about sparing his friend, Sue Green, some of the pressures of the police investigation. "So, it was a double-pronged attack?" he mused. "Green came in to rub our noses in Cortez's cock-up, and at the same time Cullen was doing the secret handshakes with Madden to get him to make us leave her alone."

"They may not have known what each other was up to."

"Of course they did. I also see, by the way, that when I decide I don't like her, it's because I've got a problem with strong women. But when she puts your nose out of joint, suddenly she's a prime suspect."

"She's not a prime suspect. And rank has its privileges," Claire said. "Live with it and get on with it."

Dave gave a weary sigh of acknowledgement and got on with it. Claire turned her attention to the incident board they had set up. Details written in marker pen and the pictures they had of the three victims and suspects so far covered the white surface, but it was the area put aside for Sue Green she focused on now. Was there something that should be up there, something so obvious they were all missing it? Or was she just grasping at straws? Momentarily, she felt a twinge of guilt. Was it worse than that? Was she just being vindictive, reacting with annoyance to the interference in her investigation? Might she not have reacted the same way herself if she had been in Sue Green's position? Sue had been helpful. It had been she who had given Claire the photos of Cullen and Thompson she had found in one of her gym's lockers.

Thoughtfully, Claire wrote the single word *Photos* on the board under Sue's name. Harsh thing to do for a friend, wasn't it? The friend who was working hard to keep the police off your back? That had to show real public-spiritedness. Claire tapped the word with her marker pen and considered. *Or something.*

"SO?"

"Well. Entering 'Green' and all the variations of 'Susan' gives about a quarter of a million results. But adding tags like 'bodybuilder' and 'gym' brings it down a lot more. Take out the Americans and pretty quickly we got to the woman we know."

"And?"

"She's a saint," Dave admitted reluctantly. "She does good wherever she goes." He pushed his keyboard away from him in disgust. "Glowing testimonials in newspapers and magazines, trade papers and online chat forums." He thought of his ill-fated venture into the Venus and Adonis. "And from anyone I've spoken to as well. She creates jobs, helps people achieve their goals, and makes the sick and lame walk again." He momentarily ground to a halt, aware of Claire's irritation. "Okay, she helps the disadvantaged and elderly take up exercise, working in tandem with Cullen and his Fitness First scheme. And—" he couldn't keep the acid tone out of his voice "—don't forget she tries to help people find true love."

"She's a veritable matchmaker," Claire agreed.

"Life is not a musical."

"You are so not gay." Claire's eyes fell on the picture of Cullen, Green and Best pinned to their board. "But that's what she does, doesn't she? Bring people together. You and Cullen. Cullen and Best." She thought of the other photo from the Venus and Adonis that Dave had described for her. "Cullen and Thompson."

"Cullen, and God knows how many more."

Claire nodded slowly. "Even miserable Marc and that girl, what was her name?"

"Alys."

"Right. She brings them together and then bills and coos over them like some tacky reality TV date show hostess." Claire leaned in towards the board and wrote another word: *manipulative.*

"Don't you mean, *strong businesswoman?*" Dave asked disingenuously. "You're right, of course, but people still seem to love her for it. Those girls at the gym were falling over themselves to big her up." He flipped back in his pad to the notes he had made at the Venus and Adonis. "Here you go. Alys said, for instance, that Mrs. Green had had 'a hard life' but she was 'very good' and 'always helped others.' That was right after I asked about Mr. Green. Which, now I think about it, she never got round to answering."

"Do you know shorthand?"

"What?"

Claire indicated his pad. "You always get every detail. I never used to get down half as much making notes for Jim."

"I write quickly," Dave said, sounding almost defensive.

"Okay. So—" Claire turned to their incident board again, pointing at each person on it as she referred to them. "The Venus and Adonis girls love her. We can assume Marc loves her in his Neanderthal way, as no one else in their right mind would employ a gorilla like him, plus she got him a girlfriend, which, I would suggest, would have been well beyond his capabilities without help." She sighed. "I'm guessing it would be the same in her other gyms too. Where were they again?"

Dave turned once more to his notepad. "The south-east, south-west and Manchester."

"Why two in Worcester but only one each in all the other places? What makes us special?"

"Worcester's quite a social mix in a relatively small area," Dave said, turning back to his computer as he spoke and pulling up the Venus and Adonis's official website. "The two gyms certainly cater for two different ends of a social spectrum. Just depends where exactly her other gyms are located, I suppose. There you go." He tapped the computer screen which was displaying the "About Us" page of the website. "Cambridge and Bristol. Big student populations in both. You'd think..."

Claire pointed to another part of the incident board. "Bristol. Paul Best came from Bristol."

"Yes," Dave agreed cautiously. "But that was a year ago." He scrolled quickly through the determinedly positive biographical information posted there. "According to this, Sue Green has been living in Worcester for the past two years, setting up the gyms. And before then, she was in Cambridge for over a year doing the same thing. So, depending on when Best actually started training, they might never have met there."

"Maybe," Clare conceded. She gestured at Dave's computer. "What else does it say about her there?"

"Sean Cullen thinks the relationship between a gay man and a straight woman is a rare and beautiful thing," Dave muttered as he searched through the information in front of him. "I doubt he was thinking about cyber secretarial work."

"Yes, well, if Sean Cullen worked for me he'd have been fired by now so think yourself lucky."

"Praise indeed. Okay." Dave quickly gave her a summary of what the Venus and Adonis had to say about its boss. Written as it undoubtedly was by the subject herself, it told them nothing they didn't already know.

Not expecting much but wanting to be thorough, Dave switched the search engine view from "Web" to "Images." Not surprisingly, the first few pictures were copies of the one from the local rag they had already seen. After those were many more, mostly of Sue with various "celebrities," many of whom Dave recognised from the wall at the Venus and Adonis. Going back further chronologically, pictures of Sue from her bodybuilding days began to emerge. Dave scrolled faster and further.

Claire sighed. "I'd have killed for her waist. But not those arms. Found something to raise your interest?" Dave had slowed in his backward journey through Sue Green's internet picture history, and Claire's comment was a small dig at the fact that this latest bunch of pictures included many with male bodybuilders alongside Sue. Some were copied from magazines, at least two from covers, and several others were photographs from competitions. "I thought muscly guys didn't do it for you?"

Dave was leaning closely into the screen, scrutinising the images. "They don't. But this one might." He clicked on the link to the webpage from which one of the images was taken and directed Claire's attention to the text.

"They do it in pairs," she said in disbelief.

"It would seem so," Dave said, "and mostly, Sue Green did it with this guy."

The article Dave had stumbled on was in a PDF of a bodybuilding magazine dating from about twelve years previously. The subject, and the object of Claire's incredulous distaste, was a vogue for paired bodybuilding competitions. Men and women competing as a team, often in outlandish though, of necessity, revealing costumes. Sue Green had had some notable successes in a number of these, and always, it seemed on closer inspection, with the one man.

"I know it's too long ago to be Paul Best, but tell me it's not Sean Cullen," Claire said, leaning in closely to study the low-resolution images. "Or, God help us, Bill Kilby."

"Neither. This guy's name is Ray Monroe and..." Dave broke off in surprise.

"What?"

"He's her husband."

Claire cast her mind back to her meeting with Sue in her house. *It didn't work out.* She looked again at the man standing next to Sue in the picture, arm raised as if lifting some invisible weight, all the better to make his massive biceps stand out. She still found the posturing and posing ridiculous. But Ray Monroe had been handsome. And obviously as fanatical as Sue Green had been about the whole physical culture thing. "So why didn't it work out?"

"Maybe because she didn't take his name after they married," Dave muttered as he skimmed the information he was downloading. "Why am I not surprised?"

"I didn't take Ian's name when we married."

"Really?" said Dave. "I didn't know that. So he's not Mr. Summerskill?"

"Only in my head. I didn't want to have a different name to Tony. Or the hassle of changing all the documentation."

"Right. So, what was your first husband's name?"

"Ian *is* my first husband."

Dave stopped what he was doing on the computer. "Right," he said, and then, "Okay." He tapped his screen, "Y'know, it says here that Sue Green beat her husband to death with a dumbbell then swore to do the same to all other male bodybuilders she could get her hands on. Police have been searching for her ever since. Guess we got lucky."

"You know I hate smart Alecs."

Dave did know. But he had succeeded in changing the subject. "Okay, but what I'm reading so far is a lot less interesting. Monroe was a competitive bodybuilder too, obviously. Less successful than her by the looks of it but then I'm guessing he'd have been competing in a bigger pool. They competed together for a while and did well at it, but the fashion for mixed competition didn't last long." He scrolled rapidly through the pages he had opened on the computer screen. "They set up the Bristol gym together, although that little fact seems to have been omitted from the official website." He quoted from the article he'd found. *"Ray and Sue are both keen to draw in budding bodybuilders, boys and girls, and train them to achieve the best they possibly can."* He scrolled on. "Here's another one. *Local bodybuilding benefactors*—what is it about cheap newspapers and alliteration?—*Sue and Ray are keen to train eager boys and girls to achieve their goals* and blah blah blah *in their new gym in Bristol."*

"Boys like Best?"

Dave squinted at something he'd just seen. "Like I said," he muttered, as he attacked his keyboard again with a speed and accuracy Claire could only dream of, "the dates don't really work out."

"But Thompson was older. And Kilby was certainly older. Maybe one of them had some connection to the Bristol gym. Maybe..."

"You got the station database open?"

"Give me a second." Claire turned to her own computer and keyed in her password. "Why? What am I looking for?"

"Ray Monroe. Turns out he would have been in Bristol at the same time as Best, but probably wouldn't have been spending much time in the gym. Not the one he'd opened up with his wife anyway."

"He's got form?" she asked, even as she entered Monroe's name.

Dave nodded slowly. "Oh yes. Though how, or even if, this fits in with what's going down here, I have absolutely no idea."

Chapter Thirteen

METROPOLIS. STEPFORD WIVES. *That episode of* Star Trek *where they stole Spock's brain.* Dave found himself running through all the science fiction films and television shows he could remember that featured beautiful female robots. The line of thought was inspired by the young girl behind the reception desk he stood at. She was smiling at him even as she dealt with a call on her telephone. She was small, and blonde, and smiley, and wore the same crisp top that Maia in the Venus and Adonis had worn. The biggest difference he could see between her and Maia was that this girl's name tag read *Sara* and beneath her name in smaller letters was the name of this gym, *Samson and Delilah*. Dave smiled back at the cheerful girl and took advantage of the moment to look around him at what had been the first of Sue Green's ever-expanding chain of gyms.

The Samson and Delilah was very like the Venus and Adonis, its fixtures, fittings and general ambience so similar Dave felt a mild sense of disorientation at the different arrangements of the desk and workout areas in the face of so much other similarity.

Her phone call finally concluded, Sara turned her full, beaming attention on Dave. "So sorry to have kept you waiting. How can I help you? Are you thinking of joining a gym today?" She tilted her head to one side and attempted what Dave assumed was meant to be a twinkle. "Or should I say *rejoining?*"

The presentation of his ID card quickly squashed the girl's hopes of enrolment and some of the energy behind her smile. Dave quickly reassured her she had nothing to worry about, that he hadn't come to arrest her but he'd just like to have a wander around the gym if she didn't mind, and maybe have a word with a few people, all in connection with a case up north. He left all details vague.

Obviously as puzzled as she had every right to, Sara showed him around and answered all of his questions. Dave learned all about the history of the gym, its successes and its plans for the future. He was also subjected to yet another barrage of praise and adulation of the gym's owner and Sara's employer, Sue Green.

"Mrs. Green is a quite remarkable woman," Sara gushed. "To be honest, she's something of a role model for me. Not in the bodybuilding way, you understand," and she gave a painfully high laugh, "but as a businesswoman. If you'll excuse me saying it but—" and Sara contrived to appear just a little sheepish "—she's living proof a woman doesn't have to be a bitch to succeed in business."

Says you, Dave thought. Enough, he decided, was definitely enough, and to cut short any further hero worship of Sue Green, he removed the photo he had tucked into his notepad and held it up for Sara to see. "Do you know this man by any chance?" Not really expecting a yes, he was caught off guard by the girl's reaction.

Sara's flow of tributes came to an abrupt halt, her smile fading into something colder and a lot less friendly. "Yes, I do," she said. "That's Paul Best, isn't it?"

"It is. How do you know him?" Sara's reaction hadn't been positive, but it had also suggested she didn't know Best was dead, far less the victim of a murder. "Did he use this gym?"

For a moment, it almost seemed as if Sara might have denied that but then she gave a curt nod. "For a while. Then he...left. Went to another gym. And then I think he left Bristol altogether."

"When would that have been?"

Sara gave him rough dates that fitted in with what Dave already knew about Best's move to Worcester. "You don't sound very...fond of Paul," Dave suggested as he replaced the picture in his notebook.

Pushed out of her recruitment-mode comfort zone, Sara became reluctant. "No. No, I can't say as I am. I mean, he wasn't a nice man, that's all. But I don't want to get him into trouble. I mean, it was a while ago now, and it's all been sorted, I suppose."

"What's been sorted?" Dave prompted, as gently as he could. "And please, trust me, you are not going to get Paul into any trouble." *Not now.*

Clearly torn between reluctance to speak and a desire to confide in the handsome, friendly police officer, Sara gave in after the shortest of internal fights. "He...took up with a girl who worked here, someone Mrs. Green had taken on before she moved on to set up her other gyms. You know she has a number of gyms the length and..."

"I know," Dave said. "Even as far as Manchester. But please, tell me about Paul and this girl."

Sara pursed her lips but went on. "He was...horrible to her. I mean *really* horrible," and as she spoke, she nodded at Dave as if willing him to understand the full import of the words she couldn't bring herself to vocalise.

Dave nodded, recalling the file they had found him, the euphemistic reference to *girlfriend trouble*. "I see," he said. How much further could he push this maddeningly vague girl? How much further *should* he? The police records on Best had suggested less than Sara seemed to be implying. Was she exaggerating? Or had the information Best's girlfriend given the police downplayed his behaviour? It wouldn't be the first time a victim in a case of domestic abuse had been reluctant, for a variety of reasons, to tell the full truth.

"It was good riddance when he left," Sara concluded before brightening and adding, "and Mrs. Green was wonderful, of course."

Saint Susan again. "Of course. What did she do?"

"As soon as she heard what was going on, she came all the way from her gym in Cambridge to talk to the girl and help her. It was Mrs. Green who encouraged her to go to the police, even though by then he'd stopped coming to this gym." Sara sniffed. "So, she did. And all Best got was a slap on the wrist." She became more vehement. "If it had been me I would have locked him up and thrown away the key, but that's the problem these days, isn't it? The police don't..." She remembered suddenly who she was talking to.

Dave had a pretty good idea how the lads in the local station would probably have dealt with the young man, and it would have been a damn sight more than a slapped wrist. But it would still have had to be within the limits of what the law allowed, and sometimes even officers like Dave had to question if that was really enough. "It's okay," he said. "I know what you mean."

Sara gave a small sheepish smile of gratitude and, for a moment, Dave considered telling her what had happened to Paul Best. He had a feeling she'd be pleased. He decided he didn't want to see that.

As they had been talking, Dave and Sara had been walking around the gym's floor space. They had stopped now, and Dave had a horrible feeling he could see why. There in front of them was a wall of pictures, just like the one back in the Venus and Adonis. *Another shrine to Saint Susan.* With a sinking sensation, Dave knew that unless he did something to stop her, Sara was going to launch into the picture by picture exposition Alys had given him back in Worcester.

"Well, thank you very much, Sara," he began. "That's all been..."

"Oh, actually, this is her," Sara interrupted, pointing to one of the pictures.

Reluctantly, Dave followed the direction she was indicating, expecting to see yet another picture of Sue Green, quite probably one he was already familiar with from the many he had seen in the course of this investigation.

"Oh," he said. Sue Green was in the picture of course, but it was the person standing next to her in a group shot of the gym's employees that had brought on his surprised reaction.

"Yes," Sara sighed pityingly. "Paul Best's girlfriend. She left us two or three months ago now. This was probably taken a couple of weeks before then. Lovely girl. Polish, I think. Her name was Alys."

"RAY MONROE?"

"Yeah, who wants to know?"

Claire held up her ID card. "Detective Inspector Summerskill. I wonder if I might have a word with you?"

When she'd decided they were going down to Bristol, Claire had said she would interview Monroe; Dave could go see what, if anything, he could pick up from Samson and Delilah. "Why don't we do them both together?" Dave had asked. It was not an unreasonable question. It was, after all, fairly standard procedure.

Claire had vetoed it, though. At the back of her mind, she saw Madden asking her why she was wasting time traipsing down to the south of the country. "We're not talking official interviews here," she said. "We split up, we save time. And time is money."

Dave had been unconvinced. "With respect, Monroe is a former competitive bodybuilder. Even if he's not training these days, he's still going to be bloody big. And you—" he shrugged with insincere apology "—are not."

"I'm going to talk with him, not arm wrestle him. You do the gym, I'll do the ex-husband. And we'll drive down separately."

"That'll save money," Dave murmured, following her as she strode from the office to the carpool.

Standing now, facing the burly man in the dirty overalls who had thrown down the tyre he was carrying and kicked it savagely, Claire couldn't help wondering whether, after all, she had made the right decision.

"For Christ's sake," the man said. "I'm checking in regularly. I'm doing every damn thing they say I have to. Is this what it's going to be like for the rest of my life?"

Dave had been right, of course. Ray Monroe was indeed still a formidable physical presence, though more of his weight now was round his waist than had previously been the case. On the lonely drive down to Bristol, Claire had mentally run through all her options for if the man was aggressive, defensive, or even physically violent. His kick at the tyre hadn't boded well, but then she'd taken in the darting eyes, the stooped shoulders, and the whining edge to his voice. Ray Monroe was visibly flinching from her presence like a beaten dog from a harsh master. She hadn't expected that at all.

Claire pocketed her ID. She could have lowered her voice to spare him the embarrassment of his workmates hearing, but she didn't. "Is there somewhere more private we can talk, Mr. Monroe?"

Monroe went to say no but then presumably realised Claire would simply have continued their conversation where they were, and so gestured for her to follow him out of the garage. "I'll be back in a minute, Len," he said to an older guy leaning over the open bonnet of a car. There was a grunted reply from deep in the engine's innards.

He led Claire round the back of the ramshackle building she'd found him in to a patch of scrubby grass and discarded packing cases. Judging by the number of butts on the ground, this was where the garage workers took their cigarette breaks. She doubted that much smoking so close to that much petrol was either safe or legal, but at the moment she had more pressing matters on her mind. Monroe circled her, and she had the sense again of having made a mistake meeting this man on his own. Then she saw what he was doing: positioning himself so that he was now facing the path they had walked along. Throughout their interview, he kept an anxious eye out over Claire's shoulder in case anyone should come along and overhear what they were talking about.

"So? What do you want?" The surliness of his question was undermined by the defensiveness of his body language.

Bloody good question actually, Claire thought. *I want you to give me something like a lead in this mess of a case, though I have no idea how you're going to do it, and if you don't and Madden ever finds out I'm indirectly harassing his friend's friend again...* She forced herself to stick to the present and let the future worry about itself, for at least the next five minutes anyway. *Just shake that tree, girl, and see what falls out.* "I've been speaking to your probation officer at Colston station."

"I haven't done anything wrong," Monroe said immediately.

The old story. "I didn't say you had."

"Then why are you here?" He jabbed a thumb in the direction of the garage. "If these guys find out I'm on the register I've had it. Do you have any idea how hard it is to find any kind of job if you've done a prison stretch, let alone if you've got...a record like mine?"

"I can imagine," she said, her face hard. He'd made a mistake. He'd been punished, paid his debt to society. But she still despised him for what he had done. "Have you seen your wife lately, Mr. Monroe?"

The big man blinked rapidly as if someone had shone a bright torch in his eyes. "What?"

"Your ex-wife, I suppose I should say."

"Susie? Is she...okay?"

Interesting. "Yes. I'm sorry, I didn't mean to alarm you." She wasn't sorry. She wanted him confused, uncertain. And, she couldn't deny, she was curious as to what a woman like Sue Green could ever have seen in a man like this.

"Not alarmed," Monroe mumbled. "Just...wanted to know."

Right. "You sounded pretty concerned there. Any reason to think something might have happened to her?"

"Yes. A police officer has turned up at my work and asked me questions about her."

Fair point. But don't get arsy with me, sunshine. "Not many men would still be so concerned about their wives after...how long has it been since you divorced?"

"Since she divorced me, you mean?" Monroe's face twisted in a bitter smile. "That wasn't long after I was convicted. Not long at all."

"But you'd been quite the team up until then, hadn't you? Winning all those competitions. Making it onto the cover of all those magazines. Getting the money together to buy your first gym."

"*Her* first gym. Yeah. Everything was coming up roses."

Claire nodded as if agreeing with him. "And then you were found guilty of having sex with an underage girl."

Monroe winced as if she had slapped him. He hung his head, eyes closed, jaw muscles bunched. She could hear his breathing as if he was labouring to control it. For several seconds he just stood there. When he spoke again his face was still turned down, eyes closed, his tone of voice that of a man repeating a too familiar mantra he no longer had any hope whatsoever of anyone else believing. "I didn't do it."

"That's what they all say, Mr. Monroe." She waited for the repeated denial, the insistence, the self-righteous anger, the bluster. She'd seen it all before and it made her sick.

"Yeah," Monroe said, so quietly she hardly heard him. "They do, don't they?"

"Let's be frank, Ray, you were convicted and punished for a crime you admitted committing."

Monroe's head snapped up, his eyes blazing. "Yes. Yes. Yes! Of course I did. One count. That's what they call it, isn't it? One count. CCTV footage of me taking the girl into a room. The girl's testimony. Who was going to believe me? My brief told me it made more sense to plead guilty, get it over with. So why are you here now, raking it all up again?"

"CCTV footage?"

"My own bloody cameras. We'd set them up in the gym. That's where it was supposed to have happened, you see. Sue was quick to hand over the footage."

Claire frowned. This wasn't going the way she'd planned. She'd meant to arrive unannounced, put a bit of a scare into Monroe, verbally knock him about a bit then bring the talk round to Paul Best and the others, see if she could find any kind of connection. But the story he was dredging up from the past seemed out of focus. Monroe's reactions were off kilter. She'd long ago lost the kind of naivety that might have led her to think he didn't look like the kind of person to take advantage of an underage girl, so she knew she wasn't being swayed by appearance alone. It was the situation that was wrong somehow: no prior; no evidence of grooming, and, if he was to be believed, and the local force certainly thought it was true, nothing since. She wished she'd spent more time on the history of his offence rather than taking in the bare details with Dave back at Foregate Street. At the time it had merely been a means to an end. But now...?

She pressed on with her questions, hoping that maybe momentum itself could push her through to some kind of result. "Have you been in touch with your wife recently?" She studied his face for signs of anger, hatred even. What she saw was a terrible longing.

"No. Sue doesn't do backwards. Always onwards and upwards with Sue. I don't suppose I'll ever see her again." He kicked miserably at the ground with his heavy working boots. "Probably for the best."

Claire pulled out the photo of Paul Best she had brought with her and held it out to him. "Do you know this man?"

Confused by the abrupt change of topic, Monroe took a second to understand what she was showing him. Uncertainly, he took it. Claire watched him, assured herself he was really studying it, before she took it back off him. "No," he said. She had the feeling he had really wanted to be able to say yes. "What's he got to do with anything?"

Claire ignored his question, furious with him but mostly with herself. What she'd hoped might have been a long shot was obviously just another inept piece of bumbling. Madden was going to have a field day if he ever heard about this. Which she had no doubt he would. She shoved the picture back into her coat pocket. "That will be all, Mr. Monroe." She made as if to walk past him but couldn't resist a final, "For now," on the way.

Monroe moved automatically to block her path, and she froze. "Has he...?"

"What?"

"Has he done something to Sue?"

Claire was surprised. She hadn't imagined he might interpret her questions that way. She hadn't thought he would have cared that much still for his ex-wife. "No," she said brusquely. "No, he hasn't."

"Is it...is it something like what I was sent down for? Is it to do with the girl?"

Something like I was sent down for? And suddenly she couldn't help herself. All her anger at this bungled investigation. All her frustration, anxieties, fears of being hauled over the coals again by Madden and found out as being incapable of carrying out her job, the gloss on her new promotion not even having had time to tarnish yet, all of it seethed to the surface in a boiling lava of fury.

"No," she practically spat at him. "It wasn't *something like what you were sent down for.* And you have no right whatsoever to ask anything about that girl."

Monroe stepped back from her anger. "I... I didn't mean anything by..."

Claire jabbed a finger towards his chest. "No. Your kind never do, do you?"

Monroe's head was down again, swaying from side to side, unable to meet her furious eyes, her righteous anger. "I didn't mean... She was a good kid. I didn't want... I didn't mean... Even after she did what she did..."

"What *she* did!" Claire exploded. "She was a child! You were an adult. Don't you dare give me your excuses or denials, Mr. Monroe, because there *isn't* an excuse. She has to live now with what you did to her for the rest of her life. And to you, she's just...a kid, a good kid. *The girl.*"

With a huge effort, Claire reined herself in, taken aback at the strength of her own reaction, and uncomfortably aware of just how close she was coming to doing or saying something that would leave her open to some nasty reprisals from Monroe and any slimeball of a lawyer he could find to support him. And there'd be many of those, she had no doubt. She took one deep breath and forced her way past this pathetic excuse for a man, back down the path to her car and away from him.

"Do you even remember her name?"

It had been an accusation, not a question. She hadn't expected a response.

"Of course I do," Monroe called after her, his face stricken. "It was Alys."

Chapter Fourteen

"ALYS PROCHAZKOVA."

Sue Green's face was unreadable. She sat on one of the threadbare sofas in Heavy Metal, facing DI Summerskill and DS Lyon who were seated on the other one opposite her. "Alys? What about her?"

"We'd like to talk with her, Mrs. Green," Dave said crisply.

"Well, as you know, Sergeant, she doesn't work here. She works at the Venus and Adonis."

"We've already been there, Mrs. Green, and she wasn't there. Your young girl there thought she might be here, probably visiting her boyfriend."

"Well, as you can see, she isn't," Sue Green said calmly. "Perhaps if you'd like to try again later. Or, as I said, the Venus and Adonis is really where you are most likely to find her. If you like, I can call Maia now, find out when Alys will next be on duty and you can..."

"We've already asked Maia, thank you, Mrs. Green," Dave said. "Alys won't be on duty for another twenty-four hours at least. And Maia was certain that if Alys wasn't at work, then she would be with Marc."

"And Marc," Claire continued, "is pretty much always at work here. So we're assuming..." There was no need to finish the sentence. "What time will Marc be back on duty?"

Both officers caught it—Sue Green's quick glance at the plain clock fixed to the wall. "Another couple of hours or so, I'd guess."

"Then we'll wait." Summerskill and Lyon settled back into the battered sofa. Both felt confident they wouldn't have to wait for long. People looked at clocks to estimate minutes, not hours.

"Perhaps you'd like to wait in my office?"

Claire smiled, a tight smile. "No thanks. As you've said before, it is just a bit small. And it'd be so easy to miss Alys coming in from over there."

"But if you happened to have a couple of those fabulous coffees to hand...?" Dave said.

Sue Green's response was steely. "Why do you want to speak to Alys?"

"It turns out," said Claire, "Alys knew Paul Best well. Very well, in fact. He used to be her boyfriend. Until he abused her."

"But you'd know about that, wouldn't you, Sue?" said Dave cheerily. "Because according to Sara at Samson and Delilah—lovely girl by the way, full of useful information—you went out of your way to help Alys. It's not beyond the wit of man to assume that she owes her job in the Venus and Adonis to you. Very public-spirited of you."

"Extremely," conceded Claire, "especially when you consider that Alys Prochazkova was the girl cited in the case of underage sex that effectively ruined your former husband."

Sue made a sound, as if she was clearing her throat, but in all other respects, she was as calm and collected as ever. She crossed one well-toned leg over the other. "What are you implying, Claire?"

Claire leaned forward. "I'll be honest, *Mrs. Green*, I don't quite know what I am implying at the moment. Why don't you tell me?" She nodded at Dave as a signal for him to retrieve his ever-present notepad from the inside pocket of his jacket. "Let's start, while we're waiting, with how you came to be such a friend to the girl who wrecked your marriage."

"My marriage was wrecked long before Ray had his little fling with Alys, Inspector." Sue stopped as if suddenly aware she might have said too much. She took a calming breath. "Alys is a good girl..."

"Just what Mr. Monroe said." *Yes, I've spoken to him,* Claire thought as she saw Sue Green's eyes widen.

"What happened between her and my husband," she continued, "is all in the past. And surely you can't think it had anything to do with the terrible things that have been happening here. Raking the past up is just painful and pointless."

"Ma'am." Dave was indicating the entrance door to the gym just a few feet away from them. Alys Prochazkova had just walked through, followed by Marc who was closing the door behind them.

"I don't know yet how she is mixed up in all this." Claire quickly got to her feet, "but I'm more and more sure she is in some way. And I think today we're going to find out how. Alys," she called out to the girl.

With the wide eyes and nervousness that seemed to be her natural state, Alys took in the sight of Inspector Summerskill and Sergeant Lyon quickly crossing the space between them. She gave a frightened gasp and turned to her boyfriend who reached out one powerful arm and pulled her close to himself for protection.

"There's no need to be alarmed, Alys," Summerskill said in as soothing a voice as she could manage. "We'd just like to have a word with you." She held her hands out, feeling absurdly like some hostage negotiator demonstrating she was unarmed. But there was no denying the tension and hostility in the room, most of the latter radiating from the scowling Marc. Alys looked up pleadingly at him. He shot a threatening glare at Claire. Claire tried to make Alys look at her. And no one noticed Sergeant Lyon quietly edging his way round the space, trying to put himself between Marc and Alys and the gym door.

"They just want to talk to Alys, Marc," Sue Green said.

"Thank you, Mrs. Green," said Claire in a clipped voice. "I'll handle this. There's no need..."

"It will be all right," Sue Green said, but it was Marc she seemed to be talking to, not Alys.

"Let's just sit down here, shall we?" Claire indicated the sofas. "And have a little talk."

Around them, the crashes, bangs, and expletives that filled the air of Heavy Metal gradually slowed and came to a halt, as one by one the gym users became aware of the charged confrontation taking place by the entrance desk.

"That's right," Claire said soothingly, as Alys went to take a step towards the sofa. Marc held onto her, but she said something to him quickly and quietly, that none of the others heard, and with obvious reluctance, he let the arm holding her drop, though he still looked poised to snatch her back to his side in an instant.

"Good girl," Claire said. "Now, why don't we...?"

It would take Claire a good hour sitting at her computer writing her report later that night to sort out and record in sequence what happened next. At the time, the rapidity and violence made it all feel like some kind of explosion.

There was a sudden, inarticulate shout from Dave as Marc darted to one side, and the table between the two sofas they had been sitting on shattered with a startling crack, the mugs and magazines on it flying in all directions. Marc spun round, the broom he had snatched up and used to destroy the table now making a whooping sound in the air as he swung it around and brought it slicing down at Dave's head. Dave half leaped, half fell backwards, sprawling on the floor.

"Dave!" Claire shrieked, with no time for anything more as Marc brought the broom scything down again onto the fallen sergeant. Desperately shoving himself out of the makeshift weapon's way, Dave crashed into the entrance desk, papers and cards showering down on him.

"Marc, stop! This isn't the way!" Sue Green yelled.

Ignoring her, Marc flung the broom handle to one side and fell on Dave. Both meaty hands wrapped themselves around Dave's neck and he dragged the officer to his feet, squeezing with all his might. "Alys! Run!" he bellowed, but Alys Prochazkova stood rooted to the spot, eyes wide, frozen in helpless denial.

"Marc! Let go of him!" Claire shrieked. "This isn't helping anyone." It was useless. A berserker rage had consumed the young man and he was throttling Dave Lyon with all the strength of those pumped muscles of his. Dave's eyes bulged as his hands clawed impotently at the constricting grip on his throat. In desperation, Claire looked around for something she could use to stop Marc. Crazy images from old movies flashed through her mind: vases, bottles, anything she could smash over this frenzied man's head. Across the gym, she saw about a dozen bodybuilders standing, watching, not really sure if what they were seeing was actually happening. "Don't just stand there! Do something!" she screamed at them.

From behind her, there was a muffled grunt. Dave was leaning against the desk, coughing and retching but free of Marc. His attacker was doubled over in front of him swearing volubly. She'd find out later her resourceful sergeant had stamped on Marc's feet and mercilessly kneed him in the groin. "Dave!" Instinctively she stepped forward to help him.

Marc lunged at her and grabbed, pulling her into him tightly and wrapping his arm around her neck. "No!" she yelled, and screwed her eyes tight shut, waiting for the terrible pressure, for him to start squeezing the life out of her too. Nothing happened. She felt Marc's breath on her cheek, hot and rapid, heard his wheezing—but he wasn't strangling her, just holding her. She opened her eyes. "Marc..." she began.

"Shut up!" he shook her.

In front of them, Dave had stepped away from the desk, eyes fixed on Marc's, arms loose by his sides, ready to react at the first sign of Marc's doing anything other than just holding his boss. "Put her down, Marc!"

No! Claire mouthed at him, unable to shake her head by so much as a millimetre. Dave nodded slightly, but his tense body posture didn't change, and his eyes stayed fixed on Marc's.

"Marc," she said again, slowly and as calmly as she could manage. "This isn't going to get you anywhere."

"Let her go," Marc said.

Claire understood. He meant Alys. "We need to talk to her," Claire said carefully. "And you. We need to..."

"No! I did it. It was me. All of them. Not her. Let her go."

Marc's grip on Claire tightened. "It's all right!" she called out as she saw Dave about to spring forward. With great reluctance, he stepped back again.

"Marc," Claire said, "there really isn't anything else you can do."

"No!" Marc's voice cracked. "Alys. Run!"

Dave tensed, ready to stop the young girl at his side if she tried to make a break for it. She hadn't moved an inch since Marc's outburst began, and she didn't move now. She stared at her boyfriend, her eyes full of tears, shaking her head. She was saying something, but her voice was so low the words were inaudible.

"Run!" Marc screamed at her, in a long drawn out howl of desperation.

"No, Marc." Sue Green stepped forward, putting herself between Dave and Marc.

"Mrs. Green, get out of the way!" Dave barked.

Sue Green ignored him. "Alys can't run away. She mustn't. And you must stop this now. Let the inspector go, Marc."

For a second, Marc stood, his muscular arm still wrapped around Claire's neck. Then slowly, under his employer's unflinching gaze, he relaxed his grip. Claire felt the rigidity of his body against hers gradually fade. When, after what seemed like an age to her, she felt it was safe to do so, she reached up, almost gently took hold of his unresisting arm and pushed it away, stepping forward and out of his grip.

Dave moved quickly towards her. "You all right?"

"I'm fine," she said, more effort than she would have liked going into keeping her voice steady. "Bloody well arrest him."

She watched as Dave simultaneously cuffed Marc's hands behind his back and read him his rights. Marc didn't resist. The fight had drained out of him as quickly as it had flared up. Unnervingly, he was crying. When the cuffs were on and Dave had shoved him, none too gently, onto a sofa to wait for the van, Alys came and sat next to him and pulled his head down onto her shoulder.

Sue Green stood to one side, watching them.

"Thanks," Claire said to her. "For your help."

Sue Green's face was unreadable.

Claire turned to the assembled watching bodybuilders. "And you lot were bloody useless!"

Chapter Fifteen

"THE FIRST THING I want to know," Claire said, as she and Dave prepared for their first formal interview with Marc, "is just what kind of lunatic we've got locked up in there and what exactly his girlfriend had to do with it."

"The link with Best is clear enough," Dave said. "Best had a bad history with Alys, Marc found out, Marc killed him."

"No. You saw what Marc was like back there. Bull in a china shop doesn't come close." Dave rubbed his throat ruefully. He had noticed. Claire continued, "Marc would have laid into him as soon as he'd found out what Best had done to his girlfriend, probably in full view of a whole room of witnesses. But Best was murdered somewhere private, late at night, and then his body dumped in a cover-up attempt that might just have worked. Not Marc's style at all."

"So do you think maybe Alys is the brains behind it, using Marc to get back at Paul?"

Claire snorted, considering the mousy beauty technician. "Not likely, is it? And then what? She found out she enjoyed it so much she got him to kill two other guys as well, like some kind of Bonnie and Clyde?"

Dave conceded it seemed unlikely. "But Bonnie and Clyde would be a cool name for a gym. Better than Venus and Adonis anyway."

"And who is it keeps coming up with those names? I think we both know who else is caught up in this mess. Okay, c'mon. Let's get the show on the road." She paused. "Has he been assigned a lawyer?"

"I don't think so."

"All right. Get Jenny to call Travers. He'll sort something. In the meantime, we can make a head start. The sooner this is started, the sooner we can..."

"Not so fast, Inspector. If you'll forgive the slightly melodramatic introduction." Standing in their doorway and smiling at them was Sean Cullen. "This is Mr. West," Cullen said, indicating the man standing next to him. "He'll be acting as Marc's lawyer."

"If you could just show me to my client, officers," West said officiously.

Dave regarded Cullen's companion closely. "I think we've met." He turned to his boss. "Mr. West represented Gunnerson in Redditch, end of last year. Not cheap, ma'am." He turned again to West in his silk suit and fashionable, top of the range, steel-rimmed glasses. "Not cheap at all."

"We were just about to have our first interview with...your client," Claire said. "If you'd like to..."

"I'm sure you'll appreciate my need to speak to Mr. Kirkwood before then, Inspector," said West primly. "Now. If I may?"

With conspicuously bad grace, Claire summoned a uniform to take West to see his client.

"Thank you, officer," he said, as he was led away to Marc's cell.

"And thank you too," Sean Cullen said, once the lawyer had gone.

"Mr. Cullen," Claire said. "What are you doing?"

"I'm sure I don't know what you mean, Inspector Summerskill."

"Why are you here, now, with a top-notch lawyer for...for him?" And she gestured in the direction of the cells.

"I'm his MP, Inspector," Cullen said.

"We should all have MPs so helpful."

"Actually, you have. I am your MP too, remember."

"I didn't vote for you."

You didn't vote at all, Dave thought, but wisely said nothing.

"Please don't play games with me, Mr. Cullen. Young thugs like Marc Kirkwood don't get lawyers like your Mr. West there unless..." She stopped short. "It's Sue Green again, isn't it?"

"I don't know what you mean by *again,* Inspector," Cullen demurred, "but yes. Sue asked me as a favour to recommend a lawyer and Toby West happens to be a friend of mine who also owes me a favour. That's how the world works. People help each other."

Dave was pretty sure what kind of friend the man he so casually referred to as Toby was. He could picture him and Cullen sharing a pleasant evening together, somewhere behind a plastic potted plant, probably.

"In certain circles," Claire said icily.

"Claire," Cullen began.

"Inspector Summerskill," Claire snapped.

Cullen held up his hands in the sort of placatory gesture guaranteed to infuriate anyone. "Inspector Summerskill. Sue Green asked for help for an employee and I was more than happy to give it." He was grave for a moment. "It's pretty obvious Marc has done...something bad. Sue doesn't doubt that. From what she told me, he nearly did something bad today." He paused. Dave said nothing. "But she still wants to help him. She is that kind of woman. Quite remarkable, actually." He waited, as if inviting them to agree with him. They did not. "And so I take my leave of you," he said and did.

"Saint Susan strikes again," Dave said, as soon as he was sure Cullen was out of earshot.

"NOW YOU JUST lie back and go to sleep, yes?"

"Yes, mummy."

"G'night, love."

"Night night, mummy."

Claire kissed her youngest on the forehead and smoothed his hair away from his eyes which were already fast closing. Sam let out the sigh he always did before finally drifting off, as if exhaling the last reserves of the energy that had kept him bouncing through the day. As she sat at his bedside his breathing slowed and deepened, and within minutes she knew she was safe to get up, turn off the light, and creep from the bedroom. She left the door ajar just enough for the landing light to give the room some dim illumination in case Sam awoke again, and for her to be able to hear him if he did.

Downstairs, Tony was slouched on the sofa, TV remote in one hand as he mechanically surfed the channels, quite obviously not watching anything. "He all right?" he asked, without turning his attention away from the screen.

"Course he is," Claire said, sitting down next to him. "He only had a bit of a tumble down the stairs. Again. I think he's getting used to it." She watched the channels change: studio-bound sitcoms with canned laughter backgrounds; grim news feeds of war and strife from around the world; garish adverts for a plethora of things she either didn't want or couldn't afford. "You could have dealt with it, you know."

"He was pretty shook up."

Claire nodded. "Yes. But you're just as good at calming him down as me and Ian. You know you are."

Tony's face was a set mask. "He wanted his mum and his dad, not his brother." His channel-hopping stopped, the screen settling on some picture of a bombed-out house as if Tony had chosen something that somehow reflected his mood. "And neither of you were here."

No, we weren't, Claire thought. *I was at work catching a killer, but I came back. Now where the bloody hell is Ian?*

DAVE LAY ON his bed, jacket and shoes thrown to one side and tie loosened to provide some relief to his still sore throat. It wasn't especially late, but he had thought, after the events of the day, that he'd fall easily and deeply into sleep. But sleep resolutely refused to come. *Guess that's what happens when someone nearly pulls your head off.*

He turned his head to one side. On the table by the bed was a police procedural manual, the latest one he had to know by heart if he was to ever proceed up the greasy pole of promotion should the opportunity come knocking. Next to it was his mobile. Almost hating himself, Dave reached for the mobile and tapped on the gay dating app. There were three messages waiting for him.

Fakehater, who was, he claimed, *29,* and an *easy-going guy* with *an interest in leather and boots,* said, *Hi.* His picture though, thought Dave, said *Goodbye.*

Wayne, 25, proclaimed he *liked older guys. Well you can sod right off,* Dave thought. Besides, Wayne's profile pic of a magnificently tanned and buffed sun worshipper on a beach screamed theft from the internet. *And I have had quite enough of bodybuilders to last me a very long time, thank you.*

Which just left *Chat2U?* No age, no pic, no bombastic piece of text bigging himself up, just that rather forlorn name underneath the generic shadowed head and shoulders of someone who wished to remain anonymous. In its way, it was probably the most honest of the lot. What was the worst that could happen? A few short messages that shattered any fragile illusions on one or both sides? But what if they didn't? What if they ended up in another of what was coming to seem like an endless string of hookups in grim pubs around the county?

Dave sighed and dropped the mobile back down on the table. *What's the point?*

He picked up the book and held it in front of him, still closed, taking in the title, the weight of it, its grey, institutionalised format. He dropped that back on the table too.

What's the point?

"I TOLD YOU, I was at a meeting."

"Till this time?"

"You're not the only one who doesn't work office hours, you know?"

"Office hours! That's bloody stakeout hours!"

"Right. Because I should be back home taking care of the kids while you're playing cops and robbers."

"I do *not*..."

"I just had one last thing I needed to sort out about these new specs," Ian said. "I knew I was only going to be an hour away. Hour and a half tops. Tony was here. He's big enough now to look after Sam for that long."

"Unless something happens, like your son falls down the stairs."

"How was I supposed to know that would happen? And it's not like he injured himself. You said yourself he was more shook up than actually hurt."

"That's not the point, Ian."

"And what is the point, then? That it's okay for you to stay out all hours of the night to further your career but not for me?"

A sharp response was on the tip of her tongue, but through sheer force of will, Claire bit it back. Fired up though she was by righteous anger that in turn had been fuelled by the mercifully short-lived fear her youngest had been hurt, now she found herself wrong-footed by this unexpected turn of the argument. This was new. Of course there had been times in the past when Ian had complained about her long hours. But he'd never made such a brutal comparison between their jobs before. And he'd never, ever been so bloody condescending. She was angry. No, she was furious. But, she realised, she was also beginning to feel just a bit guilty. She took a deep breath. "Okay," she began. "I'm...sorry. It's been another shit day. Why don't we...?"

"Why don't you ask him about Mrs. Grant?" shouted Tony from the sofa.

"HI, RICHARD."

"Dave?"

Dave had no trouble hearing the surprise in his former partner's voice over the phone, and could just as easily picture the puzzled face, the small furrow in his forehead, and the way he would incline his head slightly to one side. There were some people who had thought Richard a bit of a cold fish, but in the few months they had been together, Dave had learned to read his reactions, muted though they might have been. He smiled now at the image in his head and wondered what Richard was wearing. For a fraction of a second he even considered asking him, just so he could make the mental picture complete, then wisely refrained, realising how creepy it would have sounded. Instead he settled for, "How are you doing?"

"I'm fine." And now Dave heard the wariness behind the answer, the unspoken question: *Why are you asking? Why are you ringing me up at this time of night to ask?* "How are you?" Richard asked, just a few seconds too late.

"I'm fine too." Dave fingered his tender throat. No need to go into the details.

"So. What can I do for you?"

Dave considered. "Nothing really. I mean, there's nothing I want. I just wanted to see...how you are."

"Oh. Right. I'm fine."

Dave smiled, then realised that wouldn't cross a phone line, so laughed. He wanted it to be loud enough for Richard to hear but it ended up sounding too loud, horribly forced. "Yes. I got that."

There was second or two of dead air.

"How's the new job going?"

"It's going..." Dave had been about to say *fine* but pulled himself back from that at the last minute. "Well," he said. "Busy but well."

"Managed to get your hands down the trousers of that handsome guy in your office?"

For a moment Dave couldn't work out who he was talking about, then he remembered the conversations they'd had when he had first joined Foregate Street station, the descriptions he'd given of his new colleagues. "You mean Cortez? Nah. He's still straight. Got a girlfriend even. A trolley dolly. And no, she really is a woman." It was strange to him now to recall he had ever thought of Cortez in the way Richard remembered.

He considered for a minute going on to give a quick summary of the case he and Claire had been working on, that they were, God willing, about to finally wrap up. Richard would be bound to have heard about it in the papers or on the net. He couldn't bring himself to do it though. He knew Richard would be eager to hear about *The Muscleman Murderer*. But there was the problem, wasn't it? Richard had always been eager to see Dave's job through the prism of some bad TV show or film, and the more he had done that, the more Dave had insisted on impressing the reality, the often grim or even boring reality of it on him. In a lot of ways, it was the attempting to share his life with Richard that had pushed them apart.

"Are you seeing anyone?" he asked instead, regretting the question the moment it was out. He'd just wanted to change the subject, and now he sounded like he was checking up on his former partner. Or worse: it sounded like he was lonely and missing him.

"No," said Richard. "That is... No, not really."

Right. Dave waited. "Me neither," he said finally.

"I guessed as much."

And Dave could see that too, the slight lowering of Richard's head, the fractional raising of his eyebrows that made for his sympathetic expression. "Why? I mean, how? I have seen guys."

"Which is not the same as *seeing* guys," Richard said patiently. "You haven't got the time for it."

"I..."

"You don't *make* the time for it."

And there, Dave thought with a flash of annoyance, *is the reason we aren't still together. Because you always had to be there with the criticisms, the nagging, the neediness. You always had to be...right.* "It won't always be like this."

"Which is what I said when I started teaching. *It'll get easier,* I said. *I'll learn to cope better.*" Richard gave a dry chuckle. "And then I got promoted. And promoted again. I still had to do all the stuff I was doing before, but now there was a whole lot of new stuff to do too. Want to guess what I'm doing right now while everyone else is watching reality TV or downloading porn?"

"Marking," Dave said, at exactly the same time as Richard.

"Thirty-two essays on 'Our Day at the Zoo.' You wouldn't think so many kids could see so many animals and yet be able to name so few of them."

Dave laughed. "Guess I'd better let you get on with it. then."

"Yeah. 'Fraid so."

"Just wanted to touch base."

"Thanks. It was good to hear from you. G'night, Dave."

"G'night."

Dave took the phone away from his ear. *Call ended. 1 min 47 secs, said the display.* He closed the telephone screen and the home screen winked back. In the corner, the gay contact app icon had a red 1 in a circle next to it. The one message he hadn't deleted. *Chat2U.*

Sod it. Dave opened the app and tapped out his response.

Hi.

"SO. WHO'S MRS. Grant?"

Claire sat up, watching her husband carefully fold his trousers over the chair prior to getting into bed with her, in that way that always, inexplicably, annoyed her. Tony had been dispatched to his bed a quarter of an hour earlier. Claire had known better than to ask him what he had meant by his obviously pointed remark. She and Ian had gone through their usual preparations for bed in unusual silence. But now, Claire meant to find out exactly what was going on with her husband.

"Y'know," Ian said, even as he apparently focused on hanging his trousers just right, "I think I can name every one of your colleagues."

"Your point being?"

"You can never remember any of mine."

"Yours come and go," she said, blunt but determined to stay calm. "You've said yourself, teachers these days are like mayflies. And besides, you're only thinking of the plain clothes. The day you can name every uniform at Foregate is the day they put you in charge over Madden. But that's beside the point. Who is Mrs. Grant?"

"Maths teacher."

"You're art. So, what have you got to have late-night meetings together for?"

"She's curriculum leader for maths. I'm standing in for Lisa as curriculum leader for art. We're going through massive curriculum changes and all the leaders..."

"You're always going through curriculum changes. And when did you stop being heads of department and become *leaders*?"

"We've been leaders for years now," Ian said stiffly. "And yes, we *are* always going through changes which is why we have to keep having bloody meetings all the time. You're not the only public-sector workers who are regularly screwed over by the government." He climbed into bed, pulled the duvet over himself with an angry jerk, and turned off the light on his side of the bed, lying with his back to his wife.

Claire sat, unmoved, her light obstinately left on. "So, why did Tony say I needed to ask you about her?"

"God knows! He's just being a typical, bloody annoying adolescent at the moment."

"So, you finally accept he's not behaving properly. He can skip lessons and that's just typical teenage behaviour, but he says something about a friend of yours and..." Claire was hit by a sudden rush of understanding. "This is what it's all been about, isn't it? Tony's been upset lately because he thinks you're carrying on with some other teacher. And I'll bet that's why he's been getting into trouble at school with his mates. They'll have been talking about it and winding him up. Is that what's been going on, Ian?"

Ian sat up again and jabbed at his light switch. "Nothing is *going on*, Claire. Yes, from what I have gathered, some of Tony's so-called mates have been saying some pretty stupid things about me to him and he took it the wrong way. But that's what Year Nine boys do. They see two members of staff having a laugh and straight away it means they're having an affair. And if one of those members of staff happens to have a kid in the school, then he's going to have a pretty rough time of it."

Claire stared at him, but she wasn't really seeing him. Her new understanding of events was going round and round in her mind. New facts, new insights. If this had been a work case, she could have sorted them, processed them, made some kind of sense of them. But somehow here, now, with something so close to home, though she had apparently all of the facts in front of her, she couldn't make any sense of them. When she spoke, her voice sounded ridiculously small.

"Are you having an affair, Ian?"

Chapter Sixteen

IT WAS TWO days later when Summerskill and Lyon walked back into the Heavy Metal gym for what both sincerely hoped was the last time. There was a new lad behind the desk, blond where Marc had been dark but in most other respects a similar model. He seemed to know who they were. He hadn't got round to writing himself a badge and didn't offer his name, so they never found out who he was. With the same lack of grace Marc had always demonstrated, he went to fetch Sue Green for them. She arrived in business mode: jacket, jeans, hair tied back, as outwardly cool and perfect as ever. But Claire felt a guardedness about her. And she felt the anger smouldering within herself. It would be best, she knew, to keep a tight rein. Good thing perhaps she had Lyon with her.

"I see you haven't replaced the table," Dave remarked, as Sue invited them to sit on the sofas by the entrance desk. *And you're not offering us coffee either.*

"I've been too busy, Sergeant," Sue said briskly. "I'm coming to the end of the first phase of setting up my latest gym."

"Manchester," said Dave, an ironic echo of the awe Maia had used when she had told him about it back in the Venus and Adonis.

If she caught his inflection, Sue Green gave no sign. "Yes. And it's been keeping me very occupied. Soon, I'll be having to move up there full time."

"Please don't make any plans to move away just yet, Mrs. Green," Claire said. And there it was. A hardness in the other woman's eyes, a calculation going on behind them. Had it always been there? Had she been too ready to be impressed by this apparent success story of a woman in a man's world to see the reality underneath?

"Why not?"

"You'll be aware, of course," Claire went on, as if what she was saying was not, in fact, an answer to the question, "that Marc Kirkwood has confessed to the murders of Paul Best, Daniel Thompson, and Bill Kilby."

"Under the watchful eye of his forceful lawyer," Dave added.

"Yes, I am," Sue said. "Though I can't say I understand why you..."

"Best, of course," Claire continued, heedlessly cutting across Sue, "he murdered out of what the papers will almost certainly sum up as revenge. Not to put too fine a point on it, Best had been a bastard to Alys when they had been together." Claire shrugged. "So far, so simple. Then Thompson was murdered because he knew."

"How do you know this? And, if he knew, why didn't he simply tell someone? The police, for instance? And how did he find out?"

Right questions, Claire thought, *but wrong order.* "I will admit we are having to fill in some of the details ourselves, but Marc is being very helpful." She looked closely at Sue for signs of any reaction. There were none.

"In most areas," Dave modified.

"Dan knew," Claire explained, "because he was on the scene of the murder and saw what happened."

Sue Green took a breath, her lips parted as if she was about to say something but then held herself back, folding her hands in her lap and waiting.

"Why didn't he come to us?" Claire said. "Two reasons, really. Three, if you add the simple fact that he really didn't like Paul so wouldn't have felt any great compulsion to turn his killers over to the police. I'm going to be generous and suggest that the main reason he didn't tell us was, he was shit scared. It's not nice to speak ill of the dead, I know, but in my brief acquaintance with Mr. Thompson I wasn't struck by any strong suggestion of moral fibre."

Sue Green arched one of her beautifully delineated eyebrows. "And that's being generous?"

"Yes," said Claire, "because the other reason he didn't come running to us to report a death was that he saw some advantage in it." She paused, wondering if Sue would make a pretence of not understanding.

"Kilby," Sue said. It wasn't a question.

Claire inclined her head in agreement. "Thompson wasn't up to risking Kirkwood coming for him, but then he also realised how valuable information could be, if given to the right person."

"Kilby," Dave said, echoing Sue Green. "He was perfect. It took us a while to find out just how much of a lowlife he was..."

"Though the signs were there from the start," Claire muttered.

"But Thompson, along with quite a few others I'm sure, knew all along." He paused, as if suddenly struck by something. "I'm surprised you hadn't cottoned on he was dealing steroids at your gym Sue. You taking such pride in knowing your clientele and all. But of course, you did know he had a sideline in blackmail, didn't you?"

"What do you...?"

"Kilby was blackmailing Sean Cullen, wasn't he?"

"If you're referring to those photos I handed over to Claire, then I..."

"But Sean would have told you, wouldn't he?" Dave interrupted. "That it was Kilby using those photos. After you'd found them and handed them over to us, of course." He paused. "If not before. You and him being such good friends, I mean. I doubt he'd have kept something like that from you."

Sue Green's lips set in a thin line.

"So," Claire took over again, as if sublimely unaware of the iciness now between her sergeant and the other woman, "Thompson made his big mistake: he went to Bill Kilby who, as Sergeant Lyon has said, was perfect, not only because he was more than happy to use the information that fell into his lap, but because he was able to pay Thompson for information received in the form he most appreciated."

"Steroids," explained Dave. "Better than cash. Kind of like finding a post office that gives you a really good exchange rate for your foreign currency."

"The trouble was, Kilby's blackmailing skills were as weak as his social skills."

Dave nodded. "The man was a thug. Just ask young Robert."

For the first time in the interview, Sue Green appeared puzzled. "Robert Taylor?"

"When we started our investigation," Dave explained, "Kilby saw us talking to Robert. His main worry then was that the lad would tip us off to his steroid dealing."

"So he 'had a word' with the boy," Claire said. "You saw the black eye."

"And then later, when Thompson was murdered..."

"And Robert panicked and started thinking maybe, after all, the best thing *would* be to tell us everything he knew..."

"Kilby, who by then was blackmailing as well as drug dealing, decided he had to make his point about keeping schtum even more forcefully."

"Leaving Robert in hospital today," Claire said.

"When actually Bill's real worry should have been Marc Kirkwood."

"Quite," Claire said, grimly enjoying her double hander with Dave and the way it kept Sue Green turning her head back and forth between the two of them like some unwilling tennis spectator. "Kilby was greedy, clumsy and so full of himself he thought he could handle a lad that big and thirty years younger than him. He weighed in on Marc with a blackmail attempt and Marc responded in the way, I suspect, he's responded to most problems in his life: with brute force and ignorance."

"And a skipping rope."

"Dan Thompson was killed because Kilby had fingered him as a witness."

"And then Kilby had to go because he knew and was trying to blackmail Marc."

"End of case."

There was a moment's silence, punctuated as ever by the constant clinks of metal and sounds of exertion that were the ambient sounds of Heavy Metal. "I see," said Sue Green. "Very neat."

"No, Mrs. Green," Claire said, leaning forward towards the other woman, her eyes full of the anger burning inside her. "Not neat at all. Very bloody messy."

"Because, as I'm sure you can see," said Dave, outwardly calmer than his boss, "there are all sorts of things in this story that really don't add up."

"No, Sergeant," Sue Green said in a clipped tone that suggested she too was working hard to keep strong emotion under control. "I'm not a police officer, so I don't see."

"Let us explain," Claire said. "We told you Dan Thompson saw what happened to Paul Best. But did you ask yourself, how did he just happen to be on the scene of the crime?"

Sue Green hesitated. "I presume he must have followed Paul there."

"Like a ninja?" Dave suggested.

"Hardly stalker material, was he?" Claire said. "A big man like him. Almost certainly dressed in some sort of ridiculously eye-catching, tight T-shirt. Hard not to notice him, don't you think, tagging along behind Best through the streets of Worcester?"

"Talk about the elephant in the room," Dave said.

"And besides, why?"

"He was angry with Paul," Sue said. "You know he was. You heard what some of the lads who were here that day said. Paul had wound him up."

"You're right." Dave reached into his pocket and flipped back to the notes he had made right at the start of the investigation. *You know how it is. You know how it was.*" He flipped the book shut. "Actually, one of the witnesses claimed Best had said one thing, and another said the other, but I'm thinking he probably said both, y'know, to really rub it in."

"So yes," Claire agreed, "Thompson was angry. But what was he going to do? Have it out with Best? Hit him?"

"I suppose so," Sue Green snapped. "That is what men do, isn't it? React violently."

He treated me badly. Very badly. Claire remembered Sue's words from their late-night conversation at her place. "Some men, yes," she conceded. "And Marc Kirkwood almost certainly. But if that was Dan Thompson's intention, why follow Best unseen for the mile or so between here and the scene of the murder before doing it? If Thompson had wanted to thump Best, he could have jumped him outside Heavy Metal. Hell, he could have gone for him in the showers if he'd been worried about witnesses. No, Thompson wasn't planning to beat Best up. Or at least, that wasn't uppermost in his mind. And he didn't follow Best. He didn't need to. He probably got there first. He knew where Best was going."

"You never asked us where the murder took place, Mrs. Green," Dave said. "Although, again, I'm sure you know. Marc Kirkwood told us. In front of his lawyer. Your friend Sean Cullen's good friend. So I'm sure Mr. Cullen will have told you."

"Yes," said Claire, "that must be how you knew. Thompson knew Best would be at the Venus and Adonis because Best had dropped enough hints about what he was going to do, and Danny knew very well where he was going to go because that was where he used to do it when he had been Sean Cullen's hunk of the month."

"Now wait a minute!" Sue Green said, finally galvanised into anger. "If you're suggesting that Sean..."

"No," Claire said quickly, "I am not suggesting Mr. Cullen was present at the scene of the crime when the murder was committed. Marc has been very clear indeed that wasn't the case."

"Or rather Marc's lawyer has," Dave said.

"You can tell Mr. Cullen he needn't worry about that."

"Of course, we should have worked it out," Dave admitted, "where the murder took place, I mean. Best hadn't taken a wallet that evening, not even any cash, probably because he was expecting to be given a wad of it by the end of his photo session. But he did have his gym membership card." And now Dave took out of his pocket the small plastic rectangle that had been Paul Best's and held it up so Sue Green could see it, especially the series of black and white stripes on the back. "He wouldn't have needed this barcode to get into Heavy Metal where he always trained, but he thought he might have needed it to get into Venus and Adonis."

"So," said Claire, "here's what we think happened. Paul Best was duped into going along to the Venus and Adonis that night with the bait of a lucrative photo shoot with Sean Cullen."

"Who wasn't there at all," Dave said quickly, as if forestalling an objection.

"Dan Thompson was there too, either having arrived beforehand or followed on shortly afterwards. We know Thompson, stupidly enough, cared for Sean Cullen, or at least felt jealous about being thrown over for a younger model. My guess is, he was planning on making a bit of a scene but held back out of sight when he saw Cullen wasn't there, waiting for him to arrive."

"Not that he was ever going to," Dave added.

"But Marc Kirkwood was. Best was probably surprised. Marc's never shown any inclination to get involved in Sean Cullen's photoshoots before, and Cullen's never shown any interest in him."

"Not his type," Dave said quietly.

"But hey, why not? Best was happy to get his kit off and show his potential for cash. He probably assumed Marc was the same. So, they wait and talk. But Marc's not exactly much of a conversationalist, is he? Best would have got bored pretty quickly. He's probably restless anyway. According to our statements, he'd left Heavy Metal early. He'd cut his workout short. How does that feel Sue, not doing the—what is it—*sets* and *reps* you normally do? I imagine not doing your quota is like not getting your daily fix. Probably leaves you feeling twitchy, yes?"

"I doubt you'll ever know," Sue said, her face unreadable.

"You're probably right," said Claire, unfazed by the implicit criticism. "I hope I never do. I imagine it's like trying to resist that last biscuit in the pack. You hang on and you hang on till eventually you think, *sod it,* and you go for it. And I reckon that's what happened with Best. He starts working out while he's waiting. Probably wants to look good and pumped for when he pulls his shirt off. And maybe Marc's egging him on. Best had bench-pressed a personal best at Heavy Metal that day, hadn't he? Maybe Marc pushed him to see if he could match it. Better it even. So, Best's on his back on one of those benches and Marc's loading the weights on the bar, more and more, and Best's pressing them, and Marc's putting even more on, and then..."

"Alys turns up," said Dave.

"And things get a lot nastier." Claire paused. "Now, this is where Marc's account gets a little unclear. Best realises he's being set up, probably goes to leave. Marc stops him. They shout, threaten, posture, you know how it is. With so much testosterone between them, real and synthetic, it's hardly surprising, is it? And somehow—" Claire looked across the gym floor to a workbench and, over it, a barbell, loaded at both ends with massive black metal plates. "Best ends up on his back on the bench again with the fully loaded barbell over his head. Maybe even the same weight he had pressed earlier here. And somehow the bar gets pushed off its rest and..." She brought one hand down onto the upraised palm of the other with a chopping motion.

"Should have had a spotter," said Dave.

"Hell of a mess," Claire said. "You ought to be pleased with the quality of your staff, though. Between them, Marc and Alys did a great clean-up job. Good enough so the Over Sixties Ladies' Zumba group didn't notice anything the next morning."

"Not good enough to hide from our forensics team, though," said Dave. "Evidence everywhere, if you know how to find it."

"So, there you have it." Claire sat back on the sofa.

"Very thorough," said Sue Green.

But Claire was shaking her head. "No, Sue," she said, almost sadly. "Because it still doesn't make sense."

"What do you mean? What more do you need? Motive, method and opportunity, isn't that what it's all supposed to be about?"

Claire leaned forward again, a dangerous smile on her face. "You want to play Agatha Christie with me? All right." She held up three fingers of one hand. "Motive." She folded one finger over. "Yes, Marc and Alys both had reasons for wanting to hurt Best. But Marc Kirkwood is a Neanderthal, and Alys Prochazkova is frightened of her own shadow. He wouldn't plan some elaborate showdown like that, and she wouldn't have wanted to take part in that sort of confrontation. No, what happened has all the hallmarks of an altogether different sort of person. Someone who enjoys games and manipulation."

"Someone who sees people as just things to play with," said Dave coldly.

"Opportunity," Claire said before Sue Green could butt in, folding down the second finger. "The empty Venus and Adonis. Okay, so both of them could probably have accessed the place after hours but could either of them have guaranteed no one would turn up unexpectedly?"

"The owner, for instance?" Dave said.

"And how could they have convinced Paul Best that the invitation he'd had to go there had been genuine? Neither of them had been involved in Cullen's darkroom shenanigans before. It would have taken someone Best knew was involved, maybe even someone who had taken photos for Sean..."

"A close friend, perhaps?" Dave suggested.

"And method." Claire folded down the third finger and stopped for a moment, examining the fist she had made. There had been a vicious pleasure in making Sue Green squirm but as she came now to the dreadful method of Best's death, the image of his mangled body on the autopsy table came back to her and she felt a cold sickness again at the pit of her stomach. "I'm going to go out on a limb here. I don't think that whoever planned this vicious payback scenario actually meant for anyone to die that night. I think the aim had been to hurt Best. Scare him definitely. Maybe even run him out of town. But things got out of hand, and..." She opened her fist to show the palm she had chopped with her hand earlier. "The rest you know."

Sue Green sat on the sofa, nodding slowly. "Are you accusing me?"

"Of what, Mrs. Green?" Dave asked.

She shot him a contemptuous look. "Of involvement."

"We have no evidence, Sue," Claire said softly. Across the space between them, she felt the tension ease in Sue Green's body language. "Nothing Marc or Alys have said..."

"Through their lawyer," Dave said through gritted teeth.

"Implicates you in the slightest." She sighed. "You really do inspire a great deal of loyalty."

"They're good people, Inspector." She shot another black look at Dave. "And they deserve all the help they can be given."

Claire was nodding as if agreeing. "Alys especially."

"She is a good girl."

"I suppose you see something of yourself in her."

"I suppose you could say that."

"Really?" Claire affected surprise. "Shy, jumpy Alys similar to confident, outgoing Sue Green?"

"I didn't mean we were alike," Sue Green snapped. "I meant..."

"That you had things in common, perhaps?"

"Yes."

"A shared life experience, maybe?"

Again, it seemed as if Sue Green was going to say one thing but bit it back, taking a second to compose herself before asking in measured tones, "What are you getting at, Inspector Summerskill?"

When she spoke, there was almost a touch of regret in Claire's voice. "You do inspire loyalty, Sue, and I think that's partly because you are loyal in turn. Loyal to people you feel a kinship with. And loyal to people who have helped you in the past."

"Helped me?"

"Alys Prochazkova was cited in a case of underage sexual abuse committed by your former husband."

"What has that got to do with...?"

"He, of course, denied this. Still does, in fact, and..."

"You've spoken to Ray?"

"But this was a good girl. And there was plenty of circumstantial evidence. I believe you yourself were able to supply some quite incriminating CCTV footage."

"And I'll bet Alys had a good lawyer too," Dave murmured.

"Alys was believed. She was a good girl. Your husband was punished, disgraced, and you were able to get your divorce."

"I didn't need that sordid affair to get my divorce."

"True. You said your marriage was over before the business with Alys, didn't you?"

Sue Green stopped, all too aware of the precipice Claire Summerskill had led her to. She took a second to collect herself. When she spoke again it was so quietly Summerskill and Lyon could hardly hear her above the gym's background noise but, at last, Claire thought she caught a glimpse of the real Susan Green, the woman behind the style and the muscles, the false friendships, and manipulations.

"He deserved to be punished," she said.

"Who, Sue? Paul Best or Ray Monroe? Or that first man who made you want to rebuild yourself into someone who could never be hurt again?" Claire shook her head. "It's not for us to decide who and it's not for us to decide how." She nodded to Dave and the two of them stood. "I'm meeting with your ex-husband again later today. I have a feeling there are elements of the case made against him that need to be reviewed in the light of recent events. We'll be in touch again soon." The officers moved towards the gym door.

"Have you ever been hurt, Inspector?" Sue called out after her. "I mean, really hurt. By someone you completely loved. Don't you think a strong woman should have some right to payback?"

Dave wondered if his boss would turn and respond. She did not. Claire Summerskill walked out of the gym without hesitation and Dave followed her through the door.

But he had seen her flinch at the question.

IT WAS ALMOST a week later that Dave met Sean Cullen again at Gallery 48.

"Sergeant," said Cullen pleasantly as he took up the empty seat at the bar next to Dave.

"Mr. Cullen."

Cullen waved at the barman who walked over to them. "Would you...?" Cullen asked, gesturing towards the half pint Dave was nursing. Dave shook his head.

"The usual, sir?" the barman asked cheerily. Cullen nodded.

"Great memory that guy," Dave said, even though the man was the same one who had come on to him the last time he had been in here and who had given no sign of recognising him when they'd met again. "Remembering your usual, I mean. You not coming here very often and all."

Cullen laughed. "It's his job."

"Yeah," said Dave. *Although the fact you're cruising in here every Thursday evening at this time like clockwork probably helps.* Dave knew this because this was not his first time back in Gallery 48 since his first meeting there with Cullen. He had returned two days previously, been unrecognised by the barman, and had asked about Cullen's visiting habits. Which was why he was here now.

"Quite a coincidence bumping into you here yet again," Cullen said.

"Quite," lied Dave.

The barman brought Cullen's drink, a large gin and tonic, and Dave was amused to see he charged it to Cullen's tab—just one more little proof of regular patronage. "Shall we take our drinks somewhere a bit more...private?" Cullen suggested.

Dave nearly laughed. "Behind the plastic potted plant? I'm fine here, thanks."

Cullen took a sip of his drink. "Things aren't going well," he said.

Dave knew what he was referring to. "That depends on your point of view."

"I suppose it does." Cullen swirled his glass, watching the ice cubes circle and chink. "It seems wrong, though, don't you think?"

"That a murderer should be brought to justice?"

"No. Marc Kirkwood is a killer, there's no doubt about that. The death of Paul Best may have been an accident, but there is no doubting the intent with the others. But I still wouldn't describe him as evil. He's violent, yes, brutish even, but there are probably one hundred and one reasons to do with his background and makeup why he's like that, and there but for the grace of God..." He caught Dave's frank disbelief. "Or perhaps not. Anyway, yes, Marc has to be punished and society has to be protected from him." He spoke the words quickly, as if they were some kind of proverb. "But Alys really isn't a bad girl," he said, his attention apparently once more on his drink. "She had some tough breaks and was actually getting a good life together for herself. She doesn't really deserve to be dragged down in all this." He paused, took another sip of his gin and tonic. "And as for Sue..."

"Wasting police time."

"I'm sorry?"

"That's what we talked about last time we were here. And that's what Sue Green could be charged with now." Dave took a pull from his own drink. "At the very least."

"There's no real proof..."

"It's quite obvious," Dave said in a voice low enough not to carry but emphatic enough to convey his contained anger, "Sue Green set up the meeting that led to Paul Best's death. Even if no one is admitting it. At the moment. I find it hard to imagine either Kirkwood or Alys having the intelligence or nerve to clear up after Best's death, then carry the body to Shrub Hill station and leave it on the train tracks to make it look like suicide or an accident. But that's for others to determine. And even if, incredibly enough, Sue Green hadn't been involved, hadn't in fact been the guiding hand behind Paul's murder, she knew about the link between Alys Prochazkova and Paul Best, and should have told us about it. But she chose not to, preferring instead to try and protect the people she thought worthy of protection even as it all span out of control and people died."

"She's very..."

"Loyal?" Dave snorted. "Please don't go there. We haven't even got started on how she stitched up her ex."

"Putting that aside for a moment..."

"Because he doesn't matter?"

"For a moment," Sean said firmly. "You say Sue knew about Alys and Dave but, again, there is no proof. Their both coming to Worcester could have been the most unfortunate coincidence."

Dave shook his head. "Alys was brought here and given a job by Sue Green, the woman whose husband she helped to put away. Reward for services rendered? Who knows? Yet." He pressed on before Cullen could interrupt. "And then Best moves from a big city to a small city to further his bodybuilding ambitions? Unlikely. Unless he got wind of the, shall we say, money-making opportunities on offer here." Cullen actually gave a small smile. Dave gripped his beer glass so tightly he was worried it might shatter. "Or he heard about the ready source of steroids to be scored at Heavy Metal. Or both. And who might have made sure he heard about all that?" He took a pull of his drink. "The more we dig, the deeper your *friend*'s involvement seems to lie."

Cullen tutted. "You really don't like her, do you?"

"I don't," said Dave, "and my God it feels good to be able to say it openly."

Cullen knocked back the last of his drink and signalled for the barman to bring him another. "Fair enough. But consider this. The real problem in this awkward setup was always Marc. I imagine when he did find out Paul Best was the man who had treated his girlfriend so badly in the past, however he found out, he got very angry indeed. I gather your own Inspector pointed out he would, in all likelihood, have attacked Best at the first chance he got. Perhaps if there was, as you seem to be suggesting, someone else behind the scenes, arranging meetings and confrontations, that someone was actually trying to avoid an out-and-out fight."

"Shame it didn't work, isn't it?" said Dave.

Cullen demurred. "No, it didn't, did it? The best-laid plans of mice and...women. And you know," he said, suddenly becoming brisker, "you are underestimating the help Sue gave you." He affected a sorrowful face. "She did shop me, after all."

"The photographs?" Dave snorted again. "Oh please! There was no way your little fetish was going to stay in the closet through all this. It wasn't a question of *if* it came out, only of *when*. Her producing them, you admitting to it before you had to, it was all just your way of keeping as much control over events as you could. Because that's what you are, both of you.

Controllers. We're all just little people to you, aren't we? I'm presuming that even those cack-handed attempts to fix you and me up were just more of the same, weren't they? Keep your friends close and your enemies closer?"

"Maybe," Cullen said. "At first. You're extremely judgemental, Dave. I know, I know," he added quickly, as if Dave had been about to interrupt. "All part of your job, I suppose. But you do see everything in black and white. One action. One reason. One effect. Life really isn't so simple." He took another sip of his drink. "And I'd never think of you as my enemy, Dave."

Dave stood as if to leave but Cullen reached out and rested one hand on his arm. "Don't you think you're being a touch...naïve?"

Dave looked down at the hand on his sleeve. Cullen left it there a second, two, then removed it, still smiling. Dave sat back down. "What do you mean?"

"You talk about manipulation and control. I call it politics. Sue calls it helping people. It's what we do. It's what we are. I'm sure you appreciate the importance of being true to yourself."

"I'm not a politician."

Cullen raised his glass. "And I'll drink to that. I think you'd be terrible at it. But you'll always be caught up in politics, manipulation, whatever you want to call it, like it or not." He leaned forward, his voice taking on a confidential tone. "Take your career, for instance."

"I don't..."

"I've seen your record. No, don't start getting all conspiracy theory about it," he said in response to Dave's obvious bridling. "I'm only talking about the public records that are open to anyone—well, certainly anyone in as exalted a position as me. You're good at what you do. Very good. And yet you're still only a sergeant, aren't you? You should be an inspector at least by now, and quite possibly well en route to something even higher. And yet..." He left the sentence hanging. "Feeling manipulated much? Ever wonder why?" As he asked the question, he waved his glass around, an apparently idle gesture taking in the bar in which they sat, the groups of men and men, women and women.

"Yes," Dave said coldly. "I have thought about it. And no, before you come out and say it, I do not think it has anything to do with my sexuality. The very fact I'm here at Foregate Street is because of the Force's positive policies."

"Ah yes, promotion to Worcester," Cullen said. "That renowned hub of civilisation."

"You're its MP."

"Touché. But this is a stepping stone for me, not a layby. I've already had my slap on the wrist from my local parliamentary committee over this business. They didn't even tell me not to do it again, only to *be more careful* in future. Trust me, some of the old goats there are up to much worse. A couple of months from now and my, shall we say, tangential involvement in this affair will be forgotten and I will be moving onwards and upwards. Can you say the same? Or are you going to have to rely on the police's equal opportunities initiatives for the rest of your career?" Cullen tilted his glass at Dave, an ironic toast. "It's all manipulation." He finished his second drink and placed the glass on the bar counter. "But, it doesn't have to be that way."

Dave waited. "What do you mean?" he asked finally.

"I could be...a friend?"

"What kind of friend?"

Cullen laughed. "Not *that* kind of friend. If I'd wanted to get into your trousers, I'd have insisted on buying you another drink."

"So, what? Are you talking about some queer brotherhood kind of thing? We'll be friends just because we're both gay? You'll use your influence to get me made up to inspector just because I fancy guys? That's ridiculous. And insulting."

"People bond for less."

"And of course, you'd have a policeman in your pocket, so to speak. Another one," he added, thinking about what Claire had told him of her conversation with Madden. "No thanks. Sean. It's the twenty-first century. No one cares if I'm gay or straight."

"Right," said Cullen. "So, you're all just one big, happy family at Foregate Street?"

Dave thought of Rudge and Cortez, even of Claire and Jenny Trent, of the silences in the office when he walked in, of the solitary lunches in the station canteen. He said nothing.

"I thought so," Cullen said softly.

There was a silence between them for a moment. From the outside, it might almost have looked as if the two men were friends, sharing a companionable drink. From the other end of the counter, the barman nodded in their direction and smiled and the couple of guys he was talking to laughed knowingly.

"Why did you come here today, Dave?" Cullen asked.

"Because," Dave said, "I really didn't have anything better to do tonight."

Cullen laughed again. "Let me buy you another drink."

Dave considered.

"YOU KNOW, I'VE heard Eileen is thinking of putting a plaque on this table with your name on it."

Dave looked up from his moody inspection of the station's canteen menu to see Claire Summerskill standing by his table. "I thought you only got that sort of thing if you'd died?"

Claire pulled out a chair and sat down. "I think this would be more along the lines of *I heart Sergeant Lyon* rather than *Sacred to the memory of...*"

Dave considered. "I'd be happy with a simple, *Reserved for the sole use of...*"

Claire nodded. "Pithy. And practical." She hadn't appeared surprised to see him sitting on his own in the canteen again. "Tony told me you had a talk with him. That day you found him in the centre and took him back to school."

"Ay. Yeah." Involuntarily, Dave's eyes flicked to the canteen's exit. Could he fake an excuse and leave before this got too personal?

"It's all right," Claire said, marking the reaction. "He told me what you talked about."

Dave relaxed, but only slightly. Just as he had that afternoon in the café with Tony, he had a feeling of being sucked into a domestic against his will. On the other hand, he liked Tony and wanted to know how he was doing. "Is it okay?"

Claire hesitated. She found herself uncertain how to respond to the open-endedness of the question and uncertain how far to open up to her still relatively new sergeant. *Well, Tony seems to have opened the way.* "Yes. And no."

"You turning into a politician too?"

"God, no! I mean, Tony is okay. Ish. I wanted to thank you for talking to him. I...wasn't happy at first, when he told me."

I can imagine, Dave thought, glad he hadn't been around when his boss hadn't been happy.

"But when I thought about it, I realised he really hadn't got anyone he could confide in, poor kid. His mates were all being little shits and he could hardly talk to me or Ian about it. I'd never have imagined he'd turn to you."

"Well, not exactly turned to me."

"I know, I know. More accident than design. But you were there for him and he could talk to you. I'm grateful."

The two police officers sat for a moment. Dave couldn't help it. His eyes flicked again to the exit. But he couldn't just leave it there, could he? "And you?" he said. "You okay?"

Claire gave a small smile. "Yes and no." She took a deep breath. "Tony told you he thought Ian was having an affair, yes?" Dave nodded. "Well, Ian says he isn't." Dave waited. Claire sighed. "You're a policeman, Dave, ask the question."

Dave thought back to the moment in Heavy Metal when they'd been leaving, to Sue Green's parting shot: *Have you ever been hurt, Inspector?* He remembered how Claire had flinched. "Do you believe him?"

Claire's eyes were fixed on the tabletop, her index finger following the pattern on the hideous plastic covering Eileen insisted on putting across all the tables. "Yes," she said.

Dave considered. "Okay," he said.

"Tony's bright, but he's still a kid. And all his mates are kids. They see adults, a man and a woman, getting on, having a laugh, and they put two and two together and get three."

Or sometimes two, Dave thought, but he said nothing.

"So, that's that," she said briskly.

"Not tempted then, to frame your husband with a bit of underage jailbait?"

"There's one thing I do not have to worry about. He teaches them. That's enough to put you off wanting to have anything else to do with them."

"Unlike Ray Monroe?"

"Or perhaps not. I've just heard his case has been accepted for review. That's what I came down here to tell you. Seems there were one or two problems with the original conviction when certain new facts, that have recently been brought to light, were taken into consideration."

"Fancy. That's not going to please a certain gym owner."

"That could be the least of her worries. But I think it could definitely mean kissing goodbye to the membership deal for the station we had lined up."

"I'll stick to my fitness DVDs."

"I didn't think that was the kind of workout you got from your DVDs."

"Moving on..."

"I shouldn't think the news will please a certain gym owner's friend either." She paused. "That bother you?"

Dave felt a small prickle of suspicion. Did she know about his meeting with Sean Cullen the other night? "Me? No. Why should it?"

Claire smiled. "Relax. I know he's not your type. God, I should hope not anyway. Y'know, you really are too easy to wind up."

"Yeah. Right." Dave thought back to that final drink at Gallery 48. "Not my type at all."

"Which," Claire said, "after the considerable diversions of recent days, brings us back to the all-important matter of who exactly is your type."

Dave groaned. "No. Not again."

"Yes, again. You need someone to keep you sane through all the madness of this place. And enough of all this *two questions he should never ask* crap. Which reminds me." She drew herself up slightly in the way Dave had noted she did in interviews when she was about to spring a killer question on some poor, squirming, soon-to-be con. "You know, you never did get round to telling me. What is this second question that is such a turn-off for you?"

"You really..."

"Yes, I really do want to know, Sergeant."

Dave took one last longing look at the exit. *So near, and yet so far.* "All right. I really, really hate it when you're chatting away with a guy, it's all going well, you're starting to get to know him, he's a decent enough guy and you're thinking, *Okay, maybe I could get along with this one.* And then he comes out with it."

"The usual?"

Engrossed in the long-awaited revelation, neither officer had noticed Eileen approach with her ubiquitous trolley. "Bacon sandwich?" she prompted.

"Brilliant. Thanks, Eileen, you're a lifesaver."

Eileen's beaming became even broader. She turned to Claire, and her upturned lips turned down in sympathy. "I'm guessing you're still on your diet, Claire?"

"Yes, Eileen," Claire said stiffly. "Yes, I am. Thank you for reminding me."

Eileen nodded happily. "Good girl. Okay, Dave, I'll get right on with your sandwich."

"Thanks, Eileen. And don't forget, please: easy on the butter. One slice only."

Eileen gave him a jaunty thumbs-up and scuttled off to her kitchen.

"So come on then," Claire urged, "what is it? What is the big second question never to be asked?"

"Top or bottom?"

"Sorry?" With the weirdest sense of dislocation, it took Dave a second or two to understand that Eileen had returned, and the question was coming from her.

"Do you want the top or the bottom slice buttered?"

"I..."

Eileen shrugged. "I suppose it doesn't really matter, does it?"

Dave turned from her to his inspector, still waiting for his answer, then back to Eileen. And burst out laughing. "No, Eileen," he said. "I suppose it really doesn't."

Claire waited as her sergeant laughed on and on. "What?" she said.

About the Author

Steve Burford lives in one of the less well-to-do areas of Malvern mentioned in the novel. When not writing in a variety of genres under a variety of names, he tries to teach drama to teenagers. He has only occasionally been in trouble with the police.

Email: Summerskilllyon@gmail.com

Other books by this author

It's a Sin

Also Available from NineStar Press

Connect with NineStar Press

Website: NineStarPress.com

Facebook: NineStarPress

Facebook Reader Group: NineStarNiche

Twitter: @ninestarpress

Tumblr: NineStarPress